ABU

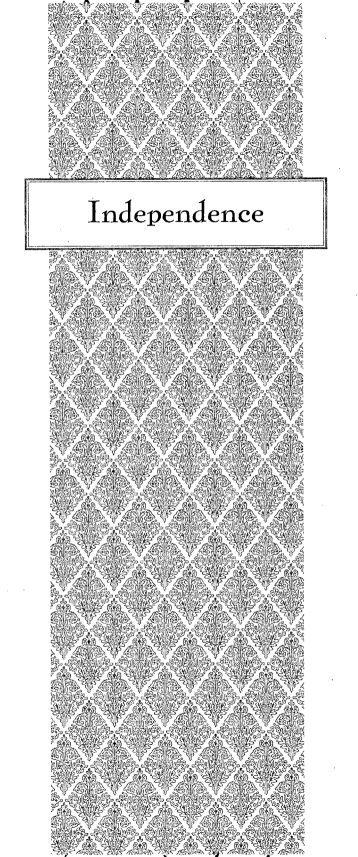

Independence

Also by Chitra Banerjee Divakaruni

The Last Queen

The Forest of Enchantments

Before We Visit the Goddess

Oleander Girl

Grandma and the Great Gourd

One Amazing Thing

Shadow Land

The Palace of Illusions

The Mirror of Fire and Dreaming

Queen of Dreams

The Conch Bearer

The Vine of Desire

Neela: Victory Song

The Unknown Errors of Our Lives

Sister of My Heart

Leaving Yuba City

The Mistress of Spices

Arranged Marriage

Black Candle

Independence

a novel

Chitra Banerjee Divakaruni

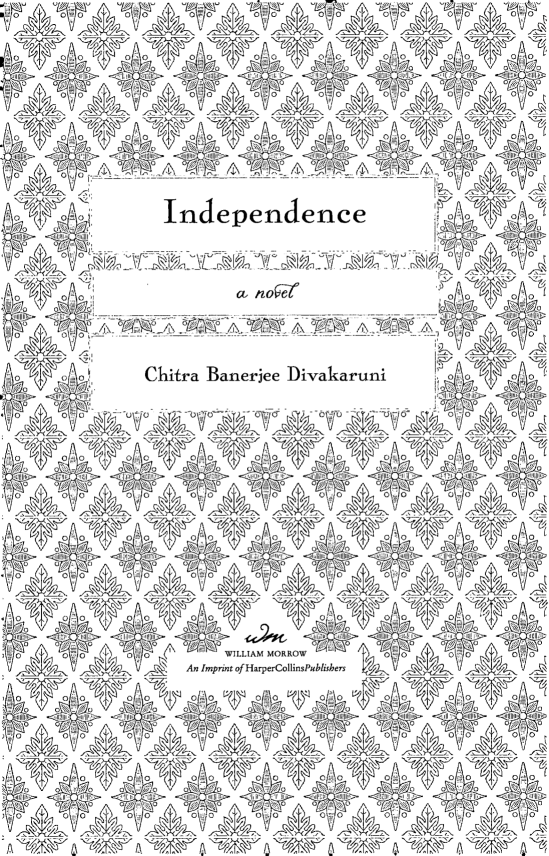

WILLIAM MORROW
An Imprint of HarperCollinsPublishers

INDEPENDENCE. Copyright © 2023 by Temple Hill Publishing, LLC. All rights reserved. Printed in the United States of America. No part of this book may be used or reproduced in any manner whatsoever without written permission except in the case of brief quotations embodied in critical articles and reviews. For information, address HarperCollins Publishers, 195 Broadway, New York, NY 10007.

HarperCollins books may be purchased for educational, business, or sales promotional use. For information, please email the Special Markets Department at SPsales@harpercollins.com.

Originally published as *Independence* in India in 2022 by HarperCollins India.

FIRST EDITION

Designed by Leah Carlson-Stanisic

Library of Congress Cataloging-in-Publication Data has been applied for.

ISBN 978-0-06-314238-1

23 24 25 26 27 LBC 5 4 3 2 1

To my grandfather, Nibaran Chandra Ghosh,
and my mother, Tatini Banerjee, who taught me independence
and my three men, Murthy, Anand, and Abhay,
who teach me love every day

[There are many] stories which are
not written on paper, but are written on the
bodies and minds of women.

— *Amrita Pritam*

Part One

August 1946

✦

Here is a river like a slender silver chain, here is a village bordered by green-gold rice fields, here is a breeze smelling of sweet water rushes, here is the marble balcony of a grand old mansion with guards at its iron gates and servants transporting trays of delicacies up the stairs, here are a man and a woman in carved teak chairs. Here is the country that contains them all.

The river is Sarasi, the village is Ranipur in Bengal, the mansion belongs to Somnath Chowdhury, zamindar. He is playing chess with Priya, daughter of his best friend, Nabakumar Ganguly. The country is India, the year is 1946, the month is August. Everything is about to change.

Chapter 1

Priya

*P*riya captures Somnath's bishop with her knight and waves it about in delight. "You did not see that coming, Kaku, did you?" He bends over the board muttering, secretly pleased. He taught her to play ten years ago when she was eight; her victories are his, too.

Somnath in his cotton kurta-pajama, a glint of gold buttons at his neck. One would not guess that he owns most of the fields in Ranipur and a shipping business and fancy mansion in Calcutta. His village home remains his favorite residence. Priya claims it is because he does not have a worthy chess opponent in the big city.

Priya in the loom-woven sari most village girls wear, her laughing face framed by curly hair escaped from her braid. One would not guess she holds close to her heart a forbidden dream.

The servants arrange the food on marble tables. Lime sharbat in silver glasses, three kinds of milk-sweets, steaming pumpkin-flower pakoras, pistachios, fruitcakes sent up from Calcutta. Guilt twinges in Priya. At home, her mother and two sisters would be eating puffed rice and jaggery, peasant fare. Money is always short in the Ganguly household. Nabakumar, a fine doctor with practices in Ranipur and Calcutta, is hobbled by a bad habit: he cannot turn away patients who are unable to pay. People take advantage of you, Priya's mother, Bina, complains. What would they have done if Bina had not been a talented quiltmaker, much in demand for her wedding kanthas? Bina is correct; still, Nabakumar is Priya's hero.

Up the stairs comes Manorama, Somnath's sister, manager of his household ever since his wife died giving birth to their only son, Amit. Manorama wears the white sari prescribed for widows, but hers is of the finest cotton. Jewelry is forbidden, but at her waist hangs a massive silver key ring proudly holding every key except the one to Somnath's safe. All in this household must petition Manorama for their needs.

The pakoras are getting cold, Manorama observes.

"Take it all away!" Somnath snaps. He descends into irritation when the game grows tense. "A hundred times I have said, do not disturb me when I am playing. If I lose to this chit of a girl, it will be your fault."

Manorama, undaunted: "If you lose it will be because Priya is a better player. At least let her eat!"

Priya bites into a pakora. "Thank you, Pishi. Unlike certain people, I can eat and think at the same time."

Manorama laughs. In her dry way, she is fond of Priya. Once she told Priya that though her oldest sister, Deepa, was the beauty of the village—fair skin, rose-petal lips, soulful eyes, hair like a waterfall—Priya was more admirable. She did not lie or think too highly of herself or deal in pettiness. Priya had thanked Manorama, but inwardly she shrugged. Life was too short to waste on trivialities when one had a goal.

❦

A commotion in the compound below. A gate bangs shut, footsteps crunch unevenly along the long gravel driveway, Priya suppresses a sigh. It is her middle sister, strident-voiced Jamini, calling her by her full and proper name.

"Bishnupriya! Ma wants you home!"

Jamini was born thirteen months before Priya, but she seems older. Perhaps it is the way she dresses: decorous long-sleeved blouses, stiff-starched saris so that people will take her seriously. Hair pulled into a severe bun that makes her look haggard. Priya can see this. But Jamini dislikes advice from her sisters, so Priya has opted wisely for silence.

Jamini likes to order Priya around; mostly Priya allows it. Jamini's left leg is a trifle shorter, she walks with a lurch although Nabakumar took her to a Calcutta surgeon when she was a child. The village women whisper that no one will marry her. This saddens Priya. She herself does not consider marriage crucial, she has larger plans, but she suspects that wifehood means much to Jamini.

Still, she will not let Jamini cut short her game. "I will go home once I am done."

"Should not take long," Somnath announces. "About to beat her."

With a vixen grin, Priya inserts a bishop between her king and Somnath's queen.

"You might as well come upstairs and have some sweets while you wait," Manorama says. She is not fond of Jamini, Priya has overheard her say that Jamini is too virtuous, but the Chowdhurys are gracious to guests, even uninvited ones.

Jamini, primly: "Many thanks, but not today, Pishi. I am helping Ma cook for Baba—"

"Baba is home?" Priya rises, jolting the chessboard in excitement. "Why did you not say so?"

Somnath frowns. "Nabakumar is back early from Calcutta. I wonder why. He does not like changing his routine."

Jamini loves being the one who knows. "Something occurred at the clinic. He will tell you tomorrow. I must leave now. I do not want to miss Baba's Calcutta stories. Priya dear, take your time, finish up the game. I am sure Baba will not mind."

Priya is too used to Jamini's taunts to react. She sends Somnath an apologetic look as he nods his understanding, casts a regretful eye on her plate of uneaten snacks, bids goodbye to Manorama.

But here are hoofbeats. The durwans swing open the great lion-crested gates, a black stallion gallops in, carrying Amit. Two years older than Priya, her best friend, recently returned from studies in Calcutta. In imported jodhpur pants and a fine muslin shirt, he is overly elegant for the village. Priya teases him for this. He is an excellent horseman, tall and sturdy, strong enough to control the wildest horse. But this she does not say; already he thinks too much of himself.

He halts the stallion with a flick of his wrist, swings down, calls her by the name he gave her in childhood.

"Pia. You cannot leave so soon. I timed my ride so I would get back just as you finish your boring game. I still have so much to tell you about my Calcutta stay—"

Jamini interrupts. "Priya must go home. Now."

Priya wonders at her tone. Jamini is courteous with everyone except her sisters, but since Amit's return, she has been thorny toward him.

"When did you become Pia's guardian?" Amit retorts. Jamini faces him, eager for altercation.

Priya puts an apologetic hand on Amit's arm. He has a formidable temper; she does not want it to flare now. "Baba has come home unexpectedly. He has been gone two weeks—"

Amit's face clears; Priya can always appease him. "You want to see him, of course. I will come with you. I love hearing Nabakumar Kaku's news. Let me hand Sultan to the groom—"

Jamini cuts in. "Today is not a good day for visits. Father wants a quiet family dinner."

Priya, bristling: "Amit is family, too!"

This time it is Amit who touches her arm. "I will see him another time."

Only the thought of her waiting father keeps Priya from argument. "He will come tomorrow to talk to Somnath Kaku. I will accompany him. We can chat then"—she throws Jamini a searing glance—"without interruption."

❀

On the way home, Jamini stops at the shrine of Pir Moyinuddin, a Muslim saint beloved of all in the village. Priya is annoyed.

"You said we were in a hurry. You would not let me talk to Amit."

It is bad luck, Jamini says, to pass a holy place without praying. As for Amit, Priya is too friendly with him. "You are not a child anymore. You need to behave appropriately, or you will bring shame on our family. Do you not see how shallow Amit has grown? He cares only about fine clothes and expensive horses and his rich Calcutta friends, every one of them idle and wasteful. I heard that he failed his exams . . ."

Priya prefers not to argue with Jamini, who is adept at twisting words, but today she is too furious for prudence. "You should be ashamed to repeat malicious gossip like that. I know Amit. He is a good human being. Also, he is right; you are not my guardian. Unless Baba tells me otherwise, I will be as friendly with Amit as I please."

She walks faster so Jamini will not be able to keep up, she kicks at the stones in her path. Fields of golden mustard flowers, silver-white egrets feeding in the rushes, things she loves. She passes them unseeing. She is good at shrugging off Jamini's jibes. How, then, did her sister get so deep under her skin today?

❀

Dinnertime. On the floor of their two-room cottage, the three sisters have gathered around Nabakumar. They are similar in build but otherwise so different that a stranger would not think they belong to the same family: Deepa scintillates in her confident beauty; Jamini is pale with virtue and suppressed longing; Priya glows, passionate with purpose. Their mother, Bina, ordinarily stern or worried, is radiant today because her husband is home. She has cooked ilish in mustard sauce, an expensive treat for which she made a special trip to the fish market. She must have taken the money from her lockbox, Priya thinks, money she is saving with difficulty for her daughters' dowries.

Dowries—or the lack thereof—is a constant cause of tension in their household. Though Nabakumar is not eager to send his girls off to the homes of in-laws, Bina feels they must marry soon. She turns accusing eyes on her husband, pointing out that most village girls their age are already betrothed, if not wed. Bina has ambitions for her daughters; she would like to marry them into affluent and respectable families. But without sufficient dowries, what chance do they have of attracting such matches? Her voice grows sharp as she reminds her husband that as they get older, their options are shrinking.

Priya has no wish to get married. Even still, the notion of dowries infuriates her. Is a woman not valuable enough in herself? she asks. When a man brings home his bride, isn't the family gaining a housemaid they will never have to pay? But it is a losing battle. Even her idealistic father concedes that the custom is too strong to fight.

But today Bina is in a good mood and smiles shyly when Nabakumar compliments her cooking. Jamini jumps up to serve everyone, though he has told her they can help themselves. Priya sits closest to Nabakumar, asking about new cases in his Calcutta clinic until Bina says, "Must we hear about blood and pus and fever-vomiting at dinnertime? Let Baba eat in peace."

Nabakumar winks at Priya when Bina is not looking. *Later,* he mouths. Their little secret.

Nabakumar loves opportunities to expand his daughters' horizons. A talented singer, he has taught them many Tagore songs. Deepa and Jamini learned quickly, they have discerning ears, but Priya—in this she is like her mother—cannot sing at all. She knows all the words, though, and loves to hear him sing, especially the patriotic songs that are his favorite. For some reason, Bina cannot stand these; when she is around, Priya has noticed, Nabakumar switches to innocuous melodies praising nature's beauty.

Nabakumar would have kept the girls in the village pathshala until they completed their final year, but Bina said, Enough, which man wants a wife who knows more than him. Still, he brought home textbooks and notes, encouraged the girls to take their examinations from home. The others declined, but Priya studied on her own and matriculated with high marks. Perhaps that is why he loves her most; he sees himself mirrored in her hunger to know the world.

Now he launches into politics, his other passion. In youth he was a freedom fighter; he insists that his family should know what is happening in their country. This exciting, difficult time: bitter-cold arguments between Viceroy Wavell and Nehru and Jinnah, Gandhi sidelined, opposing factions raising hydra heads. No one can agree about the shape that independent India should take, he ends sadly. Who knows how rocky the transition of power will be.

Priya longs to know more, but Bina interrupts. "Could we talk about something peaceful and happy?"

Into the awkward silence slides Deepa with a charming pout that no man can resist, not even a father. "Baba, when will you take me to Calcutta? You promised last year that we would go shopping in New Market."

The girls have not been to Calcutta in years. Priya's only memory of the city is of screeching peacocks in a zoo they visited while she was a child. Partly this is because, though it is not particularly far, getting to Calcutta is an enterprise. Ranipur does not have its own station.

Travelers must walk for two hours or take a buffalo cart, which is not much faster, to Baduria and wait there for a train. But this is the real reason: Bina does not like the big city, does not trust it.

Now Nabakumar, shamefaced, admits he owes Deepa a trip. He frowns, calculating. "I can take you in two weeks."

Priya begs to join them. She wants to see his clinic and Calcutta Medical College, where he studied. Jamini, too, looks up with requesting eyes.

Bina responds with a decisive no; then she relents a little. "It is too expensive to take us all. Let Deepa go with you. I will send one of my kanthas with her, to show to shopkeepers in New Market. Perhaps someone will agree to stock my work."

Deepa. The prettiest eldest favorite to whom Bina gives the biggest sweet, the best sari at Durga Puja time, who sleeps beside her when Baba goes to Calcutta. Deepa says, "I will surely find a buyer for your beautiful quilts, Ma. Pack me the bridal-party kantha. It has the best needlework."

A good choice, Priya must admit; Deepa has a keen eye. The kantha depicts a bride traveling to her husband's home in a palanquin. Waving palm trees, rivers with leaping fish, the bridegroom and his friends triumphant on their horses, the bride peeping curiously from the palanquin. It took Bina an entire week to do just the understitching, even with Jamini's help.

Nabakumar speaks decisively. "All five of us will go. We will make it a family holiday. I will ask Somnath if we can stay in his Calcutta house. It lies empty most of the time. Our only expense will be the train tickets. I can afford that."

Bina frowns. "But will it be safe? In the bazaar, people are saying there will be a big rally."

"Nothing to worry about. The politicians are always organizing hartals." Nabakumar touches Bina's cheek. "It will be a special treat. I have given you too few of those, dearest."

A smile breaks over Bina's face, years fall away. She lowers her head shyly. Priya glimpses the luminous young woman she had been, mesmerized by the dashing physician visiting her little village. They had fallen in love and married without family permission, unusual in that time.

Nabakumar turns to Jamini. He might love Priya the most, but he is fair to all his children. "What would you like to do in Calcutta, daughter?"

Dutiful Jamini startles them all. "I want to visit a cinema hall and see an English movie. Bela's father took her to the Metro Cinema last year. It has red velvet chairs and—"

Bina asks Jamini if they own a huge rice go-down, like Bela's father. She points out that Jamini barely knows English.

Jamini's face flushes. She looks down at her thala and toys with a piece of fish. Priya wishes to defend Jamini, but it would only harm her case.

Nabakumar says, "We will go to an English movie, Jamini dear, if that is what you have set your heart on."

Jamini offers him a tremulous, faraway smile. In her head, she is already at the Metro, seated in her velvet chair.

Nabakumar rises to wash his hands. Deepa says, "Looks like you are done eating, Jamini. Can I have your piece of ilish?"

Priya glances at Ma. Surely she will say no to this unreasonable request. But she does not speak, and Deepa leans over and takes the fish.

❀

The house is quiet now, lanterns extinguished, the family settled for the night, parents in the bedroom, daughters on old quilts on the main floor. As revenge for the usurped fish, Jamini has claimed Deepa's place by the window, where it is coolest. Deepa grumbles her way to the second-best spot at the other edge of the room. Priya lies between them. Such things matter little to her.

She wakes to a panicked banging, someone outside shouting, *Daktar-babu,* shouting, *Emergency.* Deepa groans and pulls her pillow over her ears, Jamini sits up in fright, Priya flings open the door. Their desperate night-visitor is a young fisherman. His wife has been in labor since morning, but the baby will not budge. The midwife says she can do nothing more.

Tousle-haired, in rumpled pajamas, Nabakumar goes to the bedroom to fetch his medical bag. Bina frowns. "It sounds challenging."

His voice is somber, his words clipped. "It does. Do not wait up for me."

Bina sighs. After traveling all day, Nabakumar needs his sleep. And the case will bring little, if any, money. Still, she climbs out of bed and puts a couple of clean old saris into a bag. After a moment she adds a baby quilt.

Priya has followed Nabakumar. "Please let me come with you! It might help to have an extra pair of hands."

Bina is scandalized. "An unmarried girl cannot be at a birthing."

Priya is afraid Nabakumar will agree. Not because it is unseemly—such thoughts do not occur to him—but because he does not like to cross Bina. Also, he might not think Priya would be of use. Until now she has assisted with only simple tasks at his Ranipur clinic, stitching up a cut, lancing a boil, prescribing malaria medication. But he nods. Bring lanterns. Two of them. Hurry. She realizes that he expects more trouble than he can handle on his own.

They walk through the sultry night to the fisher neighborhood. Narrower paths, shacks leaning drunkenly against one another. The man—his name is Hamid—leads them to the smallest one. Dim light of a smoky lamp, a pregnant woman panting on a mat. The frightened midwife tells them the baby's heartbeat is very faint.

"The umbilical cord might be tangled," Nabakumar says. He disinfects his hands, examines the patient. "I'll have to cut her open. Chloroform."

Priya pushes away fear and follows instructions. Press the chloroform rag against the patient's face until she slackens, clean the belly with antiseptics, tell Hamid and the midwife to hold the lanterns steady. Hand Nabakumar the instruments he calls for, scalpel, scissors, clamp. Do not flinch when blood wells dark from the incision in the woman's belly. The woman moans. *Calm, calm.* More chloroform, count out the drops with a steady hand, hold the weeping flesh apart. Nabakumar lifts out a baby boy. Cut the cord serpent-coiled around the infant's neck. Hold his feet, slap his back, hand him to the midwife when he cries, no time for complacency, help to stitch up the woman, clean the blood, tear strips from Bina's saris. Bandage the wound, administer a penicillin injection, tell the overwhelmed Hamid what he must do until the doctor's next visit.

Then she remembers. She rummages in the bag and hands the baby quilt to Hamid.

The fisherman's eyes well up, he runs reverent fingers over the soft cloth patterned with butterflies. It is one of Bina's simplest, but Priya sees that he has never owned anything so fine. He accompanies them back in silence, but at their door he weeps again, trying to gather words for his gratitude, trying to hand Nabakumar a handful of coins.

Nabakumar waves them away, but he does not make Hamid feel small.

"Bring us some fish when the catch is good," he says.

Hamid nods. He walks away, shoulders straighter, head high.

Priya thinks, How much I have to learn from Baba about doctoring. About human decency.

At the threshold of the sleeping house, she gathers courage. "When I took the baby from your hands, knowing that it might have died but for us—I have never experienced anything as exhilarating. Did I do well?"

"You did wonderfully. Calm and efficient—the perfect assistant."

She is light-headed with tiredness, terrified with hope. "Will you let me attend the medical college in Calcutta, then? I want to be a doctor. It is my dream."

Baba looks away. "I am too tired to discuss this right now."

This is not the whole truth. He forestalls her each time she brings up the subject. But she is his daughter, inheritress of his stubborn genes. She will not give up.

❀

On the balcony of Somnath's mansion, Darjeeling tea and Britannia biscuits. The men discuss Calcutta.

"Crowded and expensive and dirtier each year," Somnath says with a delicate shudder. "The firangi soldiers have ruined our city."

Nabakumar disagrees. "Living in the village has made you soft and provincial. And fat. I will tell Manorama, no more rasagollahs for you. She will listen to me—I am your doctor, after all."

"You are the devil, that is what you are," retorts Somnath, who is fond of his desserts.

How they enjoy squabbling, these two who love each other like brothers. Priya sips her tea and thinks happily of Hamid's wife, Fatima, whom they checked on earlier today, sitting up and breastfeeding the baby, who was wrapped in Bina's quilt. Her shy smile, her stitches clean and uninfected.

The conversation moves to the Calcutta clinic, which Nabakumar runs along with his college friend, Dr. Abdullah Khan. Because the doctors do not insist on a fee, it has grown very popular among the indigent. Always long lines outside the building, the sick standing stoically, sun or storm. But last week a woman had collapsed as she waited, had almost died.

"We must add a waiting room to the clinic, and soon," Nabakumar says. "So here I am at your doorstep once again, Somu, with my begging bowl." His laughter is tinged with discomfort. He prefers to be on the giving end of favors.

"What is this nonsense about begging, Nabo? Tell me how much you need. I will send a message to Munshiji in Calcutta. He will have the money ready in two weeks. But I do not understand why that rundown clinic is so important to you. Do you not miss being with your family—especially your lovely daughters, who will soon be married and gone? If you want to help the poor, there is no shortage of them around Ranipur."

Nabakumar grows serious. "The poor in Ranipur have a place to call home, even if it is just a hovel. They can live off the land or the river. When it is harvest time, or when a pond has to be dug or a house built, someone will hire them. Most of all, they know where they belong.

"But in Calcutta, the poor have no roots, no hope. Many live on sidewalks, constantly harassed by the police. The famine three years ago, when thousands of starving people crowded into the city, made everything worse. You do not like to hear this because you do business with the British, but they were the ones who cut off the rice supply to Bengal. A million people died. I saw the bodies, Somu, piled on street corners, nothing but skin and bone. They still come to me in nightmares . . ." His voice shakes. "That is why I have to work in Calcutta, among the faceless poor. It is my small offering to my motherland."

Priya had glimpsed the hardships of the famine in the village, but she is shocked to learn how many had suffered, and how greatly. Her father's pain pricks her heart. She makes a vow: if the universe allows her to become a doctor, she, too, will help the helpless.

"You're being modest, Nabo. Your offerings are far from small. Not only do you treat the poor for free, you also send money to Gandhi's Harijan Sevak Sangh—"

Nabakumar cuts him off; he does not like to discuss his generosities.

"I have some selfish reasons, too, for spending time in Calcutta. It keeps me in touch with what is going on politically in the country. And it keeps me from stagnating professionally. I come across unusual diseases, Abdullah shares his medical journals with me, we implement exciting new cures. For me, the clinic is like oxygen."

Nabakumar's words resonate in Priya. Has she not felt the same excitement when he brings home a new medical textbook, discusses a strange case with her? The human body is intricate, a mystery. Wresting it from death's clutches is an adventure without end.

Somnath says, "Our Priya has a solemn look. What is buzzing around inside your head, child?"

She knows Nabakumar will not like it, but Somnath's encouragement pulls the words out of her. "I want to become a doctor like Baba. Cure difficult diseases. Learn the latest treatments. Help the poor. I want to go to medical college." She bites her tongue to keep in the traitorous accusation: *but he will not allow it.*

Somnath says, "If any woman can do it, Priya, surely it is you. You are already a great help to your father in his clinic here. You even assisted him last night when he delivered Hamid's baby." He laughs at her startled look. "Oh yes, I have my sources. Nabo, let our Priya take the medical entrance examination. She is so bright, I am confident she will pass with high marks."

"You have no idea how prejudiced the administrators at the Medical College—most of them still British—are against women," Nabakumar says heatedly. "The majority of women candidates do not even pass the written exam because they are graded more severely than the men. The few who pass are usually eliminated during the oral interview, where the committee tries to intimidate them. The very few who get in—usually from influential families whom the college cannot antagonize outright—drop out soon after. Abdullah's nephew, Raza, who graduated recently, has told us horror stories. The professors are extra hard on the women, asking them things no first-year student can be expected to know, then forcing them to remain standing through the class period when they cannot answer. They are given male corpses to dissect in anatomy labs, or asked to take care of male patients with sexual diseases or madmen who might attack them. Their fellow students, too, tease and ridicule them and make off-color jokes. There are no women's toilets in the college—on purpose, I am sure. I do not want my daughter to be tortured like this."

"I do not care," Priya says. "I would not allow such trivialities to bother me. I would prove to them that I can be as good a doctor as any man." She glares at Nabakumar. "Have you not always taught me to stand up against wrongdoing? How can we accept such injustice, then? How will things ever change for us women if we—and our families— are unwilling to fight for what matters most?"

Amit, sauntering just then onto the balcony: "Who does Pia want to fight now?"

"Don't interrupt!" she snaps. "We are having a serious discussion about my future."

"Apologies." Amit executes an elaborate bow he must have learned in Calcutta. His eyes dance with mischief. She should be more annoyed. Why is it that she can never stay angry with him?

"Give the girl a chance, Nabo," Somnath says. "She deserves that. If she fails, the matter ends there."

"What if I get in?" Priya asks.

"Then we will have another discussion," Somnath replies in his calm voice.

Nabakumar, reluctant: "Very well, she can take the exam. I am not promising anything beyond that."

Priya hugs Nabakumar. She grasps Somnath's hands. But for his quiet championship, Nabakumar would have refused her outright. "I will prepare hard for the exam. I will make you proud."

"Better you prepare yourself for marriage, learning skills that men appreciate in their wives," Nabakumar grumbles.

"What if she finds a man who appreciates a wife with medical skills?" Amit quips.

She smacks his arm. "Stop joking about crucial matters."

"My deepest apologies." His eyes betray his amusement; then they grow serious. "Come to my room. I want to show you what I got for you from Calcutta."

"It had better not be something stupid," she says. Then euphoria strikes her. She is going to take the medical exam. Her dream is starting to come true. She grasps Amit's arm. "Come along, slowpoke!" They hurry to the stairs.

Behind her, she hears Somnath. "How they squabble and make up, just like the two of us."

"Indeed." But Nabakumar's voice is thoughtful. Priya can feel him watching her.

Somnath says, "All this arguing has tired me out. How about a song, Nabo?"

Her father begins. His voice, slightly husky, is the one she loves most in the world. *Ei korechho bhalo, nithuro he, ei korechho bhalo.*

"Not that one," Somnath groans. "It is so depressing." But Nabakumar continues, inexorable.

Emni kore hridoye mor teebra dahan jalo.
Amar e dhoop na poralay gondho kichhui naahi dhale
Amar a deep na jalaley dei na kichhui aalo.

You have done well, O Pitiless One,
In scorching my heart.
Until incense is burned, it does not pour out its fragrance
Until a lamp is lit, it does not give out its light.

Priya agrees. It is a dismal song. She wonders why her father likes it so much.

❧

She sits cross-legged on Amit's four-poster bed, the way she has done since the beginning of memory. It is a grand bed, over a hundred years old, so high that they had needed a footstool to climb on. How carelessly he left his many toys scattered across the floor, his games of ludo and carrom. He had cupboards stuffed with books that he opened only when she forced him to. She used to scold him for not taking better care of his things, not being thankful for how lucky he was. But he was not really lucky, was he, alone in this big house with no mother, no siblings, a father who gave him too little attention, an aunt who gave him too much. That was why Priya had become his friend; he needed her.

In some ways, Amit has not changed. His belongings are still strewn around, he refuses to let the maids or even the doting Manorama tidy them. He rummages in a trunk, discarding clothes and shoes. When Priya asks what mischief he has been up to in the big city, he says, with maddening primness, Not fit for your innocent ears.

"Found them," Amit yells. "Close your eyes."

Mock-sighing, she obeys. In the past, he has brought her wondrous novelties. A globe with fake snow that swirled up when shaken, a box with a ballerina that spun around to tinkly music unlike the Indian melodies she knew. What might it be today?

He takes her hands and slips something cool and heavy over her wrists. She finds herself wearing a pair of gold bangles studded with red stones. She frowns.

"Do you not like them?" His voice is uncertain. "I got them from P. C. Chandra, the best jewelry shop in Calcutta. The stones are rubies. I thought they would look good on you."

"Where did you get the money?" Her voice is suspicious. After certain misdemeanors occurred early in Amit's Calcutta career, Somnath had sternly limited his funds.

"I saved my allowance. Did not throw a single party all year."

She is taken aback. Amit has never been a saver, an understandable flaw in the heir to a considerable fortune.

He grins. "It was excruciating. All my friends boycotted me. But I did it for you."

Breath snags in her chest. "I cannot accept this. It is too expensive." She starts slipping the bangles off, but he holds her hands tightly.

"It would make me happy if you keep them, Pia."

She wavers. Not because she wants the bangles—she does not care for such things—but because he is her dearest friend and she does not wish to hurt him. "Ma would never allow—"

"She does not need to know. Keep them somewhere safe. It'll be our secret."

A look in his eyes that she has not seen before, a look she is not ready for. She is relieved to hear Nabakumar calling her. She slips the bangles into the pouch at her waist. There is a loose brick in the wall of the storeroom at home, behind the grain jars, and a gap behind it. As a child, she kept her small treasures in it. She will hide the bangles there until she devises a way to return them.

Chapter 2

Deepa

eepa's first glimpse of Calcutta is disappointing, frightening even. O the confusion of Sealdah Station. Arrays of ticket counters, lines of jostlers desperate to be elsewhere, crackly announcements impossible to decipher, red-uniformed coolies with holdalls on their heads yelling, Get out of the way. Most shocking are the dull, sunken eyes of the beggar children. Priya wants to give them coins, but Amit, who has accompanied the Ganguly family to the city, stops her. She will be mobbed, he warns. Also, most of them work for goondas who take their money at the end of the day. Deepa is sorry, but life is like that. Priya's eyes well up. The girl is too soft-hearted for her own good. How can this happen? she demands, as though Amit is personally responsible. Amit is saved from having to answer for the world's inequities by Somnath's driver, who runs up and leads them to the car, where Deepa is quick to snag a window seat.

This is more like it. Spacious and luxurious, the car—a Rolls-Royce, Amit says—speeds along a wide smooth street lined with flowering trees. Amit has given the driver instructions to show the girls some of the sights; he takes them alongside the Hooghly River. Barges loaded with sacks and crates, ferries crammed with commuters, fancy motor launches carrying Britishers. Deepa stares at the women in their knee-length dresses, at once excited and scandalized. She has never seen a woman expose her legs in public. All the rules are different in the big city.

Priya sits next to Deepa, leaning over her to see everything. Every so often Deepa elbows her away—she is the oldest, after all—but Priya is too good-natured to mind. Jamini is a different story. Bina offered her the window seat, but she said no, she wanted Bina to have the better view. All right, Bina said. Now Jamini is staring ahead, sweating sullenly because her sacrifice was not appreciated. When Deepa wants something, she grabs it with a smile that people cannot resist. Once, feeling generous, she tried to teach this to Jamini, but Jamini flounced away.

From the front seat, Amit points out landmarks. The tall pillar of the Monument, with two dizzying balconies up high; the racecourse, hidden from avid viewers by tall fencing; in the distance the white marble palace of the Victoria Memorial with a black angel on top.

Amit had surprised them by asking if he might join them on their Calcutta adventure. A delighted Nabakumar agreed. Another man in this gaggle of girls would be a help, he said. But Somnath frowned: You have to start managing our estates. Why do you want to visit Calcutta again so soon? But Amit, like Deepa, is good at charming people into giving him his way.

Deepa knows why Amit is here; she has seen the glances he gives Priya; she is fully in favor of a romance between them. An alliance with a family as rich as his is sure to help when Nabakumar looks for a match for her. With Somnath's help, they might even find Jamini a husband. Deepa would like that. Jamini exasperates her, but they are sisters, after all.

Now they are in Chowringhee, Amit says, the most important neighborhood in Calcutta. Motorcars, buses, horse carriages, rickshaws pulled by men who ring a handbell to warn pedestrians. See the electric trams, connected to power lines above, running on tracks? He promises to take the sisters on a ride.

They pass a building blazing white and big as a palace, porticoes and carved columns along the front. The rooms upstairs have charming balconies with flowering shrubs. The Grand, the fanciest hotel in the city. Deepa asks if Amit can take them inside, just for a look, but he grimaces.

"Sorry. Only foreigners are allowed."

Priya, indignant: "Why? This is our country, isn't it?"

Nabakumar says, "Yes, and we have been fighting to reclaim it since 1857. So many have sacrificed their lives for it. Finally, independence is coming. Perhaps when we visit Calcutta next, we will go there for tea."

Bina sniffs. Deepa knows what she is thinking because she is thinking it, too: not likely. They cannot afford it. It is wonderful that Nabakumar wants to save the world, but if he did a little less of it, the family would have a little more.

More elegant landmarks speed by. The Nizam Palace, St. Paul's Cathedral, the Indian Museum. Finally a quiet, tree-lined avenue, durwans armed with rifles salaaming Amit, swinging the gates open. Rolling lawn, exotic flower borders, fountains sending up silver spouts. The mansion's walls loom whitely; its gleaming windows are covered by decorative grilles. Two marble lions guard the entry. Inside, mosaic tiles in a lotus design, shiny teak furniture. Shefali the housekeeper, who has been with the family for decades, welcomes them with joined palms, her sari much finer than the Ganguly women's clothing. Generations of ancestors stare down disapprovingly from oil paintings at their shabby bags.

If I had a house like this, Deepa thinks, I would never live in a boring backwater village.

The parents get the bedroom downstairs, Amit is on the third floor, the girls will have the entire second floor to themselves. Amit gives Priya the biggest room—no surprise there—but all the rooms are large and bright, with enormous four-poster beds. Deepa has never had a room to herself, let alone a bathroom complete with an overhead shower. Her bed is so soft, she could spend her life lying there.

Thank God they had not canceled their trip.

Two days back, a neighbor told them that the Muslim League had ordered businesses all over India to close down on August 16 so they could have a mass meeting. There might be violence. Looting.

"It will be too dangerous," Bina said. "We should stay home."

Nabakumar said, "Hartals are always happening. They are just an opportunity for party leaders to give speeches while the common people get a day off from work. We will get to Calcutta early and have time to shop. On the day of the strike, we will stay in and relax. Once it is done, we will sightsee and find a buyer for your quilts. Maybe we will even have time to go for a boat ride on the Ganges."

He was jovial and confident. Bina had given in.

❀

A large radio sits atop a chest of drawers in Priya's room, polished wood, shiny knobs. Radios are expensive, they have never owned one. Priya touches it with a hesitant finger, but Jamini leans over and twists the knobs confidently. Where did she learn that, Jamini with secrets of her own?

A song by Tagore comes on, made popular by freedom fighters across the country. Gandhiji himself loves it. "Ekla Cholo Re." *If no one responds to your call, then walk alone.*

Jamini joins the singer, her voice clear as glass. They are too poor to afford a music teacher, but she listens when her friends are taking lessons. Deepa is a good singer, too. But she stopped practicing after Jamini said, Let me at least have this one thing.

A new Tagore song comes on. *Pagla hawar badal dine, pagol amar mon jege othe.* Usually, Tagore is too high-minded for Deepa; she prefers catchy romantic songs, like Hemanta's "Jaanite Jodi Go Tumi," but something about this one haunts her.

> *On this wild windy day,*
> *my wild mind awakens.*
> *I do not know why it longs to go*
> *beyond the known world*
> *where there are no roads.*
> *Will it ever return home?*

The sisters listen, mesmerized by the woman's breathy voice. They dream of impractical things: travel, adventure, breaking boundaries. Is it possible, if one goes beyond the known world, to return? They wait for the song to tell them. But Nabakumar calls them downstairs to meet his friend Dr. Abdullah, and obedient Jamini switches off the radio.

❖

At the round mahogany table with carved lion-claw feet, not one but two newcomers. Abdullah, crisp in a white kurta-pajama, neatly trimmed beard, white crocheted Muslim skullcap. And his nephew, Raza, brought up by Abdullah because Raza's mother died when he was young. Tall, broad-chested, dressed traditionally like his uncle, with the same kind of beard. But when Deepa sits down next to him, in the only remaining chair, he offers her a dazzling smile that has nothing traditional about it. She wishes she had thought to change her sari.

The snacks arrive, Calcutta specialties that Amit has ordered: syrup-soaked ledikenis named after Lady Canning, kachuris filled with ground dal and hing, singaras stuffed with out-of-season cauliflower. Except nothing is ever out of season in this city, Amit says proudly.

As long as you know the right people and have the right amount of money, Raza says. Is his grin a trifle bitter? Surely not. See with what courtesy he offers Deepa a shahi tukra, the dessert they brought. A favorite, he tells her, of the Mughal emperors. A dish fit for a princess. Deepa, who is used to the young men of the village mooning over her, finds herself blushing. When Raza asks what she would like to see in Calcutta, she is annoyed because she cannot think of something special to impress him.

The conversation shifts. Dr. Abdullah complains to Nabakumar—only half jokingly—that Raza is getting too distracted by politics. Though a talented doctor, he spends half his day at the Muslim League headquarters, sometimes more. He has become a youth leader. The organization is always telling him to speak at rallies, while his old uncle is left to handle the clinic.

Deepa imagines Raza tall and imposing, confident in front of a crowd. He was born to give speeches, he would know what to say, he would inspire everyone.

Raza says, "It's a crucial time in the history of our nation, Mama-ji. Remember, you were involved in such things, too."

"That was different. Nabo and I were fighting to throw off the foreigners' tyranny. How we longed for an independent India! People from every community came together. Nabo, do you remember, we used to sing Nazrul's 'Durgam Giri Kantar Moru'?"

Nabakumar nods. In a voice reverberating with emotion, he recites,

Who is it that dares ask, the drowning ones—are they Hindu or Muslim?
Say instead, they are humans, they are the children of my motherland.

Abdullah continues: "We had no idea that in a decade or two, our people would be fighting to break the country we had dreamed of into separate nations. Did you read what Jinnah said? I could not believe my eyes. 'We will either have a divided India or a destroyed India.'"

Deepa sees the stubborn look that comes over Raza's face. But respect for his uncle wins; he remains silent.

Priya says, "Please tell us about your adventures, Chacha."

Bina stiffens at this, but only Deepa notices.

"That was how your baba and I became fast friends," Abdullah says. "We were both doctors at the Medical College Hospital when Mahatma Gandhi went on his Salt March. Inspired by his vision of nonviolent resistance, we decided to join him. It was 1930. Our supervisor, an Englishman, refused to give us leave. So we quit our jobs and traveled across the country to Dandi. Men and women of all classes came together, defying tradition. Do you remember Matangini Hazra, Nabo? A poor widow, no formal education, but the heart of a tigress."

Nabakumar nods. "We used to call her Gandhi Buri because she was so much older. But she had more energy than the lot of us. She fought until the day she died, shot by the police. She was in her seventies by then. She died carrying the flag, chanting 'Bande Mataram.'" The memory silences him. Is that a tear in his eye? Finally he goes on. "She was a Bengali, Priya, as is Sarojini Naidu, one of our most important women leaders. Never forget, that is your heritage. Abdulbhai, remember how Sarojini marched next to the Mahatma on the Salt March, and we marched right behind her?"

Priya clasps her hands. She loves these tales of women at the forefront of resistance. Is Deepa the only one who notices how Bina's face has darkened? Is she the only one who cares?

A faraway look in Abdullah's eyes. "Sarojini-ji. The nightingale of India. She would recite her poems as she marched. Now there was a woman afraid of nothing. She would even joke with the Mahatma, whom we all held in such reverence. 'You are a lot of trouble, Bapuji,' she would say, 'wherever you go we have to bring goats because you refuse to drink cow's milk like normal men.' When he invited her to share his vegetarian meals, she would decline, laughing. 'What an abominable mess.' Or, 'I can't live on grass like you.' When the British arrested Gandhi during the march, she took over without blinking an eye."

Nabakumar says, "I still remember how she turned to us and cried out, 'Although Gandhi's body is in prison, his soul goes with you.' Through all the hardships, the police harassment, she kept us focused."

"But your father and I never got to the ocean to make our own salt alongside the Mahatma," Abdullah says sadly. "When we picketed the Dharasana Salt Works with Sarojini-ji, we were jailed. Your father was badly beaten by the police. I had to scramble around to find medical supplies to stitch up his bleeding head."

"You were injured, too, Abdul-bhai." Nabakumar pulls back Abdullah's kurta sleeve. Deepa sees an ugly, jagged scar along the length of his arm.

"What happened after that?" Priya whispers. "Did you get to see Sarojini-ji again?"

Nabakumar shakes his head. "No. She was jailed, too. And then she went to the Round Table Conference in London, to negotiate with the British. Maybe you will get to meet her someday."

Priya's face flushes with excitement at the possibility.

"All we got to see was the inside of the government jail," Abdullah says with an ironic grin.

Wryly Nabakumar adds, "By the time we were released, we were half-starved, with a headful of lice. When we finally got back to Calcutta, no hospital would hire us because the higher-ups—all British—saw us as troublemakers. But we had the satisfaction of knowing that we had been part of something monumental."

"And because we could not get jobs, we started our own clinic. Today we are our own masters, doing some good in the world," Abdullah says. "Even if we are not sure how we will pay next month's electric bill!"

Bina's voice breaks over them, loud with distress. "Abdullah-ji, it was fine for you to take those risks. You had no family. But your friend had three little girls. Priya was barely two years old when he quit his job without consulting me. I begged him not to go, but it was like water poured over a rock. Can you even imagine how terrified I was, left alone with the children? Every day I was sure I would receive the news of his death. After a while, I went crazy. But for the kindness of our neighbors, we would not have survived."

She begins to weep, an ugly tearing sound. Priya and Jamini stare, shocked. The men look away, embarrassed. Deepa reaches for her mother's hand under the table and grasps it. She had had no idea. When men go off to be heroes, do they even realize what it does to the women they leave behind?

Finally, Nabakumar clears his throat. "I am sorry I caused you distress, my dear. I have apologized many times. But some things one has to do, even if they bring danger and heartache to those he loves the most. I am thankful I could play a small part in our country's struggle. If I had my way, I would have joined the Quit India Movement, too. I would have been proud to die next to Matangini-di. But I thought of you and held back."

And all this time Deepa had thought her parents had the best relationship. How blind she had been.

Nabakumar continues: "That is why the clinic is so important for me, even if I never make any money from it. It is the one thing I am doing for my country."

There is entreaty in his eyes, but Bina's expression does not soften. When a couple has such deep differences, what can bridge the chasm between them?

Raza breaks the awkward silence. The women have never seen the clinic. Would they be interested in visiting it tomorrow? What about Amit? After all, his father is their main benefactor.

The downturn of Bina's mouth expresses her lack of enthusiasm. To her, the clinic is a sinkhole into which Nabakumar has been pouring money for years. As expected, Priya is eager. Polite Jamini surprises everyone by protesting vehemently, reminding her father that he had promised to take them to New Market and the cinema tomorrow. She looks toward Deepa for support. But Deepa, who cannot stand the stench of sickness, who has always hated the sight of blood, looks at Raza and says she cannot wait.

Into this impasse steps Amit. "We will take the car—that will save time. We will leave home early, see the clinic, then go to New Market. We will find a buyer for Bina Kaki's quilts and catch a movie at the Globe, which is right next to the market."

Nabakumar protests. Petrol, in these postwar years, is expensive. And surely Amit has friends he would prefer to visit instead of going shopping with a flock of females?

Amit says it is good for the car to be used. It sits in the garage most of the time. As for his Calcutta friends, they are a bad influence. Better that he stay away from them. Everyone laughs. Is Deepa the only one who notices how his glance caresses Priya, how she flushes?

At bedtime, as they make their way up the stairs, Jamini touches Amit's arm.

"I appreciate what you did for me," she whispers.

He shrugs, embarrassed. "It was nothing."

Here is a tangle. Does Jamini really believe that Amit was thinking of her when he offered them the car and his company? Deepa considers enlightening her. But finally she says nothing. Their trip will go more smoothly if their prickly-pear sister is happy in her delusion.

Chapter 3

Jamini

Jamini has always known her shortcomings. She does not possess Deepa's shimmering beauty, Priya's focused intelligence. That is why, early in life, she chose goodness. She volunteers at the Durga temple, never complaining when asked to sweep the floor or scrub the vessels. If a neighbor falls ill, she is the first to arrive with a pot of barley-and-lemon sharbat. When Nabakumar comes home from the clinic, she is ready with a clean towel and water to wash his feet. She helps Bina with her quilts late into the night, creating tiny, even stitches that hurt her eyes. And yet.

What is she doing wrong? How is it that her sisters—one vain, the other impractical—coast through life, gathering so effortlessly the affection denied to her?

Each week she prays to the Pir: *I have only ever wanted to be loved. Is that too much for a crippled girl to ask?* Perhaps the Pir is finally listening. She feels a change in the air, something ready to shift.

❀

The morning of cinema-day, Jamini comes down the stairs in her best sari, a red cotton with a gold border, her eyes darkened with kajal, her customary tight bun replaced by a soft braid. Why are you all dressed up? Priya asks. Jamini sidesteps her sister to occupy the seat next to Amit at the breakfast table. She makes sure he gets the puffiest luchis. When he thanks her, she smiles her sweetest smile.

After breakfast, they drive to the clinic, fifteen minutes from Somnath's mansion but a world apart. It lies on the edge of Park Circus in a poor neighborhood. Crowded flats flank the street, women's salwars and burkhas hang from balconies. The ground floors are divided up into narrow shops that sell betel leaves and beedis. Radios blare Urdu songs. Beyond the bus depot, Jamini spies the green minaret of a mosque. The car pulls up near a rubbish heap. Across the road is a butcher shop, flies swarming around slabs of hanging meat. Jamini does not wish to seem rude, but she cannot help scrunching up her nose. The clinic is small and squat, flaking dull beige paint. Already a long, winding line in front, men in desperate ragged clothing. Bina sighs, a heavy, hopeless sound. Baba's altruism has a price, Jamini thinks, and we are the ones paying for it.

Raza is waiting in the doorway of the clinic. Seeing him, Deepa's face lights up in a way that troubles Jamini. She reminds herself that Deepa is not the kind of girl to give in to impractical impulses. She has told her sisters many times that her life goal is to find a husband who is rich and respected in his community. She does not care if he is not handsome; a plain man will dote that much more on his beautiful wife. This, too, is true: beneath her vanity, Deepa is a good daughter, a good sister. She knows Bina has set her heart on her favorite daughter making a brilliant alliance. She knows that the marital fate of younger sisters depends on the quality of the match made by the eldest.

There is no reason for Jamini to worry.

The clinic possesses the barest necessities: two examination areas, a room for simple surgeries, a small dispensary, a cupboard for supplies, a dormitory with pallets for patients who have nowhere to go, a lone, harried nurse. Priya glows as she moves from room to room. It is a magical space, she whispers to Jamini, where lives are saved and hope is reborn. Jamini sniffs. Priya begs to watch new patients being diagnosed; granted permission, she happily disappears behind a curtain. At the end of the passage, Deepa and Bina are arguing, a rare event. Deepa frowns at Jamini, warning her away. Jamini sighs. It is going to be a long morning.

Then she sees Amit, resigned on a bench, flipping through a newspaper. She hurries toward him. *Pir Baba,* she prays, *help me.*

❦

All the way to New Market, Jamini smiles to herself. By luck—or maybe it was the Pir's doing—she had asked Amit about the Globe, had he seen any good movies there. It turned out that Amit loves movies. He told her all about *Gaslight,* the last film he saw, describing with animation the villain who manipulated his wife into believing she was going insane. Halfway through the story, Priya interrupted them, giddy with excitement because Abdullah had allowed her to diagnose the patients and she had been right every time. Abdullah told Nabakumar that Priya would make a great doctor, that he should encourage her. Raza added that she knew more than most first-year medical students. If she studied even a little, she would certainly pass the entrance examination. Priya pulled Amit up from the bench and whirled around the room with him until she was out of breath. How like Priya to interrupt without a second thought, to hog attention. But Amit apologized and promised to tell Jamini the rest of the story later.

Jamini holds his promise in her heart as the car stops in front of a building massive as a fort, its freshly painted redbrick walls topped by gleaming white spires, its tower clock striking the afternoon hour.

Deepa, too, is smiling.

Before leaving the clinic, Nabakumar had invited Abdullah to the house for dinner tomorrow, to discuss the plans for the new waiting room. Deepa had whispered in her father's ear, and he had invited Raza, too. Raza said he would be delighted. He would be on duty early tomorrow at the Monument, where Chief Minister Suhrawardy would give a speech, but everything would be over by afternoon. He offered to pick up another container of shahi tukra because Deepa had enjoyed it. Bina frowned and said he need not go to all that trouble; besides, weren't the shops closed for the hartal? Raza replied, with a quick glance at Deepa, that it would be no trouble at all, he knew the halvaikar personally and could arrange things. Deepa looked at him from under her long lashes and said with a tiny smile that she would like it very much.

Sitting in the car, Jamini can feel the displeasure emanating from Bina. But her ebullient sister, gazing dreamily out the window, seems impervious to it.

❖

Stepping out, they are engulfed by flowers. This is the outdoor phool bazaar, Nabakumar says. Buckets of bouquets in every color and size; marigold and rose garlands for Hindu weddings; lily wreaths for Christian funerals. They step through an entrance that, until a couple of years ago, was closed to Indians. Inside, hundreds of shops crowd along labyrinthine passageways lit by electric lights as though it were nighttime. Indeed, it is easy to confuse night and day in this magical space. Whatever Jamini thinks of, makeup jewelry decorations cookware furniture fruits nuts pickles medicine, it materializes around the

next bend. There are even shops shamelessly displaying ladies' under-
wear.

Bina gathers up armloads of silk thread for wedding kanthas. Expensive, but it will pay for itself once she sells the quilts. Deepa asks
Nabakumar for face powder and, daringly, lipstick. Priya wants a baby
monkey from the exotic animals market but, after a look at Bina's face,
settles for letter-writing paper, though she has no one to write to. Amit
insists on selecting the design for her, an edging of black battleships
that Jamini considers ugly. Nevertheless, she asks him to pick out a
silk-flower hair clip for her; fortunately he chooses a pink rose that she
quite likes.

Finally, a shop with an impressive display of bedclothes: matching
bedsheets and coverlets hung from the ceiling, piles of lace-edged pil-
lows, velvet bolsters. Bina shows the salesman her bridal-party quilt.
He proclaims the work to be excellent, but he is not the owner and thus
cannot make a decision. If Bina leaves the kantha with him—he will
give her a receipt—he will ask Agarwal-ji. They will be closed tomorrow because of the strike—he shakes his head at the inconvenience—
but if she comes back the day after, he will have an answer. Bina is
reluctant to leave her best quilt with a stranger, but Nabakumar says it
is only for a day.

"And now for the best part," Nabakumar announces, and Amit, with
whom he must have planned this, cries, "Nahoum's!"

They refuse to explain, so the women follow them curiously down
more narrow, twisting passages to the other end of the market. It is a
considerable distance; they are moving too fast. Jamini's leg begins to
hurt; despite her best efforts, she falls behind. No one notices except
Amit. He stops to tie his shoelace, but Jamini knows it is a ploy to
allow her to catch up without embarrassment. She is touched by his
caring.

They smell Nahoum's before they see it because Nahoum's is a bak-
ery. One of the oldest and most popular in Calcutta, Amit says. The

counter is crowded with customers. By their clothes Jamini can tell the Christians from the Muslims, the Jews from the Hindus. What an amazing city is this Calcutta, where they can all rub elbows and think nothing of it.

The glass cases are filled with glistening items: plum cake, fruitcake, cheesecake, heart cake, chicken puff, cheese puff, rum ball. The prices listed on a wallboard are exorbitant to their village eyes. Amit is ready to pay, but Nabakumar insists that the family's first time here should be his treat, so Amit respectfully puts away his billfold. Deepa chooses a cream puff and licks her fingers; Priya says her heart-shaped cake is soft as a cloud; Amit chooses a slice of fruitcake, so Jamini decides on the same. The dark, dense slab is bitter, peels mixed in among the dried fruit. But she chews on it industriously and insists she has never tasted anything as wonderful.

❀

Finally the moment she has been waiting for. Amit leads them across the street to the Globe Cinema. Jamini follows close behind him, limping in eagerness. Today's movie is *And Then There Were None*. They are in good time for the evening show. Amit goes up to the ticket counter. Nabakumar does not argue; he has already spent more than he can afford.

Jamini examines the movie poster. It is deliciously scary. The violent red slashes of the title, the terrified faces, the great mansion on a windswept island where surely terrible things await them. She squeezes her hands together in anticipation. If she is agile, perhaps she can grab the seat next to Amit.

But the movie is sold out.

"I'm so sorry," Amit says to Jamini. "I feel terrible. I know how much you were looking forward to it. I should have sent the driver to buy our tickets ahead of time."

Jamini bites her lip. She will not cry in front of him.

"Please don't be upset! I've bought tickets for the day after tomorrow, when we return to Agarwal's store. The best ones in the house, first row on the balcony. Here, you hold on to them."

Jamini gives him a tremulous smile as she takes the tickets.

"Am I forgiven?"

She draws a deep breath. What has she to lose? "Only if you sit next to me and explain the parts I may not understand."

Amit is relieved to be let off so easily. "Happy to!" He goes off whistling to find the driver.

Deepa, who has overheard, narrows her eyes at Jamini. "Are you flirting with Amit?"

But it is not a good idea to tangle with Jamini. She narrows her eyes right back. "No more than you are flirting with Raza."

❀

Jamini is dreaming. She knows this, but that does not make it less terrifying.

She is inside the mansion on the cinema poster, walking along a passage that winds like a serpent. The floor is wet and slippery. She touches it. Her fingertips come away sticky and red. Blood. Footsteps behind her. It is the murderer. She tries to run, but—o unfair universe—even in the dream she limps. His breath, hot and fetid, on her neck; his grasp on her shoulder; his knife across her throat. She screams, calling for Amit. Why does he not come? The hand on her shoulder tightens, shaking her like a rag doll.

She wakes bathed in sweat. Her chest hurts as though she has been holding her breath underwater.

Priya is patting her shoulder. "Wake up, Jamini. I heard you shouting. Was it a nightmare? Are you alright?"

Jamini should be grateful, but embarrassment sharpens her tone. "I'm fine. Go back to your room. Leave me alone."

Priya, annoyed: "Next time you scream your lungs out, I'll just put the pillow over my head, like Deepa does."

She needs to know. Awkwardly, she asks, "What was I saying?"

Priya seems to hesitate. Jamini cannot breathe. Finally her sister says, "I couldn't understand. Your words were garbled." The door clicks shut behind her.

The moon bathes the room in beauty, the bedsheets are liquid silver, a distant night bird trills its lonesome song. Jamini lies wondering if her sister heard her calling Amit's name.

❧

Direct Action Day. The Ganguly family plans to relax at home, a rare luxury. The servants have set up a table and chairs in the garden. From the upstairs balcony, Jamini watches her parents seated there. Bina points to clouds drifting across the sky's brightness. Nabakumar puts an arm around her and kisses her on the temple. At home Bina would have pushed him away awkwardly; here she rests her head on his shoulder. Happy for them, Jamini briefly forgets last night's embarrassment.

In the bathroom Deepa is singing as she showers. With a twinge Jamini admits that though her sister no longer practices since the time Jamini asked her to stop, Deepa's voice is as good as hers. In truth, they sound very similar. If someone listened to them both from another room, he would not know the difference.

At breakfast Amit says, "You look tired. Did you not sleep well? Is the bed uncomfortable?" Jamini is both pleased and flustered by his scrutiny. Before she can reassure him, he hears Priya's footsteps and turns away, and she sees that he has forgotten her. The ardent smile he offers up to Priya is so different from the polite one he gave Jamini that a wiser woman would admit defeat. But Jamini is stubborn and smitten, a dangerous combination. One small relief: Priya treats her normally; she must not have heard anything incriminating last night.

Now Nabakumar calls them to the radio in the drawing room for the latest news about the strike. Bina, unabashedly uninterested, settles in the corner easy chair with her knitting. Jamini puts on an attentive expression, though in truth she finds politics dull. She suspects that Amit does, too. He sits next to Priya, playing with the tassels of her sari until she swats his hand away. Deepa, usually uncaring of such matters, tries to figure out how soon the event will end. Nabakumar and Priya are the only ones who listen with genuine earnestness.

A large crowd of Muslims—more than fifty thousand—is already waiting at the Monument for the chief minister, and more are joining them. Nabakumar frowns. "That is an unusually large number. I did not think there were that many Muslims in Calcutta." As if to reassure him, the newsman announces that a police force has been sent to the Monument from Lalbazar Headquarters to make sure order is maintained. All is proceeding as planned.

The broadcast ends; sitar music comes on. Deepa says brightly, "It looks like the strike will be over long before dinnertime."

❀

The day passes like a dream. The parents settle down in the drawing room. He reads to her from the newspaper; she knits a sweater for him, using the dark green wool she purchased yesterday. The color will look good on him, she says.

"You think everything looks good on me," he jokes.

"It does."

The sisters walk in the garden with Amit, who picks flowers for their hair, choosing the largest, most luscious rose for Priya. Jamini battles the jealousy rising in her like heartburn. When Priya was little, she followed Jamini everywhere. Jamini made sure to hold her hand so she would not fall. She reminds herself of this.

After lunch, the parents nap. Amit teaches the girls rummy. They gamble with matchsticks, feeling worldly-wise. In a while, Deepa excuses herself, saying she needs her beauty sleep. Jamini can see that Amit is hoping she will go off, too, leaving him alone with Priya. Doggedly, she insists that they keep playing. She wins all of Priya's matchsticks. Priya pushes them across the table, grumbling; she announces that she is going to her room to read. Jamini's heart speeds up.

But Amit gets up, saying he, too, needs a nap. He yawns elaborately, a fake yawn if ever there was one. He follows Priya up the stairs.

The bright, stifling afternoon presses down on left-behind Jamini. She is weary of being good. What has it given her? A wish rises in her, a crazy wind. *Let something change. Let something break. I don't care what. I don't care how.*

Chapter 4

Priya

he sun sets, Shefali lights incense, the maids bring snacks. Deepa joins the family in the drawing room luminous with lipstick and anticipation, her shampooed hair curling charmingly around her face. Bina glares at her and asks Jamini for music. But there are no songs on the radio, only an announcer who speaks too fast, nasal with panic. Riots have broken out all over Calcutta, Muslims and Hindus attacking each other. The fights began as soon as the morning's meeting was over. Clearly things had been planned ahead. Lorries full of armed Muslims sped across town to loot Hindu shops. The Hindus retaliated, especially in the North Calcutta neighborhoods where they were higher in number. Violence continues to escalate as vigilantes from both communities seek revenge: shops and homes are burned, people hacked to death. A curfew has been imposed, but the rioters are ignoring it. The police are overwhelmed. Governor Burrows has not yet responded to appeals to send in troops from the Sealdah Rest Camp.

Snacks forgotten, the family listens, horrified. The announcer lists places where the fighting is the worst: Rajabazar, Kolutola, Park Circus.

"Park Circus—Baba, isn't that where your clinic is?" Priya blurts out. She claps her hand over her mouth, but it is too late.

Nabakumar springs up. "You are right. Abdullah lives in that area, too. I have to phone him. Make sure he is safe."

It takes him a long time to get through. The lines are jammed.

"Thank God I got hold of you, Abdul-bhai. I want you and Raza to come here right away, before things get worse. All the houses in this area have armed guards. We will be safe. You can stay here until things calm down."

His face fills with worry as he listens. Finally he replaces the receiver.

"Abdullah is not coming. Raza phoned him from the clinic—I guess it was the closest place where he could find shelter when the riots broke out. Many injured people have shown up at the clinic. More keep coming. Raza cannot bear to turn them away, but he cannot handle so many emergencies on his own. Men are dying in front of his eyes. Raza is in shock. He has never seen anything like this. We cannot leave him alone there. Abdullah is on his way to the clinic. I am going, too."

"No, please." Bina clings to him, panicked. "It is too dangerous. People have gone mad in this city. You will get killed even before you get there. You cannot do this to yourself—and to us. You owe more to your family than to strangers who are probably going to die anyway."

Deepa and Jamini add their tearful pleas. Bina gives Priya a push. "You tell him, Priya. He always listens to you."

Her mother is right. But Priya hears herself saying, "Let me go with you, Baba. I can help."

Bina makes a strangled sound. Nabakumar smiles but shakes his head. "No arguments, my girl. I do not have time for that." To Bina he says, "You want me to be a coward? To crawl into a hole like a dog to save my skin? To abandon Abdullah and Raza when they need me most? I could not live with myself if I did that." In a gentler tone, he adds, "I will be very careful, dearest. I know the back roads between here and the clinic. I will make sure to stay away from any rioters."

Amit pulls on his shoes, but Nabakumar says, "I need you to stay here and take care of my family."

Bina has collapsed, sobbing; but dry-eyed Priya finds Nabakumar a dark gray kurta-pajama from Somnath's almirah to help camouflage him. Amit opens a safe, takes out a pistol. It is the first gun Priya has seen. Snub-nosed, black as a cobra, it belongs in a movie, not in her father's hand. But Nabakumar checks to ensure that it is loaded and tucks it with frightening familiarity into his waistband.

How many mysteries are locked within the people we think we know. Priya has a hundred questions to ask her father once tonight is over.

Nabakumar kisses his family and promises to call as soon as he reaches the clinic. They accompany him to the gate. Priya has chosen his clothes well; within moments, he disappears into darkness.

Bina turns on Priya. "If something happens to your baba, I will never forgive you."

What can a daughter say to that?

Back in the house, Deepa crouches in a corner, face in her hands; Amit paces grimly; Bina rocks back and forth in the armchair where Nabakumar was sitting; Priya stands at the window, looking into darkness. Should she have begged her father to stay? Jamini turns on the radio. Men and women sliced open with swords, citywide looting by thugs from both factions, tenements set on fire, their occupants forced to remain inside until they burn to death.

"Turn it off," Bina shouts.

When the phone rings, they stare at it, paralyzed; fear tightens its claws around Priya's throat. Finally Amit lurches forward to pick it up.

It is Nabakumar.

They crowd around the receiver, listening to his voice, faraway tinny beloved. He reached the clinic without mishap, he will stay there until it is safe to return. There are many injured people; he is taking care of them. "Eat dinner," he says. "Get a good night's rest. We'll be together sooner than you think."

Priya is ravenous, they are all ravenous. They eat without words the dinner prepared for guests who never came. They take second and third helpings, bend low over plates, shovel in food. In their relief, everything tastes marvelous. Immediately after, they go to bed. Deepa offers to sleep with Bina. Priya is certain she is too agitated to sleep, but she plunges into oblivion.

She is awakened by a hand shaking her. It is Jamini, in an ironic reversal of last night, tear-streaked and babbling that something terrible has happened.

❧

Dr. Abdullah had phoned the house soon after they went to bed. Bina stumbled through the dark to the ringing, Deepa close behind. Dr. Abdullah spoke bluntly. He had harsh news and not much time to tell it. A wounded man had collapsed on the street outside the clinic door and was screaming for help. Nabakumar could not stand it. Dr. Abdullah begged him to wait. But he stepped out to drag the man into the building, got caught in crossfire. Bullets to the chest and stomach. Raza and Dr. Abdullah did the best they could, but he was still losing blood. Things did not look good. Nabakumar was conscious at the moment—would Bina like to say something to him?

Deepa told her sisters that Bina had been astonishingly calm. She informed Dr. Abdullah that she was coming to the clinic. He said it was too dangerous, but she was adamant. "You can't stop me from being with my husband at this time. Perhaps I can help pull him back from death's grasp. If not, at least he will not die without any family by his side."

Defeated, Dr. Abdullah said he would send Raza to bring her.

When the girls insisted that they, too, needed to see their father, Bina did not protest. She said nothing when Amit announced he would join them. Perhaps she did not hear them. Her attention was elsewhere, her lips moved silently.

It seemed forever before Raza arrived, gasping as though he had run the entire way, his kurta splotched dark with blood and sweat, a brightness gone from his face. He handed them clothing. Quick. Quiet.

Now they hurry down the alley, six of them stepping shadow to shadow, startling at every sound. Raza in front, Amit behind, the women huddled in the center. Raza had brought a skullcap for Amit, and for the women, burkhas that belonged to Nurse Salima. They will be safer this way because they are crossing a Muslim neighborhood. Priya's burkha smells of clove and garlic. Through its net veil the world shimmers unreal. Deepa supports Bina. Jamini clutches Priya's hand damply. Priya hears Bina whisper; she is telling Nabakumar to hold on until she arrives.

They have reached the street where the clinic is located, the last most dangerous stretch. They will have to cross a major thoroughfare, many streetlamps, no opportunity to shelter in shadows. There has been some heavy fighting here recently. Priya sees bodies spread-eagled on the ground. Some have fallen into the drains that line the road. At her feet, a hacked-off arm covered in blood. Hindu or Muslim? In death there is no difference. She doubles over, retching. Assisting Baba over the last few years, she had believed herself inured to blood. Limbs lost to accidents. But the slaughter here is deeply, differently dreadful. The men, too, are shocked into stopping. Behind her, Deepa and Jamini moan. Only Bina remains fixed on her goal. Hissing at them to be silent, she picks up her pace, giving them no option but to run after her. Lucky that the rioting has moved away. Else no burkha could have saved them.

Even as Priya thinks this, a group of men comes around the corner. Seeing Bina's small party, they begin to run toward them with frenzied yells. Their leader wields a sword; his forehead is streaked with vermillion.

A Hindu mob.

The girls are frozen. Raza and Amit take a stand in front of them, hands fisted, but they look dismayed. The men are carrying rods and knives. One wields an ax. If only I had the gun, Amit mutters.

Then Bina—how is she able to think so calmly, so clearly?—removes her burkha and drops it to the ground. She orders her daughters to do the same. She pulls the caps off Raza's and Amit's heads and throws them down. She pushes Raza behind Amit. Then she joins her palms and speaks loudly, addressing the leader. "Dada, Goddess Kali Herself must have sent you. My children and I are trying to get to my husband, a doctor who was badly wounded trying to save lives tonight. He is in the clinic down the road. Will you help us get there?"

The leader is taken aback. One of his men points to the burkhas and whispers.

Bina says, "We were scared to come through the Muslim neighborhoods, so we disguised ourselves. But see, we are Hindu." She looks the leader in the face and holds up her hands.

The leader notes the marriage sindur, crimson on the parting of Bina's hair, the iron and conch-shell bangles on her arms. The men mutter among themselves, giving the rest of the group only a cursory glance. Finally, the leader nods. "Very well, I will take you to the clinic. But do not venture out again. The next group you meet might not be so kind. Follow us. Quickly now. We have much to accomplish tonight."

Priya shudders to think what these accomplishments might be. Still, for the moment these men are their saviors. They hurry behind them, Bina leading the way. Behind her, Deepa has slipped her hand into

Raza's. Priya prays the mob will not notice this questionable gesture. The short stretch of road takes forever. Jamini pants. Priya takes her by the elbow and pulls her along to help her keep up. Amit follows last of all, keeping a wary eye on the shadows behind.

At last the clinic entrance. The mob melts into the night. Raza knocks on the door, calls to his uncle. His voice shakes. Is he thinking the same thing that keeps running through Priya's head? If the mob had realized he was Muslim, he would not be standing here now. The rest of them might be dead, too, for fraternizing with the enemy.

Dr. Abdullah cracks open the door. Hurry, hurry. Just before Priya ducks inside, something makes her look up. The sky is a dull red. Calcutta is burning.

Wounded men everywhere, on pallets, on the floor, propped against the wall. Priya has to step over their legs. Many are groaning. The clinic must have run out of sedatives. A few have fallen over and lie strangely still. She cannot pull her eyes away. Metallic stench in the air. She knows what it is. How carefully Nabakumar had protected her from death when she worked with him, sharing only the healing side of medicine. The deceased she had seen were neighbors passed away from old age or long sickness, their garland-bedecked bodies. Now these corpses, toppled on the floor, no one to even cover them with a sheet.

In the examination room Nabakumar lies stretched on a table, the bright red of the bandages covering his chest and stomach. Dread chills Priya. If Abdullah has been unable to stanch the bleeding, the bullets must have hit a crucial organ. Her father's eyes are closed, his face pale, his chest still. Are they too late?

Bina grasps Nabakumar's right hand, whispers in his ear. Perhaps it is the urgency in her voice, perhaps it is the injection that Dr. Abdullah is administering. Nabakumar's eyes flutter. Priya sees how hard he strains to open them. Deepa holds her mother steady. At Nabakumar's feet Jamini gabbles incoherently. *I made this happen.* But no, it is Priya's fault. She should have stopped her father from leaving the house.

Nabakumar's left hand twitches. He is trying to raise it. Priya rushes to him.

"Do not give up, Baba," she urges. "Is that not what you always taught me? Please try. Please. For our sake."

His lips tremble. "Sorry." Even that is too much effort; his eyes fall shut.

She clutches Nabakumar's hand as though that can stop him from leaving. Another hand closes over hers, startling her. Amit. In her distress she had forgotten him.

Nabakumar speaks so softly that Priya and Amit must both bend closer. "Take care of—"

Priya forces back tears. "I will, Baba. I will take care of them. Don't worry."

Amit speaks at the same time. "Be at peace, Kaka. I promise you, I will keep your family safe."

Priya knows she should be grateful to Amit for being here; instead, she is furious at his presumption. Nabakumar is talking to her, not to him. She is the one he trusts to watch over the family. She can do it. She will do it.

She needs to make sure Amit understands this. But not now. This moment is for her father. She focuses on his face. She must hold it inside her always.

Nabakumar makes a sound. Is it relief, is he trying to say something else, is it just getting harder to breathe? He turns his head toward Bina; his lips attempt a smile.

"Sing Mother," he whispers. He is getting confused, Priya thinks. Like her, Bina is tone-deaf, she cannot sing.

Jamini is the only one who understands. Silent watchful Jamini, no one's favorite, wipes her tears and sits up straight. Tremulously she begins.

Aji Bangla desher hridoy hote kokhon aponi
Tumi ei aparup p rupe bahir hole Janani
Ogo Ma tomay dekhe dekhe ankhi naa phire . . .

Her voice grows strong, flows through the room, the corridor, the clinic. Everyone is listening now, lifted for a moment from calamity.

O Mother, when did you emerge from the heart of Bengal,
O beautiful, O splendid,
I cannot take my eyes from you. O Mother . . .

Nabakumar sighs. "Mother," he says. Then he is gone.

Part Two

August–October 1946

The river recedes, exposing muddy flats; the days grow rainless and brittle. The village is shaken by death's abrupt swoop; the city still burns with hate. The trains are crammed with those who fled, the crematoriums and graveyards with those who could not flee. A man trudges barefoot through ashes for the sake of peace. Blame is thrust from leader to leader in a pass–the–package game.

The river is Sarasi, the village Ranipur, the burning city Calcutta, though the crazy wind is blowing sparks elsewhere too. The dead are nameless, impossible to count. The barefoot man is Gandhi, ill and battling despair; the leaders are Jinnah, Burrows, Suhrawardy, Nehru, Wavell.

The month is still August, the year still 1946. But the change has begun.

Chapter 5

Deepa

Nabakumar's funeral takes place by the river, in the village burning-ground. A quiet event, just the women, Somnath, Amit. Bina said no to everyone else, friends neighbors patients who wanted to pay their respects. When Somnath tried to arrange a funeral feast with eulogies, she refused.

Bina has been acting oddly since the death. Understandable. Still, it worries Deepa.

The prayers are done. Time for the body, shrunken under the white sheet, to be set on fire. According to the shastras, the priest says, a man must perform this act. Unfortunate that the deceased only has daughters. Ah well, perhaps a friend of the family?

Amit steps forward, but Priya says, "Baba never believed in such senseless customs. We sisters will do it." Deepa tries to reason, to just get it done; Priya is adamant. Deepa looks around for support, but Jamini is mute and Bina stares at the river. Amit and Somnath take

Priya's side. The priest is forced to compromise. Amit helps the sisters set the pyre alight.

The stench, the blast of heat, the charring flesh. Deepa forces herself to stand there and watch after her sisters have turned away weeping. Because although no one has accused her of it, she knows Nabakumar's death is her fault.

⚜

After the funeral, Somnath takes them home in his carriage. Deepa is grateful. Their house is at the other end of Ranipur, and they are in no state to meet the villagers' curious stares, face their commiseration. Her mind, lulled by the rocking carriage, travels backward. The day after Nabakumar's death, Abdullah and Raza had come to the Calcutta house with condolences, offers of help. Bina would not let them in. From the doorway she shouted that they were responsible for her family's calamity. *My husband went to help you, and then your people killed him.*

The look on Raza's face, as though he had been punched in the gut.

When Bina went inside, Deepa ran to the gate. She was afraid that they were gone, that she would not get a chance to apologize for her mother's behavior. Abdullah had left, but for some reason Raza was still standing on the street corner. When she tried to say sorry, he stopped her. He gave her his address and phone number. "Contact me if you need anything," he said. "Anything at all."

The touch of his fingers. A small solace.

When they get down from the carriage, Somnath asks, "What can I do to help you at this time, Bina? Please don't hesitate to—"

Bina cuts him off. "I would like you to leave us alone."

The girls stare. Somnath frowns, confused. "Why do you say this? Nabakumar was like my brother—"

"If it was not for you supporting his folly," Bina says, "he would have given up on the Calcutta clinic long ago. This misfortune would never have fallen on us."

Somnath flinches. Guilt pounds in Deepa's chest. Priya, incensed, says, "How can you be so rude to Kaku? It is not even true, what you said. That clinic was Baba's life. He would have found another way."

Amit says, "Let it be, Priya. Bina Kaki is going through a lot . . ."

True. In just one week, Bina has lost weight. Purple bruises bloom under her eyes as though someone had pressed hard with his thumbs. She never cries when awake—the girls wish she would—but every night she rouses them by sobbing in her sleep.

Now she tells Amit, "You, too—I must ask you not to visit us anymore. It will hurt the girls' reputations if a man keeps coming to spend time with them."

And Amit, baffled: "My visits will hurt your daughters' reputations? But I have been coming to your house all my life."

Bina's voice is firm. "It was different when their father was alive. We are now a house of only women. We cannot afford gossip."

Jamini draws a sharp breath. Priya's face flushes. Deepa shakes her head at them. *Ma is not herself. We cannot be angry, we cannot argue with her.* Jamini controls herself, but Priya is incapable of backing away from injustice.

"What are you saying, Ma? Have you forgotten how much Amit helped us after Baba's death? All the things he handled? The police, the coroner, the death certificate, the bribes. The hearse to bring back the body. We would never have been able to do it on our own."

Now Somnath: "Hush, child, calm down. We will discuss all this another time. Let us go, Amit, Manorama will be worrying."

Deepa watches the carriage disappear around the bend with apprehension. Cutting their family off from the Chowdhurys is the worst thing Bina could have done at this time, when they need support more than ever before.

Bina moves like a sleepwalker into the bedroom. The end of her sari trails on the floor, gathering dust. "Deepa," she calls. "Can you shut the windows? The light hurts my eyes. And rub some Amrutanjan on my temples. My head feels like it is going to explode."

Deepa rubs the balm into Bina's forehead, over the new worry lines. Twice in the last week Bina had fainting fits. Where is the efficient and indulgent mother Deepa has known all her life? The intrepid woman whose quick thinking saved their lives on the night of the riots?

Deepa has done something that would infuriate Bina if she found out. She has written to Raza. She had struggled hard against her longing, but in the end, she could not stop herself. She had to tell someone the things that were choking her, the sorrows and fears that she could not share with her family because they had enough problems of their own. She asked Raza to send his reply to the home of her friend Malini, the only one who has stuck by her through her misfortune. Malini was apprehensive about the whole affair. But finally she promised to keep Deepa's secret.

"What will happen to us now?" Bina whispers, startling Deepa out of her reverie.

Deepa does not know. The not-knowing terrifies her. She is not religious; still, she says, "We will pray to God, Ma. He will take care of us."

Bina's lips twist. "Which god should I pray to? The god who made the men of Calcutta go mad? The god who allowed your Baba to be butchered?"

Her words pierce Deepa like a spear of ice. My fault, all of it. If I had not cajoled Baba into taking us to Calcutta, he would be alive.

Deepa buries her face in her pillow. This way Bina, who has finally fallen into a fitful sleep, will not be wakened by her weeping.

❀

The sisters have divided up duties. Jamini cooks, cleans, goes to the bazaar. Priya sits in Baba's clinic all day, though so far no patients have appeared. Deepa stays with Bina, begging her to get out of bed, eat something, work on a quilt. She borrows old *Desh* patrikas from Malini and reads the melodramatic serials to Bina. But Bina pulls the cover over her head. Is she coming apart, the way she said she did when Nabakumar went on the Salt March? Deepa in terror pushes away the possibility. Just once in the evening she leaves her mother in Jamini's care, claiming she needs a walk to clear her head. She hurries to Malini's house, where almost every day Malini receives a letter from Sagarika, her new pen pal in Calcutta. Malini is a good friend. Though she is increasingly uneasy about this deception, she hands the letter to Deepa without berating her folly. She leaves Deepa alone to devour and then destroy Raza's words of consolation and friendship—and, recently, love.

Yes, Deepa is in love. The infatuation that would have died away in the course of time here has sent its roots, watered by tragedy and shared trauma, deep into her heart. She has no idea where it will lead. She only knows she cannot bear to give it up.

The sun has set over the shal grove in front of the Ganguly home by the time Deepa returns. She calls to Jamini, who has been cooking, to find out what there is for dinner. Jamini steps out from the kitchen, wiping her hands on an old, turmeric-stained sari, her eyes red with smoke because they have been using cheaper coal recently. Or perhaps she has been weeping. Deepa is afraid to ask.

A fortunate distraction: down the street comes Shibani Talukdar with two of her friends. Shibani's husband owns the grandest sari shop in the village. She is picky and prideful, but a staunch customer. Before the family's ill-fated journey to Calcutta, Shibani had ordered, for her daughter's trousseau, a quilt with twenty-one good-luck symbols stitched on it. That was why Bina had bought the silk thread from New Market. A tendril of hope uncurls in Deepa. Shibani's support would be most precious at this time when many neighbors have stayed away as though misfortune were an infectious disease. Deepa will request Shibani to talk to Bina, get her stitching again.

She smiles and joins her palms in a namaskar, but Shibani does not respond. From the other side of the street she shouts that she will not be needing the quilt after all, she wants Bina to return the advanced money.

Deepa tries to explain that her mother has already spent much of the money buying supplies, but Shibani will not listen. Her voice rises, her friends join in, neighbors peer avidly from windows. Jamini, too, enters the fray: "Is this the time to harass us, Shibani Mashi? Have you no shame?"

Faltering footsteps behind Deepa, Bina so weak she has to hold on to the doorjamb. But her tone is firm. "Return the money, Deepa."

This is a bad idea. Deepa fears it will encourage other customers to make similar demands. But Bina glares until she goes to the lockbox. Jamini helps her mother back to bed, then joins her sister. Deepa can hear Bina mutter, "They think our misfortune will taint the quilts. Maybe they are right."

In the lockbox is a stack of rupees, thinner than Deepa expected.

Jamini says, "Baba took out money for the clinic, saying he would replace it once Somnath Kaka gave him funds." Also in the box: three slim gold chains that Nabakumar gave the girls when each turned eighteen, and the necklace from Bina's wedding. Everything else has gone over the years.

Jamini's face is pinched with worry. "Will we have to sell these?" She wants Deepa the elder sister to reassure her. But Deepa can only say, Not yet.

Jamini's gaze flicks to the storeroom, where supplies are running low. She knows something, Deepa is sure of it. But when she asks, Jamini shakes her head.

Chapter 6

Jamini

*J*n the airless alcove that serves as a kitchen, she cooks rice and dal—the only items left in the storeroom—into khichuri for dinner. She has added more water than she should in order to stretch the meal. Even so, she will have to take money from the lockbox tomorrow. More women came to their house after Shibani left; they, too, wanted their advances back. Only a few rupees are left in the box. She hopes Priya will come home soon; she hopes the girl will remember the water spinach Jamini asked her to pick from the pond near the clinic. Jamini has used up everything edible in the pond behind their house. Not a single patient yet at the clinic. Jamini is unsurprised. Why would they trust their lives to an inexperienced girl? She hopes Priya will hurry. The cook-fire is dying, and Jamini cannot afford to add more coal. Maybe she can talk Priya into taking on a tutoring job. All those books she spent hours reading should be good for something.

She misses her father, levelheaded, generous, fair, the only one in this house who cared about her. She never got a chance to tell him how much she valued that. She remembers guiltily the wild wish she sent into the world on the day he died: *Let something change. Let something break. I don't care what. I don't care how.* Can wishes bring destruction? A stupid question. She pushes it deep into the dark space inside her.

If only Bina had not cut off ties from the Chowdhurys. Having Amit come by—even if he mostly mooned around Priya—would have made a difference.

A knock at the door. Her breath quickens. The village women say you can pull a man to you with love, if it is strong enough. Or maybe the Pir has finally turned his eye of mercy toward her. She straightens her wrinkled sari, thinks longingly of the pristine clothes of her past, puts on a winsome smile. But it is only their next-door neighbor, a young mother whom everyone calls Leela's Ma. She hands Jamini a bowl of potato curry, claiming she cooked too much. An untruth, but a kind one. Sometimes she leaves two-year-old Leela with them, saying she needs to run to the market. Jamini suspects it is because she knows the toddler will take Bina's mind off her troubles for a while.

Back from her walk, Deepa is outside at the well, washing her feet, taking a long time. Jamini peeks out and sees her sister staring at the moon, a glow on her face. Deepa is hiding something, Jamini is sure of it. Why do her sisters insist on keeping secrets from her even now, when they need to come together? No matter. Jamini will unearth Deepa's secret, just as she did Priya's.

❀

A few days before the trip to Calcutta, Jamini noticed Priya going into the storeroom. Priya did not see her; Jamini was changing sheets in the bedroom. Jamini could hear pots being moved around, boxes pushed out, then pushed back. When Priya left the house, Jamini went to look. In a while she found the loose brick. The space behind it was filled with silly things that Priya had scribbled over the years. Jamini did not bother to read them. She picked up the bangles that had been hidden under the papers, hefted them. Enough gold to keep a family comfortable for a year. She knew who had given them to Priya. Her heart twisted even as she tried to be happy for her sister.

She put the bangles back. She told no one. Now Priya's secret was hers, too.

❖

Dispirited disheveled Priya returns in the dark. Jamini is sorry but also annoyed. The girl would be better off if she admitted that she cannot keep the clinic going. Priya has forgotten the kalmi shaag. It takes all of Jamini's willpower to not scold her. A good thing Leela's Ma gave them the potato curry. They sit silently around the cheerless meal, a single lantern throwing shadows on the wall. Bina eats a few mouthfuls, but only because Deepa has said, If you do not eat, neither will I. Priya pushes her food around. Deepa swallows mechanically. Does anyone recognize how hard Jamini worked to create this meal out of almost nothing? She stores the leftovers carefully and hopes they will not spoil by morning. She hurries them to bed so that she can blow out the lantern and save on kerosene.

❖

Deep night. Jamini wakes to the sound of the door unbolting. Bina at the threshold, ghostlike in her widow's white. She steps out, moving with surprising speed. Jamini's heart thrashes around; she shakes Priya awake, whispers to her to get Deepa, runs to catch up with her mother.

"What are you doing, Ma? Where are you going?"

Bina stares ahead, eyes unfocused. She is sleepwalking. Deepa and Priya call to her. She hears nothing, twists away when Deepa puts an arm around her.

"We have to get her back home," Jamini says. "There are three of us. We can do it, even if she resists."

Priya hesitates. "I read in one of Baba's journals that it is dangerous to force sleepwalkers to wake up. They can go into shock. Let us just follow her."

Bina moves fast and unhesitant through the dark, as though on her way to a crucial appointment. The girls follow, stumbling. Past the familiar neighborhoods, the village school, the panchayat building, the fisher colony with its narrow paths.

"She is going to the cremation grounds," Jamini says.

Deepa begins to sob. "She is planning to drown herself in the Sarasi and join Baba."

Terror makes Jamini turn on Priya. "We should have stopped her right away. We should not have listened to you. It is not as though you are a real doctor."

Priya flinches. But she says, with admirable calm, "Let us stay close to her. We will grab her if it looks like she is in danger."

They flank their mother as she steps into the eddying water. Ankle, calf, knees, thighs. Jamini's teeth chatter. She is certain she will drown. Her sisters learned to swim in the village pond, but she was too ashamed of her leg to join them.

Waist-deep, Jamini panics, turns to flail her way back. But Bina has stopped. She stretches out her arms, she is holding something invisible, she is tipping it over.

"She is scattering Baba's ashes," Deepa says.

Bina pours until the pot in her mind is empty. She sets it afloat on the current. The girls tense, ready to grab her if she attempts to follow it. But she turns away and starts for home.

Gray dawn by the time they get to their neighborhood, Bina still sleepwalking. But she no longer struggles when her daughters grip her arms. Jamini trembles with exhaustion relief fear. What if Bina does

this again? She does not think she can endure it. They must buy a pad-
lock this very day and secure the door from the inside.

Early risers—farmers, milkmen, old folks out for their morning
constitutional—stare and whisper as they stumble homeward. Hair
askew, faces streaked with mud, saris flapping wetly about their legs,
look, look, the strange and unfortunate women of the Ganguly family.

Chapter 7

Priya

At the clinic Priya runs her hands over the stacks of medical books Nabakumar collected over the years. How many nights father and daughter stayed up reading them to each other. Earlier today the landlord appeared, sympathetic but firm. She must leave by month's end, a doctor from another village wants the space, unless she can pay the rent, and how can she? A bit of luck, the landlord said upon leaving. The man is willing to buy the equipment, the books.

She buries her face in the pages. They smell of her father; selling them would be like losing him a second time. She cannot stop the tears though she despises herself for them.

More rapping at the door. She snatches at her sari to wipe her eyes. Finally a patient—and look at her, sniveling.

But no, it is Amit's voice. "Priya? I have been thinking about you every day. I tried to stay away because your mother insisted, but I cannot."

She does not want him to see her ugly with weeping and no sleep last night and her stomach growling because all she ate since morning was leftover khichuri. She should pretend no one is here.

She opens the door, flings herself at him. His arms come around her, he lets her weep.

After she has poured out all her problems, he says simply, "Marry me."

Priya is dizzied and silenced by the suddenness of his words. She is not sure what they are, request or command or pragmatic suggestion. But when he kisses her, she is struck by how right it feels. His firm mouth, his warm cinnamon breath. Their entire lives arrowing toward this moment—how had she not seen it before? She leans into him, teetering on the sweet edge of agreement. O if she could remain like this forever.

He says, "I will take care of you, Pia."

Suddenly she is back inside the memory she has been running from all this while. Odor of blood and fear, dimly lit corridor, wounded men groaning, her father's blood-soaked bandages, the urgent entreaty of his eyes.

Take care of them, you said to me, Baba. I made a promise. I must keep it. Stand on my own feet like the women you admired: Matangini Hazra, Sarojini Naidu. Carry the flag of my independence. It is what you would have wanted for me. It is what I want for myself.

She pulls away.

"What's wrong, my sweet?"

She cannot articulate the emotions roiling inside: relief love reluctance resolve. She will have to tell Amit that she cannot let him solve her problems, she needs to do it herself. But not today.

She says, "Thank you, my dearest friend."

"Since when have we started thanking each other?"

"Will you give me a little time?"

Other men would have balked at such indecision. Amit says, "Take as much as you need."

He helps her close up, latching the windows, sweeping the floor, winding the clock. Then he says, "Can you come by sometime soon and check on Baba's health? He sits on the veranda all day, not talking. I know he misses Nabakumar Kaka—and you."

A pang goes through Priya. Distracted by despondence, she had not thought of Somnath, had not realized how deeply she missed him, too. "First thing tomorrow, I'll give him a thorough checkup."

She picks up the bag Jamini gave her for kalmi shaag. What is that for? Amit asks. She is embarrassed; then she shrugs. Is he not her best friend? If he is shocked by their financial predicament, he does not reveal it. He walks with her to the pond, helps her pluck a large armload. Soon both are splotched with mud and laughing.

It is the first time she has laughed since her father died.

❦

Jamini is delighted by the shaag and compliments Priya on her unexpected efficiency. Priya does not mention Amit. Why ruin this rare moment of sisterly amity? When she goes to the well to wash, to her surprise Deepa follows her.

"More women came today to cancel quilt orders. They want us to pay back the advances, but we have run out of money. One of them shouted that Ma's quilts would bring them ill fortune. No one disagreed. Mother heard the commotion and came out. She threw her gold chain on the ground and told them to fight over it like the vultures they were."

Has it come to this? The neighbors who welcomed them into their homes, setting out mats, serving them coconut sweets, are turning on them? Priya cannot imagine her levelheaded mother acting so rashly. The gold chain, Nabakumar's wedding gift to Bina, was the most expensive item they possessed.

Except the bangles that Amit gave me.

She feels guilty for not having told Deepa and Jamini about the bangles. But she is determined to return them, and her sisters will pressure her not to. That is also why she will not tell them about Amit's offer of marriage. They will grasp it as the perfect and immediate solution to their problems, they will keep pecking at her to agree. They will not understand why she must say *not yet*.

Deepa pats her arm. "Don't worry. I picked up the chain before any of them could grab it. I told them I will have the money for them in two weeks. I threatened to call the havildar if they continued to harass us, and after some more muttered curses, they left."

"You can sell my chain. I do not mind." A wrenching lie. She remembers her father placing it around her neck on her eighteenth birthday.

Deepa shakes her head. "Even if we sell all our chains, how long would the money last? No. We have to go, you and I, to New Market."

❀

At night the sisters weave their whispered plans. Deepa will persuade Bina to let her go, along with Priya, to Calcutta, carrying more merchandise. She will convince their mother that the city is safe, even if that is not quite true. They will stay in Somnath's house—Priya will ask him for permission—and visit the shop where they left the quilt. Perhaps it has been sold. Perhaps the shop will take a few more pieces. Jamini will stay at home and take care of Bina.

Priya worries that Jamini might feel left out, but she seems content. "I will keep the nosy neighbors away and make sure Ma is safe," she says. "That is the most crucial thing, after all. I will keep the door padlocked. I will not leave her alone even for a minute, especially at night. In fact, I will start sleeping with her from tonight, to get her used to it." She goes off to the bedroom, a spring in her step. This is what she has always wanted, Priya realizes: to be indispensable to their mother.

She herself is chagrined to discover that she is nervous about going back to Calcutta. "Should I ask Somnath Kaku to send a guard with us?"

Deepa yawns. "It is a short train journey. Just ask if the chauffeur can pick us up from the station."

"Good idea. He can go with us to the shop, too."

"Not necessary. I have friends in Calcutta who have offered to ac-company us."

"Friends?" Like Priya, Deepa has taken only one trip to Calcutta in her adult life. What friends could she have there? And how would they know about their plan?

Deepa lies still, pretending sleep, keeping her own counsel.

❀

At the Chowdhury mansion, Priya finds Somnath listless in a planter's chair on the upstairs balcony, hair unkempt, breakfast untouched. It hurts her how thin he looks, how old.

He scowls in response to her greeting. "Took you long enough."

She sets down her father's medical bag; she knows that in this mood Somnath will refuse to let her examine him. "I was waiting for your chess to get rustier so that I could beat you in record time."

A small gleam in his eye. "Dream on!"

"Words are cheap. How about we test that claim?"

A game that Somnath wins by a hair's breadth, then a hefty lunch served by a grateful Manorama, better fare than Priya has had in weeks. Priya tells him of Deepa's plan; as expected, Somnath offers them his house and car. Shefali will make sure they are comfortable and well-fed, he adds. Then he hands Priya the newspapers he has saved all these weeks for her. He warns her that the information in them is distress-ing; but it is important for her to know the truth.

It took more than a week for order to be restored in Calcutta af-ter the riots. The death toll was estimated at ten thousand; a hundred thousand people were left homeless. Several papers claimed that more Hindus than Muslims were killed; the Muslim League disagreed, claiming that Muslim casualties were equally high. The Congress Party blamed Suhrawardy, whom people were calling the Butcher of Bengal, for obstructing the police from doing their job. The Muslim League pointed out that the fault lay with the British: they had not deployed the army in time. Nehru blamed Jinnah for calling for a Direct Action Day. Jinnah pointed out that in most cities in India, there were only peaceful talks and marches. Numerous cases of rape were reported; no one knows how many were suppressed. As always in such matters, the poor suffered the most.

The photographs are the worst, streets filled with bodies, charred skeletons of buildings, slums where hundreds died in fires. Priya has to push away the papers after she sees the ruins of the Lichu Bagan bustee, where three hundred laborers were burned to death. But at least Calcutta is protected now, Somnath points out. Bengal has been placed under Viceroy's Rule; nine battalions of British and Gurkha soldiers are patrolling the city; Priya and Deepa should have no problems if they are careful and observe the curfew. He offers to send Amit along, but Priya tells him that Deepa and she wish to do this on their own.

Finally, reluctantly, Priya gets up. She must go to the clinic.

Somnath looks at her. "I know the situation there, Priya. I am sorry about it. But who will come to you unless you have a medical degree?"

His voice is not unkind, but his blunt words force Priya to face the truth she has been avoiding. She struggles with tears.

"That is why you cannot give up on your dreams of becoming a doctor," Somnath continues. "For your own sake—and to carry on your father's legacy. You must study for the Medical College entrance exams as you had planned. If you get in, I will pay your fees. If Bina objects, tell her it is a loan. You can pay me back after you start earning. No, no, do not thank me. It is the least I can do for my dearest friend."

Priya's body feels so light she might float away.

When she turns to leave, Somnath says, "Aren't you forgetting something? Didn't you come here to do your doctoring?"

Delighted, she takes out Nabakumar's stethoscope and examines him. Somnath seems healthy, but there is an irregularity in his heartbeat that troubles her. His blood pressure, too, is high. She prescribes a barbiturate, a brisk morning walk, less oily foods, a low salt diet, and bitter-melon juice.

"I hate bitter-melon juice."

She tells him not to whine. It is unbecoming in a man as old as him. "Walk downstairs with me. The exercise will do you good."

On the way down, Somnath stops at his safe and pulls out a fat envelope. "Your first doctor's fee."

There are too many rupees inside, but when she sees the love in his eyes, she cannot refuse. She touches his feet. He lays his palm on her head as her father would have done.

Chapter 8

Deepa

heir sisterly adventure starts well. They leave Ranipur early, get to the station, find window seats in a ladies' compartment of the train with enough space for their bundle of quilts. They point out interesting bits of scenery to each other, they share the rutis and molasses that Jamini packed. Priya, in high spirits, tells Deepa a secret: she is going to pick up textbooks for the medical entrance exam she intends to take. Deepa promises to support Priya when she informs Bina of her plan. Deepa is tempted to share her own less innocent secret: Raza is going to meet them at the house tomorrow and accompany them to New Market.

Before she can say anything, the train lurches to a stop at the edge of an empty field. No one knows what the problem is, though the three Hindu women sitting across from them mutter that it is probably Muslim hooligans; since the riot, they have taken to tying cows to railroad tracks. They stare accusingly at a Muslim woman sitting on the other side of the compartment.

Deepa stiffens, though she should be used to it. In Ranipur, too, remarks like this have grown common. In their own house, Bina curses the Muslims daily for Nabakumar's death. Levelheaded Priya tells her eldest sister that similar dialogues of blame must be occurring in Muslim households, but that does not console Deepa. Once she could not stop herself from telling her mother that the bullets that hit Nabakumar might have been fired by either side. Bina did not speak to her for three entire days.

The accusers grow louder. The Muslim woman shrinks into her corner. Deepa's face grows hot, but she takes a deep breath and allows common sense to wash over her. Their own situation—two young women traveling alone—is precarious enough without her drawing more attention. Fortunately the train starts, and the conversation turns to other matters; at the next station the Muslim woman moves to another compartment.

Somnath must have sent instructions; at the house, a solicitous Shefali serves them a lavish dinner, though neither girl can eat much. A few weeks ago Nabakumar had sat at this same table. When Deepa looks at his empty chair, her throat closes up. She apologizes, saying she is too tired to eat. Shefali nods sympathetically. As Deepa goes up to her bedroom, she hears Shefali telling the cleaning woman, Poor fatherless girls.

Her pity irks Deepa. What does Shefali know of violent bereavement?

When all is quiet in the house, Deepa tiptoes downstairs and dials Raza's number. They speak hurriedly, whispered words tumbling, urgency vibrating between them like a wire. How terrible this separation has been, how wonderful now to talk and, tomorrow, to see and touch, even if only fingertips, only for a minute. He calls her dazzling, intoxicating, more beautiful than the full moon—compliments that make her shiver with delight. She is too shy to speak the words she says silently each night: *life, heart, my only one.* They must not talk too long,

Shefali might come by on night patrol. When they hang up, she kisses the phone.

A sound behind. She swivels, heart thrashing. Priya on the staircase, her face furious with accusation. Deepa sighs. She will have to explain everything now. It will take forever because Priya always has questions. She walks toward her, practicing apologies.

Close up, Deepa sees that she was wrong. Priya is not angry, she is frightened—Priya the bravest of them all.

❊

In the morning Priya says, "Raza should not come to New Market with us."

"He knows the way of the city. He can bargain with the shopkeepers better than us."

"Ma will be most upset."

Deepa holds her glance. "Only if she finds out."

She is asking for a lot, she knows. She adds, "Last night I told Raza about your medical college examinations. He is bringing you his textbooks, old exam questions, even his notes. It will be a big help, and not just financially. Raza was one of the top students in his class. His notes are sure to be excellent. He has offered to go over them with you."

But Priya is a tough one. "Don't try to bribe me," she says.

At breakfast Shefali hovers, offering second helpings and encouragement. You look smart and businesslike, you will do wonderfully at New Market, your mother will be proud. Interrupted midsentence by a knock at the door, she frowns. "Who could it be at this hour?"

Deepa runs to the door. Raza, just as she has dreamed all these weeks, handsome and smiling in his kurta-pajama and skullcap. His eyes are electric with the memory of their shared night of trauma. She falls into their depths.

Priya thanks Raza stiffly for the notes and exam questions. "You must let me pay you for the books."

"Please," he replies, "don't say that. I cannot tell you how terrible I feel about your father's death. Helping you in this small way would help me, too."

A long moment. Then Priya nods.

Deepa, relieved, calls to Shefali to bring some more tea before they set off for New Market.

Shefali brings out a tray with cups, bangs it down on the table, and retreats to the kitchen without responding to Raza's thanks.

Deepa shakes her head. "What is wrong with her?"

Raza, rueful: "Maybe she thinks it is inappropriate for me to visit unchaperoned young ladies."

Deepa shrugs. "She makes great tea, so we'll forgive her old-fashioned views."

Raza agrees and takes a sip, but Priya stares frowning at the kitchen door.

❀

Standing outside New Market, Deepa is suddenly dizzy. She had not expected the memory of their last visit to sideswipe her with such force. From every direction Nabakumar's face smiles at her. Disoriented, she cannot remember where Agarwal's shop is. Priya, too, looks confused. Good that Raza is with them. He finds a coolie to carry the quilts, asks for directions, and masterfully navigates the labyrinth of the market. Is it less festive here today, people in clumps, frowning and whispering? But not just here; even on the streets the bridges the train station Deepa has noticed more policemen and gun-carrying gora soldiers driving up and down in trucks.

The entrance to Agarwal's is narrower than before. A collapsible metal gate has been drawn halfway across so that only a few people can enter the store at a time. Raza waits in the corridor outside with the coolie and the quilts while the sisters go in. Fortunately, the attendant recognizes them; when Deepa hands him the receipt, he brings out Bina's quilt from the back and tells them that Agarwal-ji liked it. "You're in luck—he's here today. Let me call him."

Plump Agarwal, holy mark on his forehead, prayer beads around his neck, compliments the authentic subject matter and the elegant stitching. He offers twice as much as what Bina would get in Ranipur. Deepa controls her glee and asks if he would like to see more pieces. He agrees, and she signals to Raza to bring in the bundle.

"Touch the baby quilts," she tells Agarwal. "You will see how soft they are. Ma has a special washing process—"

But Agarwal is staring, instead, at Raza's skullcap. "Who is this?"

Deepa, surprised: "Dr. Raza Khan is a friend of our family. He is helping us out because—"

Agarwal shoves all the quilts back toward them. "I will not do business with you. Muslims burned down my brother's store during the hartal. He barely escaped with his life. I do not want anything to do with you people—or your friends."

Flushed and distressed, Priya gathers up the quilts. But charming Deepa, who hates scenes and the people who create them, finds herself shouting at Agarwal. "On the night of the riot, while you were safely barricaded in your house, Dr. Khan was risking his life to attend to every wounded man who came to his clinic. He never discriminated between Hindus and—"

Agarwal cuts her off. "Our Hindu brothers would not have been wounded in the first place if those Muslim dogs had not incited the riot. Leave before I order my employees to throw you out."

Deepa wants to argue further, but Priya pulls her along. Agarwal's voice follows them. "Good Hindu girls like you should not be associating with men like him. Does your father know what you are up to?"

Is it the reference to Nabakumar, is it the humiliation? Deepa dissolves in tears. She tries to apologize to Raza, but he says, "It is my fault. I should have foreseen this. Ever since Direct Action Day, there is a lot of fear and hatred. On both sides." He lifts his hand to wipe away Deepa's tears, then notices the gawkers gathered around them and stops.

Deepa wants to go back and berate Agarwal. For the first time she understands why Nabakumar had left the family to join the Freedom Movement. Sometimes you have to fight injustice whether you win or lose. But Raza says, "He is not worth the trouble. Let me take you to another shop. Not as big or as fancy, but they might buy your quilts."

The women have learned their lesson. At the next store, a small one in the back of the market, with a photo of Goddess Kali hanging from a wall, they leave Raza around the corner and act perfectly the part of meek Hindu girls. The shopkeeper buys a few items. He offers less than Agarwal, but it is still more than village prices. He tells them to leave the bridal quilt with him. They can check back in two weeks to see if it has sold.

An elated Deepa invites Raza home for lunch.

Priya looks uncomfortable. "Shefali will not like it."

But Deepa cannot bear to be separated from him so soon.

❧

At the house, dour-faced Shefali bangs down an extra plate on the table and disappears. The food is cold. Deepa fills Raza's plate and chatters gaily to keep awkwardness at bay. Afterward she says, "Maybe Raza and I will take a little walk in the garden. The weather is so nice."

The afternoon has grown unpleasantly humid, but Raza says enthusiastically, "It is indeed! Maybe you can tell me the names of some of those beautiful flowers?"

"Of course." Deepa, abysmally ignorant of botany of any kind, is careful not to meet Priya's sarcastic glance.

In the garden Raza and Deepa walk decorously past the flower beds, but once they turn the corner, they hold hands. Under a fragrant kadam tree, they exchange their first kiss. They talk and talk, storing up love words for the dry weeks ahead. The hours pass like a single breath. Too soon it is time for Raza to go to the clinic, where he handles the night shift because Abdullah no longer likes being out after dark. Raza now lives in the quarters above the clinic where Nabakumar once stayed. "I've left all of your father's things as they were," he tells Deepa. "Maybe one day you can come and see them."

When Deepa comes back to the house, Priya looks pointedly at the clock. Deepa tells her that once he is done with work, Raza will phone the house and be happy to answer all Priya's questions.

"I have no questions," Priya says. The rest of the evening, she answers her sister in monosyllables. She and Shefali form a fine, morose pair. But they cannot dampen the delight in Deepa's heart.

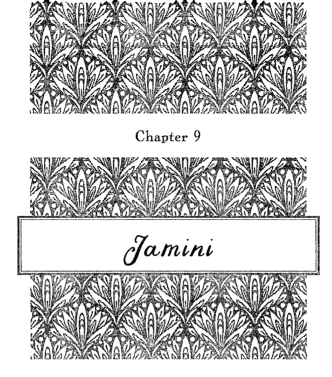

Chapter 9

Jamini

$\mathcal{L}$ ike the heroes of ancient tales, the sisters return triumphant, bearing treasures. Deepa hands Bina a purse fat with money and describes their adventures in colorful detail. Bina hugs Deepa, so clever, so courageous, and asks again what the shopkeeper admired most about her work. Jamini has not seen her this happy since before Nabakumar's death. Bina is less enthusiastic about Priya's decision to sit for the medical college examinations. But she says, with an effort at kindness, If this is what you have set your heart on, then go ahead, get it out of your system. She adds that it was smart of Priya to find secondhand textbooks. Jamini picks up a battered volume. The front page, which must have had the previous owner's name, has been torn out. She wonders if Priya did that, and why. Priya snatches the book away.

Bina claps her hands. "Stop dawdling, Jamini. Your sisters are hungry."

Jealousy sears Jamini. The last three days she dedicated every moment to taking care of her mother. She cooked her favorite dishes—pumpkin

with black chickpeas, masoor dal with green chilies—bargaining can-
nily with the grocer. She gave Bina the larger portions, and when her
mother said the food was good, Jamini was so happy that it did not
matter that she was still hungry. She massaged coconut oil into Bina's
hair, scrubbed her feet with a pumice stone, sang her favorite Tagore
songs. At night she slept lightly as though Bina were a newborn, waking at her least movement, her smallest groan. She rubbed her back
until she sank into slumber again. When she was sure Bina was asleep
and would not push her away, Jamini put her arm around her mother
and prayed to the Pir, *Make her love me as I love her.*

She had been sure it was working, that finally Bina saw the truth:
Jamini was the faithful daughter who remained behind while the others went off adventuring, the one she could count on.

Folly.

She serves the family—only rice dal greens in spite of the rupees
Priya had given her because she was unsure how Calcutta would work
out. Bina chides her. Couldn't you have fried a few potatoes at least for
your hardworking sisters? Jamini looks down to hide the resentment
in her eyes. But she need not worry. No one pays her any attention.

Deepa says expansively, "No matter. From tomorrow we will eat
better. And when we go back in two weeks, the owner will have sold
the quilts we left with him and will order more."

Bina kisses her cheek. "Such a brave girl, to go back to that devilish
city only for my sake."

Modest Deepa: "Happy to do this small thing for you."

Jamini catches Priya shooting her eldest sister a strange look. What,
she wonders, could it mean?

❀

After dinner Bina claps her hands. "Enough lazing around, girls! Clear
the dishes. Wipe the floor. Deepa, Priya, help your sister. Fetch the

chalks, Jamini dear. We must plan our next quilt. Deepa and Priya, you can watch, but don't disturb. Jamini, help me come up with something to astonish the Calcuttans."

Jamini, herself astonished, scrabbles for the colored chalks. *Thank you, Pir-Baba.* Until now Bina has done all the designing herself; she has allowed Jamini to complete only the tedious understitching. "How about a harvest scene?" she ventures. "You have never done one. It is sure to seem exotic to city people."

"Excellent idea." Bina outlines harvesters and drummers on the floor; Jamini adds dancers, goats, sheafs of rice. She suggests untraditional colors: oranges, purples, blues—the shades they bought for Shibani. The colors will surprise everyone, the quilt will be one of a kind. Additionally, they will save money because they already have the silk threads.

Bina frowns, considers, nods.

They color until the drawing gleams in the light of the lantern that Priya has lit. Where did the day go? Bina decides on a simple dinner, puffed rice mixed with onions and green chilies. "Jamini cannot possibly cook after doing all this work."

Priya makes the mix; Deepa brings out a box of sweets they picked up in Calcutta. Bina tells them to give Jamini an extra sweet. She tells them Jamini has a talent for designing. Once dinner is done, she says, "Come, Jamini. Bed. We have a lot of work tomorrow."

Jamini's chest expands with victory. She glances at Deepa to see how she is dealing with this dethronement. But Deepa has a faraway smile on her face. Is she relieved? Or is she distracted by something she considers more important?

Deepa and Priya unroll their mats along the edges of the room, careful not to smudge the drawing. The lantern is extinguished. Bina is asleep already. Jamini lies awake, unwilling to yield the triumphs of this day to oblivion. She hears Priya and Deepa arguing in urgent whispers. Something has happened during their trip to Calcutta. The old Jamini would not have rested until she dug it up. The new Jamini presses her cheek against her sleeping mother's back and falls into a dream. In it she is chosen as the most talented quiltmaker in Ranipur. The prize is a fragrant garland, and the person who places it around her neck is Amit.

Chapter 10

Priya

The examinations are in two months; Priya prepares day and night. She used some of the money Somnath gave her to pay the rent for the clinic. It is the perfect place to study, she thinks with wry resignation. No patients ever come.

But today, a surprise. Hamid the fisherman at the door, left hand wrapped in a bloody rag, an accident on the boat. She cleans the wound with Dettol, stitches it, hands him antibiotic pills, instructs him to rest. "Come back next week so I can check it," she says. "Don't worry about payment." But he offers her a bag of long beans from Fatima's vegetable plot. Then he stammers that he is very sorry for what happened to Nabakumar-babu. Her father's name, unexpected, hits her like a hammer. She bites her lip, unable to speak.

Hamid says, "He was a good man. He—and you—saved Fatima. If it hadn't been for the two of you, my little Bashir would not be here today. Anything I can do for your family, you let me know."

❦

One month left before the examination. Priya's days have grown more hectic. Patients are coming to the clinic, only the poorest ones, but still. She suspects Hamid has spread the word. Fortunately their illnesses, though sometimes severe because of delay, are mostly easy to cure. Little money comes in; the patients, if they can pay at all, do so in kind. Still, it boosts her morale. If the dead look down on the living—she would like to believe this—then Nabakumar, too, is pleased. Afternoons, Deepa stops by. She has decided it is safer for Raza's letters, written under a woman sender's name, to be addressed to Priya at the clinic. He is a prolific writer; each afternoon the mailman drops off a hefty packet. Deepa takes over Priya's desk to write her own lengthy reply, which she deposits into the squat red postbox down the road. It fills Priya with unease to be an accomplice, but she knows that otherwise Deepa will choose a more dangerous option. When the sun dips low, Amit, done with estate supervision, comes by. They share triumphs and frustrations, he quizzes her on Raza's notes, and yes, they kiss.

Each moment in between, she studies. She worries it is not enough.

❦

Every two weeks Priya must accompany Deepa to Calcutta; it makes her lose at least three days of study. They now supply four stores with quilts and embroidered bedcovers. Priya is amazed at how deft Deepa is at cajoling the best prices from shopkeepers, how meticulously she keeps track of profits and expenses. They have returned the advances to all the village women. Deepa made them sign receipts; those who could not write had to dip their thumbs in ink. She told them it was a good thing they canceled, the stores in Calcutta are keeping Bina so busy that she has no more time for village work. Her smile was like steel when she saw how they regretted their decision. Priya amazed remembers how flighty Deepa used to be: saris, jewelry, facials, new ways to braid her hair. Now, of the three sisters, she is the one taking most care of the family, fulfilling Baba's last request.

For Priya, the tensest times in Calcutta are the afternoons, when Raza shows up at the house. He no longer eats with them; even so, Shefali glowers as Deepa runs to the door, as they disappear into the far reaches of the garden. Against her will, Priya finds herself liking Raza. He spends a portion of each visit going over difficult test materials with her, though it shortens his time with Deepa. He is a good man, filled with the steadiness Deepa needs. Still, when she sees them together, Priya's heart constricts with fear. In this world, she has learned, goodness is not enough.

❖

Bina and Jamini have finished the harvest quilt, jewel toned and finely worked. Their best piece, it is sure to fetch a high price. Everyone is excited except Priya, whose examination is in two weeks. How can she afford the time this trip will cost her?

Deepa pulls her aside. "Listen, I can go to Calcutta by myself. I will take Somnath Kaka's chauffeur to New Market with me. This way, you can study in peace, and I can stay for a week and meet some shopkeepers in the Gariahat area."

It is true that the extra time will help Priya, true that it would be good for them to look for additional opportunities in the affluent Bengali neighborhood of Gariahat. But Priya fears that these are not the real reasons. What is Deepa planning to do in Calcutta when her sister's vigilant eye is not on her? But when Priya looks at all the chapters she needs to go over, panic drags her under. Pushing aside misgivings, she says yes.

Still, when it is time for Deepa to leave, she is torn. "Don't upset Shefali. She does not like Raza coming to the house. Especially this time, with you alone, it will be most inappropriate. Maybe I should go with you—"

Deepa pats her cheek. "Stop frowning, you crotchety old thing. If it makes you feel better, I will tell Raza not to come over."

"Really? You would do that for me?"

"Yes. Now you can study without worrying."

Blithe Deepa, waving from the bend in the long road that leads to the station; grateful Priya, waving back. Deepa is a good sister to make a promise like that. To give up seeing Raza just so Priya will not be distracted by anxiety. Priya thinks, I must do something special for her in return.

❖

Three days before the examination. At the clinic Priya gathers up her notes for the last time. She will leave for Calcutta tomorrow, just to be safe. Deepa will come along for moral support, even though she returned from the city only a week ago. After the examination, they will check on the harvest quilt. It has not sold yet, but perhaps this time they will be lucky.

Shuffle-steps outside the door. Jamini agitated, her breath uneven. "Manorama Pishi stopped by."

Priya is taken aback. Many people visit Manorama, but she rarely deigns to go to anyone's house. Why would she visit the Gangulys after Bina spoke so harshly to Somnath? Has Amit in his exuberance given away their secret? Might Manorama have come over with a proposal? She is at once excited and disquieted. She loves Amit, but she is not ready to be shackled by wifehood.

Then Jamini says, "Deepa is in terrible trouble."

Priya's heart flings itself about in her guilty chest.

Jamini gives her a knowing, accusing look. "We need to find her and warn her."

They look for her in all the places they can think of: Malini's house, the bazaar, the riverside where lately she sits daydreaming. But Deepa is nowhere, and then it is too late.

❖

The sky turns red, then violet, then black. Priya and Jamini wait on the porch for Deepa. They have not dared to approach Bina, who is raging inside.

"That Manorama thinks she's so much better than us, how dare she lie, how dare she accuse my Deepa of such shameless, shameless things."

Here comes Deepa walking like a song, her face bright with what she will do in Calcutta tomorrow, who she will see. Priya runs to intercept her, but she is too late. Bina at the flung-open door, calling and crying all at once, reaches out and grabs Deepa's arm, pulls her into the house, slams the door in her younger sisters' faces, locks it. She ignores Priya's and Jamini's entreaties to let them in. But they can hear her.

"Tell me it's not true, my dearest girl. Tell me what that woman accused you of is a lie. It hurts me to tell you this, she said in her prim-and-proper rich-woman voice, but you need to know what your daughter is up to. Our housekeeper Shefali tells me Deepa has been meeting with a man. A Muslim. At first it was in the house, but now they meet secretly in New Market."

Sweat prickles Priya's armpits. So that was what Deepa did when she promised Priya that Raza would not come over to Somnath's house. The chauffeur must have found out. Perhaps Shefali had instructed him to follow Deepa, Deepa who thought she was being so clever.

"I put that Manorama in her place," Bina continues. "Impossible, I said. My Deepa would never do such a thing, especially after Muslims killed her father. She is my most responsible one, honest and level-headed; she would never cause me such grief."

Deepa says nothing.

A long silence, then despair in Bina's voice. "It is true, isn't it? You did slink around behind my back with a Muslim. A Muslim, of all people. Have you forgotten what they did to Baba? Do you care nothing for him, for me? While I was blessing you for saving our family, you were ruining us all." She rallies. "No. It is not your fault, my innocent girl. That evil seducer set a trap for you, and you fell into it, believing all his sweet lies."

Priya and Jamini look at each other. Bina is giving Deepa a way out. There is still a chance for their sister.

Then Deepa's voice, frightened and entreating but resolute also: "It was not like that. Raza is a good man, better than anyone I have met. He only wanted to help. That is how he is. Baba could see that. He liked Raza when they met. Do you not remember how he risked his life to come and fetch us the night Baba died? Without his help, we would not have been able to see Baba one final time. Please let him come and talk to you. We love each other—"

A garbled yell from Bina, a roiling of furious words. Don't you dare bring up your father, you snake in my bosom, you don't deserve to say his name. The thwack of flesh on flesh. Is their gentle mother, who never raised a hand against any of them, hitting Deepa the most beloved? Bina's breath is a keening whistle; not a sound from Deepa. Priya bangs on the door, Jamini too, they are crying begging please stop please don't you will kill her.

The door flies open so hard, it crashes into the wall. Bina pushes Deepa out, panting. "Pack your things and leave. Now. I do not want you under my roof another moment."

Welts rise on Deepa's beautiful face, scratches mar her throat. She stares with unfocused eyes into the night. The outlines of the trees black on black are like outstretched claws. Where in this looming darkness, Priya thinks, can her sister go?

She must try again, though she has little hope. "Please, Ma, it is not like you think. Shefali exaggerated things, made them seem dirty. Raza has been a support to Deepa. We would never have sold the quilts without his help. Please forgive her."

Bina turns on Priya. "You knew all this time? You kept it secret from me? You could have prevented this disaster, and you chose not to? Stupid, wicked girl. I will deal with you later."

Now Jamini kneels and clutches Bina's sari. "I know you can't let Deepa live here anymore. But don't throw her out like this. Let her stay until morning."

"Never."

And clever Jamini: "If you send her away now, Deepa will be forced to go to Malini's house and ask if she can sleep there. There will be questions, she will have to explain, someone will gossip, the whole village will learn about this scandal. It will ruin Priya's reputation and mine as well."

Finally Bina gives grudging consent. "But no one is to talk to Deepa or give her any food. The two of you will sleep in the bedroom with me. She will sleep alone so she cannot corrupt you girls further, though I fear it is too late for Priya. Deepa must be gone before I get up. I do not want to see her face. Not tomorrow, not ever."

Slam of the bedroom door. Priya hears sobs. Beneath the armor of anger, her mother's heart is breaking.

❀

Later Priya tiptoes to the outer room and lies down next to Deepa. She touches her sister's swollen face, weeping soundlessly. She thinks of Deepa alone in the world. Deepa's arm comes around Priya, Deepa dry-eyed unrepentant having used up all her tears. She apologizes for getting Priya into trouble, for leaving her to bear the brunt of their mother's fury. In the uncertain light of the moon, she writes down Raza's number. "Call him when you come to Calcutta. He will tell you how to get in touch with me."

Priya presses a stack of rupees into Deepa's palm. When Deepa demurs, she says, "This is my doctor's fee from Somnath Kaku. Take it. Women without money are forced to make bad choices. I do not want that to happen to you." Her voice breaks. "Will I see you again?"

"Yes, I promise. Now forget about me and do well in those exams. I want to be able to boast that my sister is a doctor." Deepa forces a laugh. Priya thinks it is the saddest sound in the world.

When she wakes up, Deepa is gone. Priya stares at her bedclothes, Deepa who always scoffed at housewifely skills. Today the small pile of sheets is perfectly folded, the rush mat rolled tight.

❀

It is almost time for Priya's train. Yesterday the thought of getting on it had filled her with nervous excitement. Today she wonders only whether Deepa is waiting at the station, whether they can travel together one last time. She picks up her suitcase.

At the door Bina, shadow eyes, steely mouth. "Where do you think you are going?"

Priya is perplexed. They had discussed the train timings the day before. Bina had even wished her luck. "Calcutta. My examinations are the day after tomorrow, remember?"

"You are not sitting for any examinations. I have learned my lesson, trusting you. You will stay home from now on."

Disbelief rises in Priya, then desperation. "But I *must* take the exam. I studied so hard—"

Bina cuts her off. "You should have thought of that before you deceived me. I am getting you married before you do something worse. I will call on old Durga the matchmaker today. Not that I have high hopes for you, without any dowry. Perhaps a widower—"

Priya recourseless must turn to the one reluctant weapon left in her arsenal. "You don't have to worry about finding me a husband. Amit has asked me to marry him."

Bina's mouth falls open, Jamini is a study in shock. Bitter satisfaction pushes Priya to a half-truth. "And I said yes."

Regret fills her as she speaks. She had planned to accept Amit's offer after she became a doctor, caretaker protector equal to any husband.

Bina, still suspicious, dispatches Jamini to fetch Amit. Jamini drags her feet until Bina snaps at her to speed up. An endless, wordless age of waiting on the porch before Priya hears the familiar welcome hoofbeats. Amit flies around the bend on Sultan, Jamini white-faced in front clutching the saddle. It disquiets Priya, Amit's arm around Jamini. But how else could they have arrived so quickly?

Amit, her best, most dependable friend. If he knows of Deepa's disgrace, he does not reveal it. "Yes, I proposed to Pia and was overjoyed when she agreed," he tells Bina. His eyes twinkle at Priya, holding their secret. "We were waiting for the mourning period to end before asking your permission."

His words have doused Bina's anger. Perhaps all she wanted was good matches for her daughters. Still, she asks Amit, What if his family had a different kind of wife in mind?

"No such fear." Amit laughs. "Baba is fonder of Priya than he is of me." He adds that Somnath and he both want Priya to take her examination. "We would love for her to carry on her father's legacy—as surely you do, too. I can escort her to the city tomorrow—"

Priya interrupts. She would prefer to do this on her own.

Bina ponders awhile. Finally, grudgingly, she says she will allow it—but only if the engagement takes place as soon as Priya returns from Calcutta. After that, no more trips to the city for Priya until the wedding. Once she is married, Priya will be the Chowdhurys' headache, not Bina's. They will decide what she can or cannot do. Priya bristles at this statement, but she knows to remain silent. Bina ends by stating that from now on, Jamini will take charge of all business dealings. *She is the only daughter I trust.*

Words spoken in anger, aimed at Deepa as much as Priya. Still, they hurt.

At night Priya, sleepless in the dark, hears the shuffle of Jamini's feet. Jamini kisses her sister, she whispers congratulations. She is trying hard to be happy for Priya, but Priya feels her failure.

Jamini loves her, Priya knows this—just as Priya loves Jamini. The problem is they both love Amit more.

❀

In Calcutta Priya sits at her examination desk surrounded by young men; some ignore her, some fling condescending glances, some stare rudely and wonder aloud as to what she is doing here. She takes out pen and inkpot and thinks of the people who believe in her, Amit and Deepa and Somnath. Still, as the exam paper is handed out, the hall tilts dizzily and she has to shut her eyes. Then she remembers Nabakumar. *Baba, how you stepped into the rioting night because you believed that was what a doctor must do. Be with me.* Calmer now, she sees that the questions are not as difficult as she feared; she pierces through their tricky wording to what the examiners want to know. The patients in the test cases take shape in her imagination, she understands how they may be healed. The room recedes, she writes. When the bell rings she is satisfied.

Now anxiety for Deepa rises up to engulf her. Back at Somnath's house she paces, waiting for evening when she can phone Raza. Guilt-faced Shefali calls her to dinner; Priya ignores her; in any case she is too nervous to eat. To distract herself she picks up the paper. On the front page is an article about Sarojini Naidu. She is in Calcutta to give a speech on behalf of the Indian National Congress, whose first woman president she had been in 1925. Priya is drawn to her photograph: far-seeing eyes, uncompromising mouth, hardships etched across her brow. A simple khadi sari that she wears with dignity. A longing to see her—even if from a distance—shivers through Priya. But other duties must take precedence.

Finally after many attempts she gets through to Raza. He sounds out of breath, as though he ran up the stairs. Clearly distracted, he repeats himself as he gives her directions to a small eatery at the back of New Market. Deepa will meet her there early tomorrow, a short visit so Priya can return to Ranipur at the right time, without causing suspicion. When Priya inquires about Deepa, how she is doing, where she is staying, he only says, "She will tell you everything herself."

He does not remember to ask Priya how her examination went. That is when she realizes how stressed he is.

❀

At New Market Priya sternly orders the driver not to leave the car, then follows Raza's complicated directions into the maze of alleys. The shops grow smaller and dingier, the customers rougher. Men leer. Priya must don her blackest scowl. At the eatery she almost misses Deepa hunched in a corner, her head carefully covered, the end of her crumpled sari tucked behind her ears as is customary among Muslim women. Deepa, who was always dressed with elegance. Deepa, who had asked Baba to buy her lipstick. She pulls Priya to a curtained booth in the back with such practiced ease that Priya realizes this is where she used to meet Raza. Angry words rise to her lips—*besotted, deceitful, careless*—but she will not spend their brief time in recrimination. She holds Deepa's hands.

Deepa grips her back. Crumpled clothes, hair pulled into an untidy bun, the radiance that made strangers turn to look gone from her face. She speaks rapidly, as though time were water in a sieve.

"I am staying with Salima, the clinic nurse. Raza persuaded her. Paid her, too, I think. She is nice, but it is a small flat, she has two children. I am always in the way. Still, I am thankful I have a place at all. Raza is trying to find me a job. But I am not trained to do anything."

Priya is not good at lying. Still, she tries to encourage Deepa.

"Something is bound to turn up soon, you are so smart, people would be lucky to hire you."

A wan, unconvinced smile on Deepa's lips. She changes the subject. "Raza is the one light in my darkness. Every night after his shift he comes over and we go for a walk. It is the only privacy we get."

Fear sharpens Priya's tone. "A walk? Openly, the two of you?" Calcutta is in no mood, since the riots, to embrace cross-religious romance.

Deepa looks down. "Salima has loaned me a burkha. I wear it whenever I go out." She pulls an old black robe from her bag. "We decided it would be safer for everyone if people believed I was Muslim."

Deception upon deception. Deepa's house of cards is sure to tumble down at some point. What will she do then? And what will they do to her, the people whom she is tricking?

Time already for Priya to leave. She gets Deepa's address; they promise to write. Then she tells Deepa the news she has been saving, like dessert. Deepa claps, the shining back in her eyes for a moment. "Engaged! I knew Amit was in love with you. The two of you are perfectly matched, stubborn as rams. I wish I could be there to see your fights!"

But she will not see them. Nor will she see the engagement or later the wedding, not if Bina has her way.

Deepa, hesitant: "How is Ma doing?" Her unspoken question: Does she miss me?

Priya, who cannot lie, says, "Sometimes she weeps at night." Her silent answer: You cannot come back, not yet.

They say goodbye at a side entrance, far from where the chauffeur lurks. From the opposite pavement Priya looks back at Deepa, motionless in her black burkha, not smiling, not waving.

Baba, our family is breaking apart. You, then Deepa. Soon I, too, will be leaving home.

A red double-decker hurtles around the corner, honking as it screeches to a halt in front of Priya. By the time it disgorges its passengers and takes off, Deepa is gone.

Part Three

October–December 1946

❖

Season of goddess festivals, the months gentle and flowering, the music weaving through the air. Heat and dust recede, the rivers flex their muscles. But the sparks did not die. Now the crazy wind blows them across the land. Cities begin to blaze, entire districts combust. Now there is a new river of blood, and instead of music, cries of death. Worse than death. Laments of widows, tears of raped girls. A man prays and fasts, fasts and prays. Mutinies explode. The leaders of India circle each other, baring their teeth. Across the ocean a prime minister realizes that a prize is slipping from his grasp, it is about to crash to the ground. He must find a strategy, hand it over before it shatters, shift the blame.

The goddesses are Durga and Lakshmi, the rivers are Sarasi and Feni, the months are Kartik and Agrahan. The crazy wind sets afire Noakhali, sparks Magadh, Patna, Garhmukteshwar. Gandhi traverses the land, fueled only by prayer. Jinnah and Nehru search for chinks in each other's armor. In England Attlee worries about the transfer of power. Wavell is recalled. Pethick-Lawrence heads a Cabinet Mission to India; he recommends breaking the country in three. A name is heard: Mountbatten. 1946 is coming to a close. The wheel of change spins faster.

Chapter 11

Jamini

$\mathcal{T}$he planning for Amit and Priya's engagement is in full swing. Jamini watches Bina and Manorama battle each other with sword-sharp words. Bina insists that the ceremony should be held in the Ganguly home as a tribute to Nabakumar. Manorama has set her heart on having it in the courtyard of the Chowdhury mansion. She narrows her eyes. Where will they fit the extended family, the priests, the musicians, the servants carrying the betrothal gifts? And what of Kesto the cook with his assistants and their pots and pans. She has a point, though Jamini would never betray Bina by agreeing with her.

This is not a celebration, Bina says, only necessity. No guests, no gifts, no cooks either. "My Jamini is just as good a cook as your Kesto. She will prepare a simple meal for the six of us."

Jamini stares in dismay. She could never match Kesto, who has been cooking from before she was born. She imagines herself sweaty, crumpled, reeking of spices, while Priya looks like a princess.

But Amit, entering with clothes for the event, intercedes, holding up a gleaming yellow silk. "Look at this beautiful sari I got for Jamini, Bina Kaki. How can she possibly cook in this? We will have the ceremony here, no guests, but let Kesto bring the lunch. You can make the menu as simple as you wish." He pauses. "Has anyone thought about asking Pia, the most important person, what she wants?"

Priya smiles vaguely and says whatever the elders decide is fine. Jamini feels a stab of anger. Does the girl even appreciate Amit's concern? Then she is ashamed. Priya, distracted since her return, must be worrying about Deepa alone in the city. No one at home mentions Deepa, but she is always on their minds. Last night Jamini heard Bina calling Deepa's name in her sleep. The thin sound tightened its noose around Jamini, Jamini who is furious with Deepa and also terrified for her.

In her own nightmares, Jamini is lost in the black blind alleys of New Market, where she must soon venture alone.

Amit hands Jamini the yellow sari. She has never owned anything so soft, the orange-and-gold border a perfect complement to the yellow. She sends Bina a beseeching glance. Perhaps it works. Or perhaps it is Amit's smile—dazzling, irresistible—turned on Bina and Manorama. Bina mumbles her consent; Manorama, too, capitulates. The wedding must take place in the Chowdhury mansion, she warns Bina. "Do not give me a hard time then."

Bina sniffs. "Long time left for the wedding."

Now Amit hands Priya her sari, muslin-wrapped to keep it safe. Dawn pink embroidered all over with gold vines, a sari for a queen. Next to it, Jamini's looks garish.

The look on Amit's face, the tender uncertainty with which he asks Priya if she likes it, the blaze of joy when she says it is beautiful. How stupid Jamini has been to be charmed by the smile he offered her. It was only politeness for a relative by marriage, pity for a girl with a limp. Jealousy grasps her heart in both its fists.

As Amit is leaving, Jamini says, "Ma wants me to go to New Market from now on. I am happy to do it but—" Her voice falters, her eyes flicker helplessly. "Perhaps, just the first time, someone could go with me?"

And Amit, chivalrous as she had hoped: "I will take you. I do not think anyone will object, since I am your brother-in-law-to-be." Bina nods assent. Manorama is thin-lipped and silent. Jamini does not look at Priya.

Later when she is alone, Jamini goes to the almirah where Priya has put away her sari. She takes it out, careful not to disturb the folds. She jabs Bina's embroidery scissors into the part that will be tucked into the waistline of the petticoat. On the day she wears it, Priya will not notice the tiny hole, but Jamini will know. She will know the sari is no longer perfect, and it will give her bitter satisfaction.

❀

On the train to Calcutta, the picturesque Bengal countryside dances past Jamini in vain. Dark tamaal trees, thatched huts emerald with pumpkin vines, a cowherd playing a flute, a line of women balancing pots on their heads. She sees only Amit studying the sheaf of papers Somnath has given him to pass on to Munshiji. His soon-to-be-married status has made Amit newly responsible. His forehead creases as he rereads a page. Jamini wants to smooth away his frown.

You are a fool, Jamini.

There was thunder and lightning on the day of the betrothal. In spite of umbrellas, the Chowdhurys were drenched as they hurried from their carriage into the Ganguly house. But Manorama had planned well; behind them a servant brought engagement clothes in waterproof canvas bags. Manorama requisitioned the bedroom so they could dress. Amit emerged regal in his cream silk tunic, a lovely complement to Priya's pink, everyone said. Diamond buttons at his throat, rain-curled hair. During the ceremony he held Priya's hands, slipped on the bangles that Jamini had discovered in the storeroom. Priya must have returned them to him for the occasion. Now they were hers legitimately, another secret snatched from Jamini's grasp.

The train approaches the city, the swaying green of rice fields giving way to brick warehouses and factories spewing smoke. All of a sudden Jamini remembers her last fateful trip to Calcutta, Baba laughing at her as she moved from window to window, unwilling to miss anything.

Priya gave Amit a ring with a small ruby, his birthstone; she had sold her chain to the village goldsmith for it. Jamini had waited for Bina to scold her for the extravagance, but Bina said, It is good, the Chowdhurys should not think we are cheapskates. How long Amit held Priya's hands after the gift exchange, even after the elders finished throwing holy rice on their heads. *I will cherish this ring until the end of my life.* Finally Jamini could not stand it any longer and brought them platters of sweets. *Eat, eat.* Then she had to watch while they fed each other, as was the custom.

The chauffeur is on the platform, punctual, polite as ever. At the house, Shefali fawns over them, bringing hot tea and the rose sandesh Jamini enjoyed last time. Hard to believe that the two servants had betrayed Deepa like that. Perhaps they considered it not betrayal but duty. Jamini knows it is easy to confuse such things.

After the ceremony, Amit gave Jamini gold earrings in the shape of birds. Because you sing so well, he said. Aren't they pretty, Priya said. Will you sing something for Pia and me, he said. Jamini wanted to grind the earrings into the mud of the yard, to run into the storm. She smiled and said thank you and sang "Amaar Poran Jaha Chay."

You are the one my soul longs for.
In this entire world, there is no one else for me.

Everyone clapped; even Manorama said she had a voice like honey. At New Market, Amit and Jamini follow Priya's directions; still, they get lost twice. She laughs a lot, some would think from embarrassment, but in actuality it is joy. Once she stumbles and Amit grasps her elbow. She wants to stumble again, but she does not want him to grow suspicious. She has worn the bird earrings; Amit says they look very nice. *Very nice* is a lukewarm compliment but she will take it, beggars can't be choosers.

When the ceremony was over, Priya took off her jewelry. Manorama had given her a seven-layer necklace from her own wedding dowry. Somnath had given her diamond earrings and gold anklets with bells. She handed them all to Amit to keep in their mansion, where they would be safer. But he would not take the bangles. Wear them, Pia, just as I'll wear my ring, so people will know we belong to each other. Priya tilted her stubborn head. Jamini could have told Amit what she was thinking. *People do not belong to others. We are each our own.* But then Priya said, Very well.

At the store Jamini astonishes herself with her acumen and charm, her ability to bargain. She had thought only Deepa possessed these gifts.

"I hope one of your other sisters comes next time," the shopkeeper jokes. "You are too good at this." He looks at Amit curiously.

They speak both at once.

"This is my friend."

"I am her brother-in-law-to-be."

The shopkeeper raises his eyebrows. Jamini's face prickles with embarrassment.

❧

Afterward Amit asks if there is something she wants to do before they head back home. This is the moment Jamini has been waiting for. She tells him.

"You want a funny movie or a scary one?"

She should choose laughter, it would be a good break from her life. "Scary," she whispers.

Inside the Globe Cinema, air-conditioned breezes caress Jamini, the velvet chair holds her lovingly. It is a weekday afternoon, the auditorium is almost empty, they have an entire section to themselves. Amit buys popcorn, which Jamini has never tasted. She sucks butter and salt from her fingers like a child and watches him smile.

When he had refused to take the bangles back, he could have just handed them to Priya. Why did he have to hold her hands again, to slip them on carefully as though she were made of glass? Afterward he kissed her palms. Jamini waited for Bina to reprimand him, but she was looking elsewhere.

The film is *Leave Her to Heaven*, the story of two cousins who fall in love with the same man. O irony. Why of all movies is this one playing in Calcutta now? The immense figures fill the screen with their exotic American customs. At first Jamini thinks it is a romance; then it turns dark. The heroine, a wife now, grows madly jealous of anyone close to her husband. She allows his brother to drown, she accuses her cousin of plotting to steal her husband, she writes to a lawyer friend that her cousin and husband are planning to kill her. Her last act is to take sugar laced with arsenic so that her death will be blamed on them. It is: he goes to prison, she has her revenge.

Jamini had planned to act frightened, maybe shrink against Amit's seat. Surely then he would put an arm around her. But by the time the heroine dies, she is sobbing in earnest. The woman's hatred and jealousy were the real poisons that killed her, she thinks. She closes her eyes, not wanting to watch anymore.

Amit pats her shoulder. "Look, look, it is not so bad. The husband went to prison, but now he has been released. The cousin was waiting faithfully for him, and now they are happy together." But she cannot stop crying. How well she knows that jealousy, that wish for a rival to disappear so that one might fully possess what one longs for.

Outside, Amit says, "You are too gentle a person, Jamini. Too innocent for this world. You must learn to be tough like Priya. See how she goes full force after what she wants?"

O Amit, you are the innocent one. If only you knew.

"Come, let me buy you ice cream."

She has never eaten ice cream, so he chooses his favorite flavor for her. She does not tell him that the cold hurts her teeth. Bittersweet of chocolate on her tongue long after they return to Ranipur, to Bina's praise, to Priya of the glittering bangles watching her with creased brow.

Chapter 12

Priya

$\mathcal{E}$ach morning she escapes to the mansion, where Manorama is teaching her how to become a proper daughter-in-law of the Chowdhury household. She had hoped that her engagement—and the fact that she has let the clinic go as Bina had demanded—would make her mother happy. But an inexplicable coldness continues to emanate from Bina, so Priya is thankful for this refuge.

Priya's time at the Chowdhury home is more pampered holiday than rigorous training. A brief visit to the kitchen where she watches Manorama discuss the menu with Kesto, a beauty treatment or two, a head massage with perfumed coconut oil, then off to chess with the eagerly waiting Somnath. The three eat lunch together. Most days Amit cannot join them; he is taking his estate management duties very seriously.

"It is because he is going to be a married man," Manorama declares, "and perhaps a father soon after, God willing."

Priya smiles. She does not plan to have children until she finishes medical college and establishes a practice. But she does not tell anyone this. Why invite arguments before they become unavoidable?

Baba, I think you would agree that finally some wisdom is seeping into your daughter's stubborn skull.

❧

In the afternoon while the elders nap, Priya reads the papers. Somnath started having them sent regularly from Calcutta after Nabakumar died. Perhaps he felt guilty that he had not paid attention to the news earlier, had not known enough to warn his friend to stay away from the city during Direct Action Day. Over tea he and Priya discuss events, though sometimes they do not agree. He believes in Nehru and Vallabhbhai Patel, their pragmatic approach to power; she is unwilling to relinquish Gandhi's vision of a united India, utopian though it might be. The papers are guardedly optimistic about a possible separation that will satisfy Hindus and Muslims and give autonomy to both Congress and the Muslim League. The new nation will be called Pakistan, land of the pure.

But there are disturbing rumbles, a riot here, a burning there. Women abducted. Men shot. Already, people are taking precautions in case things get worse. The rich and canny exchange mansions in Dacca or Lahore for garden estates in the Calcutta suburbs or stately residences in Delhi. The less fortunate abandon generations-old dwellings and make their way across the border—or where they think the border will be, because no one quite knows—their possessions reduced to the bundles on their heads. Bus owners and lorry drivers grow fat on the hopes and fears of passengers; people perch precariously on the tops of speeding trains.

An uneasy time. Priya wonders how much worse it will get before it gets better.

❊

When the vermilion ball of the sun grazes the treetops, Amit comes cantering home virtuous and sweaty. He is spending a lot of time outdoors; Manorama complains that he is getting sunburned. Priya thinks he looks dashing with his bronzed skin and the new mustache that he has decided to cultivate so that he will look formidable and husbandly. After tea, Amit and Priya walk to the river. He asks about her day, but she has little to report and prefers listening to his adventures: figuring out why a field is not yielding the usual amount of rice, determining whether he should reduce taxes because a tenant has been ill. It is tough to make decisions that affect lives, Amit says. Priya agrees; soon she will have to make life-and-death choices about patients. She likes it best when she and Amit walk silently hand in hand, listening to the waves. She wishes she did not have to return home to Bina's displeasure and Jamini's scrutiny.

❊

Here comes Kashiram the postman, sweating in the airless afternoon.

"Didimoni, for you." He examines the large envelope curiously before handing it over. He is used to delivering Deepa's letters to Priya, but this one is different. Official. Her hands shake as she takes it. She knocks on Somnath's door, too nervous to open the letter on her own. She is certain she did well in the examination. Even so.

Somnath touches the letter to the framed picture of Goddess Durga on his wall, opens it carefully. Then he looks up, eyes mute and bewildered.

She knows. But how can it be? She checked her answers afterward. Every one of them was correct.

"They were unfair," he says in low, furious tones. "We will contest it. I will hire the best lawyer in Calcutta. We will make them dig up your paper and show it to us."

She sits down heavily on his bed. "It will do no good, Kaku. Even if they are forced to allow me to proceed to the next stage, they will surely fail me during the oral exam. There is no way to gainsay that. This is the end."

She weeps, she does not know for how long. How to accept the explosion of the one dream she has had for as far back as she can remember? How to admit that she cannot keep the promise she made to her father, *I will take care of the family*?

A sturdy arm comes around her, holding her tight. Lost in grief, she has not heard Amit enter.

"Hush, dearest. We will find a solution, one way or another."

She is the kind of woman who prefers solving her own problems, but today she sags against his chest.

He takes her home on Sultan, uncaring of village gossip. He asks her to wait outside while he breaks the news to her family. Sultan nuzzles her face, whickering. She leans against his warm, comforting flank. She hears Bina's voice, raised sharply in a question, and Amit's low, unhurried response. When Amit calls her inside, Priya steels herself for Bina's rebukes. But Bina only says she is sorry things did not turn out the way Priya hoped. Jamini, too, murmurs consolations. This unexpected kindness makes Priya weep again. Bina's arms come around her, awkward at first, then firmer. It is something she has not done since Nabakumar died. Priya collapses against her gratefully. "Don't distress yourself, daughter," Bina says, her voice confident and maternal. "All will turn out fine. Jamini, make your sister some tea."

What could Amit have said, Priya wonders, to work this magic?

❀

The day is gray and rainswept, a lone mynah calls from the eaves. Shock and an attack of gout have confined Somnath to his bedroom, so they meet there to map the future, now that Priya's plans have crumbled like mud walls in a monsoon. It takes Bina, Manorama, and Amit only a few minutes to reach a decision: Amit and Priya must be married as soon as possible, a simple ceremony, a few guests. They decide this with such alacrity that Priya suspects they have discussed it among themselves already. Was this what Amit said to calm Bina yesterday? This possibility bothers Priya, it makes her feel like a child.

Here is something else that troubles her. With all her heart she loves Amit. But she had intended to come to her bridal bed bearing success like a gift, not as a beggar maid from some outdated fairy tale.

Can no one understand this?

She tries to hide her agitation, but she is no Jamini. Amit reaches over to clasp her hand. "This is not the end of your dreams, Pia, just a deferment. In a year—some say sooner—India will become independent. The British administrators of the Medical College will return to their own country, leaving things in the hands of Indian doctors. They will understand how important it is to welcome women into this field because so many Indian women refuse to be treated by a man. In two years, you can take the examination again. You are sure to be successful."

Manorama says, "You will have another advantage then. The examiners will think twice before they interfere with the results of the daughter-in-law of the Chowdhurys."

Priya cringes. Manorama means well, but Priya wants her success to be the result of her work, not her in-laws' influence.

"Meanwhile," Amit adds, "you can reopen your father's village clinic."

Bina says, "You are lucky that Amit is so supportive."

Priya admits the truth of this. But two years in a village clinic, stitching up cuts and prescribing cough medicine, seems like a lifetime. And what if there is a baby? How would Priya undertake the long hours of training in Calcutta, the overnight duties? She feels her dream slipping further away.

Certain of Priya's consent, Amit, Manorama, and Bina are orchestrating details: when and where the wedding should take place, who must be invited and who may be ignored, which purification rituals must be observed to shorten the yearlong bereavement period. Jamini, blank-faced, examines her nails. Only Somnath looks at Priya. Then he says, "I am delighted to welcome Priya into our family, but I do not want to rush the wedding. I am still mourning my best friend's horrifying death. I sense Priya is, too, and maybe the rest of you as well. I wish to observe the full bereavement period. Then I will conduct a proper wedding, with the rituals and ceremonies that my only son deserves."

Everyone looks surprised, but the usually mild-mannered Somnath has spoken so definitively that they hesitate to contradict him. Priya sends him a glance of deep gratitude. For the moment, he has saved her.

All the way home, Bina grumbles at the postponement of the wedding. Jamini keeps her own counsel. But Priya's heart sparkles. She does not know what the future holds. However, uncertainty is better than the definitive click of a door closing.

❈

The next day at chess, Somnath says, "With all my heart I want you as my daughter-in-law. But I cannot bear to see your dream snuffed out. I want you to try for admission elsewhere. All the medical colleges in India will have similar prejudices toward women applicants. You must apply abroad. Do it as soon as possible. If you get in, I will pay your expenses."

Abroad? Priya has never dreamed such a thing. She feels the world opening for her like a flower. But what about Amit?

"Amit loves you," Somnath says. "I am sure he will understand. Besides, you can get married before you leave."

"Didn't you want a traditional wedding with all the rituals and ceremonies?"

"I only said that because they were pressuring you. You know me—I hate grand affairs where I am forced to wear heavy, itchy clothes and greet hundreds of people whose names I can never remember."

Game abandoned, they start planning. She will not apply to British medical colleges; that would be a betrayal of her father. Europe would be problematic because of the language difference; also, everything there is in disarray after the World War. America, Somnath says, is the right place. Socially advanced, more accepting of women, and friendlier to India.

Priya remembers snippets of conversations with Nabakumar. "Didn't Franklin Roosevelt demand that England should give India her independence? I think he and Churchill had a big argument about that. And America has been a sanctuary for several of our freedom fighters."

"It sounds perfect," Somnath says. "What are you waiting for?"

❀

Priya asks Bina for permission to join Jamini on her next trip to Calcutta. Somnath and she have come up with a good excuse: he wants an expensive Kashmiri shawl, and he trusts only Priya to choose it for him. Priya braces herself for cross-questioning, but Bina, gentle and permissive nowadays, says only, "You must do what your future father-in-law wishes." Jamini is more suspicious, but Priya smiles at her with bland innocence.

At night in Somnath's Calcutta house, Priya calls Raza for news of Deepa. But no one picks up the phone. At midnight she gives up, she needs to be rested for tomorrow's adventure, but she is filled with foreboding.

After the driver takes Jamini off to New Market, Munshiji hails a taxi and accompanies Priya to a tall white building on Chowringhee Road, home of the American Library. He waits in the lobby; Somnath has said Priya must appear independent, Americans like that. Sweaty-palmed and short-breathed, she goes upstairs to ask Mrs. Avery the librarian about medical colleges. But she is distracted by the books, shelves upon shelves, over a thousand books, and here is the medical section, so many shiny bound volumes, so much knowledge waiting to be drunk. She runs her hands over the spines in envy and delight, and Mrs. Avery, walking up, observes her face and smiles. *You love books. I do, too.* They get to talking: Priya forgets her awkwardness, she trips over her English words but does not care; Mrs. Avery's accent is strange, she has not seen many Bengali women up close, but she understands what Priya wants. She pulls books off the shelves, she flips through pages, points finally to an article.

"You should apply to the Woman's Medical College of Pennsylvania. You will feel more comfortable there than in coeducational institutions, which only admit a few women anyway. The Woman's College has a three-year program, it would suit you better than spending the traditional four years abroad. Additionally, they welcome foreign students. Look, an Indian woman has graduated from there already."

Priya stares at the photograph of a woman in a sari with a large nose ring, her hair tied back in a braided bun. She looks no older than Priya, Anandibai Joshee who graduated in 1886. If she could do it more than half a century ago, maybe Priya can, too.

The good news, Mrs. Avery says, is that Priya will not have to take an entrance exam. Instead, she must write an application letter in which she explains her education, her medical experience, her source of funding, and the reason she wants to become a doctor. "You will have to convince them that you will make a fine physician. That you will not give up halfway, as women sometimes tend to. Can you do that?"

Priya nods, but she is unsure. Why would the professors—in photos of the college they are stern-faced and bespectacled in their long dresses—care about the dreams of a girl from a small Bengal village?

Mrs. Avery says, "Maybe you can talk to me about what you want to write. Let us start with why you want to be a doctor." She leads

Priya to a table in a corner. Behind her tortoiseshell glasses, her eyes are sharp but kind.

Priya begins hesitantly, but then it spills out, her longing, her love, the father who was her inspiration, her little village, the clinic where she worked with him. How together they saved lives, how he died so suddenly and meaninglessly, how she is doing this for the both of them. "If I get the right training, I can help thousands of women, un-educated, poor, who would never go to a male doctor, women who are dying . . ."

Mrs. Avery wipes her eyes. "Write what you told me. Write from the heart. I think your story will persuade them."

❀

In the evening Priya tries Raza's number again. And again. Tomorrow they leave for Ranipur. If she cannot contact him tonight, she will not know how Deepa is faring. When she has almost despaired, there is his voice, tired and harried; she is afraid to ask why. She only tells him that she and Jamini want to meet Deepa in the little New Market eatery at nine tomorrow morning. He agrees to pass on the message.

Now Priya retreats to her bedroom to write her letter. She pours into it her determination her anxiety her hope. All her stories about working with her father. She is honest to the bone. She seals the letter. Now it is in the hands of the universe.

Suddenly parched, she decides to get water, but Jamini's door is open. Seated on her bed, she waits to accost Priya.

"What are you up to? You did not come all the way to Calcutta to buy a shawl. What were you doing all this time in your room?" Her voice softens. "Tell me. I promise to keep it to myself." She cajoles until Priya gives in because a part of her longs to share her dream.

Jamini does not seem displeased. "How about Amit?" she asks. "What will he do if you get accepted?"

Priya does not want to discuss Amit with Jamini. But Jamini stares at her until she says, "In that case we will get married before I leave. Somnath Kaka said so."

"Oh." A flat sound. But then Jamini leans forward and gives her a kiss. "I wish you all success, little sister. I know how much this means to you. And don't worry, I will keep your secret. I will—" She breaks off, suddenly businesslike. "It is late. We should go to bed. We have to get up early to meet Deepa."

Priya thinks, Will I ever understand this sister of mine?

Chapter 13

Deepa

Crunched together in the narrow, curtained booth in a dark corner of the greasy little eatery, Priya, Jamini, Deepa. She chose it because it is farthest from the cash register, out of earshot, she hopes, of the young man on duty today. Already he has been staring with too much curiosity at the three women so similar to one another in height and build but so different in clothing: two saris, one burkha.

In the dark booth Deepa lifts her veil but leaves her burkha on. She does not want her sisters to see Salima's salwar kameez too large on her, does not want to tell them she had to put away her beloved handloom saris, the frowns of the women in the building when she wore them.

Lukewarm tea in cracked cups. No money to spare for snacks. Her stomach growls; she had to leave Salima's flat before breakfast was ready to get here on time. She does not blame her sisters; they have a train to catch. Proud excited indignant they are telling her their news: Priya was made to fail the exam unfairly, she is trying now for America, she might be marrying soon; Jamini is helping Ma with new designs, the New Market shopkeepers like her, they joke with her and give her good prices. Deepa commiserates congratulates wishes them the best of luck. She means it—how can she not? She loves her sisters. But their lives have moved on. The Deepa-shaped hole in them has been covered over the way scum takes over a pond until one forgets there used to be shining water underneath.

And her life: How can they, sleeping secure in their own home, imagine it? She offers them half-truths out of love, out of pride, out of the fear that they will say *you brought this on yourself.* She has a job at the Muslim League office, thanks to Raza. She writes the speeches the leaders make, she pens the slogans the workers paint on walls. She is efficient, she works hard, the office people like her, they are kind. She does not tell her sisters that everyone thinks she is Salima's cousin Aliya from Burdwan who came to visit and liked the big city so much that she stayed on. That the political mood in the office grows more militant daily, that she makes too little money, that Raza must still pay part of her rent. Lying in her narrow bed in Salima's tiny flat in the storeroom that Salima emptied out for her, she sometimes feels she is suffocating.

Fortunately time runs out before Jamini and Priya can pick out the holes in her story, before they can ask her the question to which she does not have an answer. *Where is this leading?* The three women grip hands across the sticky table and promise they will keep in touch. Deepa leaves first so she will not be late for work. No, it is so that she will not have to watch her sisters depart, so that she will not be the one left behind.

❀

The Muslim League's office, a crowded room in a Park Circus alley, is filled with chatter and friendly smells: steaming tea, roadside pakoras.

On feast days, the richer members bring biriyani, cutlets, seekh kebab garnished with onions and green chilies, halal of course. Deepa fills her plate with other things but carefully, so no one notices her not eating beef.

The League is mostly men, though luckily for Deepa there are women, too, because all must work for the cause of independence. Today kind and motherly Zaahira beckons to Deepa to sit by her in the alcove where the women work. Deepa manages to pick up two pakoras; they will have to do until lunch break, when she will run back to Salima's flat and eat the breakfast that she hopes Salima has left for her. Soon she grows busy writing a speech for Aminul Miah, a militant member of the League, to deliver tomorrow at Islamia College.

When Raza enters, Deepa feels it even with her back to the door, his glance like a cool breeze. He will take his time to cross the room; he has risen high in the organization and must greet everyone, must check on important correspondence, handle emergencies, and answer questions before he can walk to the women's area with an assalamu alaikum. They have kept their relationship secret in the office. Deepa's coworkers know only that Salima from Raza's clinic asked if he could find a job for her cousin and Raza helped. People approve of Deepa because she is quiet and useful and does the tedious jobs. She keeps her burkha on—even the veil—with charming small-town modesty. Best of all she expresses no opinions, and who does not like that in a woman?

Today, though, Deepa struggles. One of the men is late, he comes in cursing the idiot Hindus who blocked his road. They were transporting materials to build a pandal for the upcoming Durga Puja, the back of the lorry fell open, poles and tent canvases all over the road; it took the dolts forever to clean things up. It will only get worse, someone else says, until the celebration is over, hordes traipsing across the city to gape at heathen images. Others add comments and complaints. Some make fun of the Durga idol. A female who stands on a lion, battling a bull-demon? Preposterous.

"This is why," Aminul hisses, "we must have our own country where such haram practices are forbidden. My friends in Noakhali have been pushing hard for it. They have the right idea. Here in Calcutta we are a bunch of wimps."

The hatred in his voice makes Deepa stiffen. She has always loved Durga, a no-nonsense goddess who does not wait for a man to solve her problems. In Ranipur they would be cleaning the Durga temple now, decorating the steps with alpana symbols: flowers birds elephants butterflies. Priests would polish brass platters and bells, lamps that held a hundred wicks. Prayers, plays, songs, a feast sponsored by Somnath, khichuri and fried brinjals served on banana leaves. Why would people hate such a happy celebration?

Her throat aches with loneliness. Can a man—even Raza, whom she loves with all her heart—make up for the loss of culture, family, community, generations of tradition woven into her blood? Perhaps it is not too late, perhaps she can go back and beg Bina's forgiveness.

No.

"Are you coming to evening prayers, Aliya?" Zaahira asks. It is Friday, when the entire office goes to the Masjid-e-Mohammadi close by to take part in the Maghrib at sunset. Deepa always joins her co-workers in the ladies' section. At first she was terrified about making a mistake, but Salima made her practice over and over, and now she no longer has to think. Stand, kneel, bring the forehead to the ground, turn the head side to side blessing the world, do not worry about the words, just move your lips, modest women pray in silence. Now she even enjoys crowding into the little bathroom, whispering and giggling as the women wash before entering the mosque. But today she does not have the energy for so much deception.

"Not feeling well," she manages.

"Ah, time of the month, is it? Stomach hurts? You want an aspirin? Shall I request Raza to let you go early?"

She nods. "Please, could you ask if I may leave as soon as I finish Aminul Miah's speech?"

"I'll do that. I know he'll say yes—and he'll worry about you, too."

Deepa makes a startled movement and Zaahira chuckles. "What? You think people haven't noticed how he looks at you? Ah, young love!" She bustles off, amused.

Deepa lays the speech—the usual exhortation to good Muslims to come together in service of their brothers, demand their own country, and support the League with donations—on Aminul's desk. He frowns, but she raises her hand to her forehead in a quick adab and escapes before he can insist that she use sterner words.

❧

The bell rings. Deepa—showered, combed, dressed in her nicest sari—runs to the door of the flat, but Raza is not alone. His uncle is with him.

Deepa has seen Abdullah only once since she moved to Calcutta. He stopped by Salima's to give Deepa a modest stack of rupees, told her to let him know if she needed more. She could see he was torn between wanting to assist his friend's daughter and wishing that this trouble had not descended upon his nephew. Deepa appreciated his help—Raza had told her that Abdullah was the one who persuaded Salima to take her in. But she was hurt by his clipped tone, his obvious disapproval. She did not contact him again, though sometimes she wished for his advice. Raza was wonderful intelligent ebullient; he helped her get through her days. But he was as inexperienced as Deepa in the art of deception.

It seems her wish is about to come true.

Abdullah waves away Salima's offer of snacks and tells her to keep the children in the bedroom. He does not want them to hear what they are about to discuss. He tells Deepa that the situation between Muslims and Hindus is getting worse. A repetition of Direct Action Day is waiting to happen—maybe not in Calcutta, where the army is vigilant, but surely in other cities with large Muslim populations.

Raza nods, his face dark. "Secret messages have been going back and forth."

Abdullah says, "If someone at the League office or here in the building guesses that you are not Muslim, only pretending, they will immediately think that you are a spy, and Raza and Salima are collaborators. I am afraid to imagine what they will do to all of you."

Salima, sharp and scared: "I cannot risk that, Doctor Sahab. Who would take care of my children if something happened to me?"

Deepa's hands begin to shake. She knows what is coming.

"I am sorry." Abdullah's tone, though not unkind, is firm. "You have only two choices. One is to go back to your family in Ranipur. The other is to convert right away."

Bina's furious face rises in her mind. She cannot go back.

Raza takes her hand. He, too, knows returning home is impossible for Deepa. "Once you convert, dearest, we can get married. That would make me so happy."

Abdullah says, "I know a small masjid in North Calcutta. The mullah is a friend, very discreet. Raza will take you there for conversion. The actual nikah should take place in the Park Circus mosque. Raza will invite the League members for the celebration. The League is getting more powerful each day, more dangerous. But once you are one of them, once they have eaten your salt, you will be safe." He adds, devastatingly, "If your father knew the trouble you are in, this is what he would advise, too."

Deepa, numb-lipped: "I need some time to think, please."

Raza's eyes are full of sympathy. He has dried her tears often as she described to him how Bina threw her out for loving him. He knows Deepa has not stopped loving her mother in spite of that.

Abdullah says, "You have until tomorrow. I cannot allow you to endanger Raza longer than that."

They leave, Salima serves dinner, Deepa cannot eat. She pleads a headache and goes to her room, but she cannot rest either. When Salima takes the children to bed, she comes out and sits on the floor. She feels she does not deserve a chair; she has brought everyone in her life nothing but trouble. Salima comes and sits beside Deepa, she rubs her back, her wet face glimmers in the broken light from the window.

Deepa knows then what she must do.

❖

The following night on their walk, Deepa tells Raza that she cannot convert. "I am not religious, but being a Hindu is deep in my bones. Also, if I became a Muslim, there would be no reconciliation with Ma ever. She would see this as the ultimate betrayal—of her, of Baba. I cannot bear that."

The burkha hides her agony, but it cannot protect her from his. His face looks like an extinguished lamp.

"Is this the end? Are you saying goodbye? Were you only playing with me all this time while I put my life in danger for you?" His voice is furious, then worried because he is a good man. "But what will you do? You cannot go back to the village—"

"I am not going anywhere. I love you." Deepa has never been so afraid, not even when Bina threw her out. She prays that he will see the reason in her plan, simple and intricate at once.

When he hears it, he argues hotly. Foolish impractical dangerous, like something out of the movies, impossible to carry out. It will fall apart under the slightest scrutiny.

She remains silent until he has run through all his objections. Until—because he loves her—he starts thinking about how to make it work.

On Monday, Raza and Deepa both call in sick. They know this will cause gossip; that is what they want. They take the train to Burdwan, where they visit a dilapidated mosque Raza had come across in the course of his political trips. They go to their separate sections. It is not the prescribed time for Salat, the mosque is almost empty. After prayers, Raza greets the imam, converses for a few minutes. They leave, again separately. Later in a curtained booth of an eatery, they sign the nikah contract that Raza had obtained earlier in Calcutta. He has already faked the other two required signatures, using different pens. Now he adds the imam's name. Perjuring my soul, he says, only half joking. The contract is in Urdu; Deepa has no idea what she is agreeing to. Too late now, Raza says. She smacks him, he grabs her and plants kisses along her arm. Deepa is too nervous to eat, but when the chicken biriyani arrives, she discovers she is famished. She finishes her share and part of Raza's, too.

Next morning they arrive at the office together. Raza confesses to their coworkers that they had a small private wedding in Burdwan because Aliya wanted it to be in her hometown. Deepa's is the easy role; she stands with bowed head, face hidden in burkha. Raza explains: because of a recent death in her family, they did not want any fanfare. The room fills with commotion, everyone talking at once, congratulating, complaining, insisting on a belated celebration. But of course, says Raza. There will be a feast for his League family.

The Walima banquet is small but festive, Deepa next to Raza on an ornate sofa, dressed in a silk burkha. She wipes nervous palms surreptitiously on her robe. What if someone has figured out their deception? Maybe someone here is from Burdwan and will ask her questions that she will fail spectacularly to answer. What if someone knows the little mosque, the old imam? But the evening flows smoothly. League members call her bhabhi and offer envelopes of rupees, the women wish her a houseful of children, everyone agrees the food is delicious.

Then Abdullah steps up to felicitate them. Raza had gone to his home and explained that it seemed safer to perform Deepa's conversion in a different city, there were fewer chances of League members coming across the imam. "Since we were there already, it seemed easiest to get done with the wedding, too. Neither of us wanted a big ceremony."

Abdullah had not challenged the story, but Raza could see he was suspicious and unhappy. "A mistake," he said. "A public wedding in Calcutta would have been better." And then, "Do not call her Deepa anymore, not even when you are alone. You must both think Deepa never existed."

Good advice, but it sent a chill through her when Raza told her. *Deepa never existed.* She watched Raza's mouth shaping the words and felt a bit of herself dying.

Abdullah speaks the traditional words of blessing and hands her a hefty decorated envelope. He responds politely to her thanks, but his eyes are cold. They say, *I know what you did—or rather, what you refused to do.* They say, *You will be the ruination of my nephew.*

Chapter 14

Priya

*T*oday after weeks of waiting, she hears Kashiram calling. "Letter for you, Didimoni. From Amereeka. If it is good news, I expect big baksheesh!"

The paper smooth and expensive, the color blue as infinity. Her name typed in neat black capitals. She has never received a typed letter. Never received a letter from another country. Colored stamps line the top, soldiers in helmets, guns ready: Guadalcanal, Tarawa, Coral Sea. Raised letters proclaim the sender's name: Woman's Medical College of Pennsylvania. Her breath hitches in her throat. She is halfway up the stairs when he calls her back. "I forgot. You have another letter. It has no sender's name."

Priya recognizes the handwriting. Deepa. Her breath catches again. Priya has written to her sister twice since they saw each other in Calcutta over a month ago, but this is the first letter Deepa has sent. Priya had worried about her; she had missed her, especially during Durga Puja. It was their custom to go to the temple, all three sisters together.

This year, walking with Jamini, Priya felt as though part of her body had been amputated. She slips the letter into her batua for when she is alone.

Once again she must wake Somnath from his nap. His yawn gets cut off halfway when he realizes what she is handing him. His fingers shake as he tears open the envelope; he has aged over these last months. Then he gives a bark of triumph. "You have done it, my girl!"

The letter from the admissions committee is short and businesslike. Priya senses that they do not like to waste time. She does not like it either; they should do well together. They write that the Woman's College is impressed with her personal statement. They will grant her probationary admission if she can cover the costs of travel, tuition, and board. The next academic term will begin in January, she needs to arrive in Pennsylvania before then. If she can keep up with the other students, who have been in the program for some months already, she will be allowed to continue and get her degree. The letter ends, *Your case was greatly aided by a letter sent to us by Mrs. Avery from the American Library in Calcutta. She advocated warmly for you, stating that she has rarely met a more sincere and determined young woman. Perhaps you will be a second Anandibai for us!*

Gratitude wells up in Priya. She must make a special trip to Calcutta to thank Mrs. Avery.

Somnath, equally excited, ticks off items on his fingers. "The journey will take you a month, you will take a ship from Calcutta to Bombay and go through the Suez Canal, I hear it is open again now that the war is over. You will change ships somewhere in Europe and then cross the Atlantic. You must leave by the end of November, in case there are delays. That leaves us only three weeks. I must tell Munshiji to start making arrangements, getting you travel papers, putting funds together. You will have to get the right clothes, these flimsy saris will not do; in many places in America the streets are covered in ice until

March or April. We must find a good tailor in Calcutta. Munshiji will need to locate a trustworthy Indian to meet your ship in New York, and—"

Her heart labors in her chest, her throat feels like sandpaper. "Kaku, before we do any of this, we have to let people know."

Somnath, sobering, knows who she is thinking of.

"Some of them may not be too happy about this," she continues.

He reaches for her hand. He knows he will face his share of disapproval for having encouraged her in this madcap endeavor, so inappropriate for a woman who is about to be married. Then he grins mischievously; years fall away from his face. "We will deal with them together—but tomorrow. Tonight, let us enjoy your well-deserved success."

❖

Priya, halfway home, weightless and jubilant, remembers Deepa's letter and digs in her batua. She needs to keep it secret from Bina. She must read it here, under the tamarind trees. The letter is unsigned, addressed to no one. The first sentence reads, *Burn this as soon as you have read it.*

O chilling subterfuge. Her eyes blur, her hands shake; she must hold the tree trunk for support. How could Deepa believe such a precarious scheme would work? How could the levelheaded Raza go along with her? Does love derange you like that? Priya hopes she will never need to find out.

This is how Deepa's tear-splotched letter ends:

The world believes me to be a devout Muslim, R's wife. I am neither. Please tell Ma that it was for her sake that I did not convert—because I knew it would pain her more than anything else. Thus I could not marry R, although I am living with him in the little flat that used to be

Baba's. In sin, the world would say, although I do not feel particularly
sinful, only desperate. I love him so much and I have endangered him.
The deception is an arrow in both our hearts.

Ask Ma to meet me just once—wherever she wants. I need to see her,
even if for the last time. To look her in the eye and tell her how much she
means to me. For this, I have put both R and myself in grave danger.
Persuade her, dear sister. Better yet, ask J to help you. She has the most
influence over Ma these days.

Burn this now.

Priya runs the rest of the way home. She pulls Jamini out into the
shal grove, swears her to secrecy, shows her the letter. Jamini's mouth
thins with worry. They enter the house, clutching hands as though they
were children again. They beg and beg, but it is no use. Their mother
stands at her window, sharp stiff adamantine, face turned to the night.
Perhaps even if she wishes it, she no longer knows how to turn back.

❀

"Such a huge decision, and you hid it from me?" Amit's voice is not
loud, but his tone makes Priya flinch. She tries to read his expression,
but it is evening already in the garden by the river, and his face is a
plane of shadows.

Perhaps she should have listened to Somnath when he said, Let me
tell Amit. Let him take out his anger on me. After he calms down, you
talk to him.

But she refused. That is the coward's way, Kaku. Amit deserves
better.

Somnath had sighed. He told her she was too idealistic, like her
baba. He warned her that the world was not kind to people who place
principles before practicality.

Now she tells Amit, "I did not think the Woman's College would accept me. I saw no point in upsetting you needlessly." She hates that her voice sounds apologetic.

"So you knew it would upset me, and still you went ahead? Even though I had promised that you could continue your studies at Calcutta Medical College? You couldn't wait two years? Or is it that you felt marrying me was less important, less glamorous, than living in America, rubbing shoulders with the whites?"

Priya, bristling: "I have never been fascinated by foreigners, you know that. And I do not care about living abroad. But I have already been burned by the Calcutta Medical College. I cannot wait for two years, hoping that their admission policies will grow equitable. Becoming a doctor is too important for me to take a chance like that."

"But it is okay to take a chance on me—because you think I will always be here panting after you."

The harsh words so unlike Amit knock the breath out of her. When she can speak, she says, "I have to do this. I promised Baba I would take care of the family. You were there. You heard it."

"I heard Nabakumar Kaka asking *me* for help—and I said yes. If you had married me, that help would have flowed to your mother and sisters in the most natural way. I will keep my word to him in spite of what you have done. I'll take care of them whether you are here or not. But you—you have twisted the facts to suit yourself. Your father never wanted you to be a doctor. He said so many times. Can you deny that?"

Amit is wrong. Nabakumar's words, rising from caution, were not his real truth. Priya had seen the pride in his eyes when she diagnosed a difficult case correctly, sutured an ugly wound, lifted a newborn out of the gaping hole in his mother's stomach. Still, Amit's accusation echoes in her ears.

She takes a deep breath, she places an entreating hand on his arm, she honeys her voice. "Marrying you means everything to me. I love you. Nothing about that has changed. We will get married before I go." A new idea strikes her. "Maybe you can come with me to America—"

He flings off her hand, his lips a thin, angry line. "You were not willing to compromise even a little, but now you want me to turn my whole life around for you? Shrug off my responsibilities and abandon my family, like you are so ready to do? Follow you like the pet dog you think I am? And what would I do in America, while you are busy running around fashioning yourself into a lady doctor? Sit at home hankering after whatever time you can spare for me, while back here my aging father struggles to manage his affairs?"

Priya's face burns. Perhaps she *is* as thoughtless as Amit is implying.

Still she says, because a portion of her heart is breaking, "Maybe you could come just for a month? Please? It would be far less scary if you were there with me in the beginning . . ."

Amit does not deign to answer.

"We can still get married before I leave, can we not?" Her voice is a trembling thread.

"I do not want a wife who puts me last, after all the other things she considers important. And you do not want a husband who would keep you close to his heart; to you it would seem like he is holding you back from your life's goal. It is best we end our engagement." In one swift motion, Amit pulls the ruby ring she gave him off his finger and throws it in the river mud. Priya has to force herself to remain still, to not scrabble through the dark for it.

The lights have come on in the mansion. Glittering flecks play on the water, in Amit's eyes. His tone is no longer angry, and that frightens her more. "I am freeing you, Priya. This way, you can focus on your destiny, and I can fulfill my responsibilities as the heir of the Chowdhurys."

Her world is breaking into fragments. Amit my love companion of my childhood my dearest friend. He swivels sharply, strides back to the mansion. She is left with the dark swaying grasses, the mud soaking the edge of her sari, the invisible night birds crying.

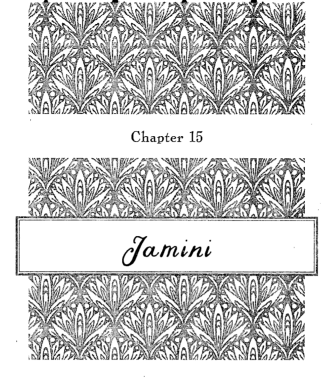

Chapter 15

Jamini

When Priya made the most foolish decision of her life, Jamini was afraid the disappointment would shock Bina into ill-ness. Already Deepa's defection had shaken her mother to the core. But after a fiery outburst berating Priya's stupidity and a declaration that she was washing her hands of her, Bina busied herself with a new bedspread. When Jamini asked if she was upset, she shrugged. "That match was too good to be true." Then she asked Jamini's advice as to whether the sun on the bedspread should be red or orange or yellow.

Jamini does not trust Bina's demeanor. It is too calm, considering the immense loss to the family's fortunes and the ensuing wildfire of gossip that is certain to rage through the village. She vows to watch her with vigilance, to guard her—from herself, if necessary. As for Jamini, every nerve in her body buzzes with excitement, though she is careful to conceal it. Now that Amit has chosen to break the engagement, perhaps she will finally have a chance at love? A bonus: she will be the only daughter at home, the claimant to all of Bina's affection, the one who stayed back devoted, ignoring the pull of the crazy wind.

Yet this, too, is true: she is happy that her sister, who in childhood would crawl under Jamini's quilt if night noises frightened her, is following her lifelong dream.

When Jamini wishes Priya success in America, she means it. She is less sincere when she says she hopes Priya will return soon. She loves Priya, but in her shadow she will always be the stunted sapling. If Priya makes a home for herself in America—a happy one, of course—would that not be the best for both of them?

❀

Priya is the one who brings home the horrifying news. In spite of her break with Amit, she has continued to visit Somnath each day, though she leaves the mansion well before Amit's return. This evening she carries the *Anandabazar Patrika*. In itself, this is not surprising. She often brings back newspapers to share with Jamini, though Jamini mostly uses them to start the cook-fire. But today Priya grips Jamini's arm and will not let go.

"You need to know what has happened, and you need to tell Ma." Her face is pinched, her voice tear-rasped.

She is so dramatic, Jamini thinks, always incensed about things that are none of our business.

But looking at the patrika, Jamini is shaken. A month earlier—this, too, she had learned courtesy of Priya—the governor had passed a law forbidding papers to print news of communal violence, possibly for fear of more uprisings. But the owner of this paper has defied him, and after reading the article, Jamini understands why.

It is too dreadful a disaster to keep hidden.

Noakhali, East Bengal, ten days ago. Armed groups of militant Muslims came together under two Muslim League leaders, Ghulam

Sarwar and Kasem. They named themselves Sarwar's Army, Kasem's Fauj. It was a holy day for Hindus, Lakshmi Puja, no one was ready. The militants burned shops schools government buildings private homes, even the mansions of prominent Hindu leaders. They beheaded Hindu men, raped women. The death toll was in the thousands and rising. Thousands more had been forcibly converted. Even more had fled the region, leaving everything behind. Many had come to Calcutta; more were arriving each day. Governor Burrows and Prime Minister Suhrawardy had flown to Noakhali, but the reports they brought back, stating that the violence was now under control, seemed vague and suspicious. One of them had remarked—though both denied it later—that it was not surprising that so many Hindu women were raped since they were more attractive than Muslim women. The photographs in the paper—charred remains of bodies and buildings—bring back horrifying memories of the Calcutta riots to Jamini.

She crushes the paper into a ball, she cannot read any further. She tells Priya she is not going to traumatize their mother by telling her any of this. It does not concern her life here in small, sleepy Ranipur. Priya argues that it might make Bina realize the danger Deepa is in, she might allow her to return home. But Jamini says, "Deepa is smart. She has created a good alibi for herself. If we interfere, we might put her at greater risk."

❧

At the Durga temple the next morning, Jamini overhears two women talking about a couple who had arrived at her friend Bela's home two nights ago, distant relatives that escaped from Noakhali with immense difficulty. Bela's father, Mahendra, has called the heads of the important Hindu families to his home today to listen to their story and decide what needs to be done.

Jamini drops her errands and hurries to Bela's house, impatient with her leg for always slowing her down when speed is essential. Jamini and Bela are no longer as close as they were before Nabakumar died. For a while Bela would not talk to Jamini; perhaps she, too, believed the Ganguly women were bad luck. But after Bina's work started selling well in Calcutta and Priya got engaged to Amit, she began inviting Jamini to her home again. Jamini accepted the invitations. She would never again feel affection for Bela, but she did not let her know that.

An excited Bela pulls Jamini into the house. The inner courtyard is filled with men; women crowd the doorways of the women's area. Jamini follows Bela, trying to gauge what is going on. The prominent patriarchs sit on rope cots; the others have made a space for themselves on the floor. Jamini peers around two plump village aunties and sees a man and woman huddled on a rope cot, facing the audience. Bela's father, Mahendra, sits next to the man, patting his arm encouragingly.

Jamini is surprised to see the woman in the middle of the assembly. In Ranipur gatherings, women keep strictly to their side, men to theirs. This woman is not veiled either; she holds on to a corner of the man's fatua as though she were a child. She does not seem to notice everyone staring at her. Bela whispers that she has been like that ever since they arrived.

Suddenly the man starts speaking, his voice flat but clear. "We were praying when the Muslims kicked down the door. They came with knives and sickles, swords and guns. Ransacked our house and set it on fire. We rushed out. Every hut in our neighborhood was burning. Some of our men tried to fight back; they were chopped down. We knew many of the attackers, they bought groceries from our shops, worked in our fields. We heard gunfire. We hoped our zamindar, Rai-moshai, was coming to rescue us, but after a while the shots stopped. Later they boasted that they had stormed his house and beheaded him.

"They herded us into the cattle pen in the middle of the bazaar, which they had looted. They picked out the girls and young women—

including our daughters, Uma and Hema—and took them away. I can still hear them screaming."

Jamini sees the man's shoulders shake. Then he continues in that toneless voice which is worse than grief. "The Muslims beat up any men who tried to resist—that was when I got the cut on my head. They killed quite a few, leaving the bodies lying in the pen. Sometimes they wounded a man but did not kill him, and we had to endure his screams until he died. Their leader told us that he would have been happy to kill all of us kafirs, but their mullah had said that we should be converted to Islam instead. He taunted us, saying they were already cooking vats of beef to force-feed us tomorrow. I rushed at them—I wanted them to kill me, too. Then I thought, What will happen to my wife if I am gone? That made me stop.

"Late at night friends managed to loosen some of the stakes of the pen. The guards were sleeping, they were sure they had broken our spirits. We knew we had to leave right away. Escape would be impossible later. Some were too scared, but I dragged my wife out—she was already the way she is now. Perhaps that was lucky. She would never have come with me otherwise, leaving our girls behind.

"We did not know the way, but a couple of men guided us west. We kept to the forests, even at night, though we were afraid of tigers. There were crocodiles in the rivers we had to swim across, they got some of us. After several days, I am not sure how many, we made it to the Ichamati River. There were some boatmen there. Luckily they had not heard about the massacre in Noakhali. We told them our village was destroyed in a wildfire. They took us across. I paid my boatman with my wife's earrings. Once we reached this shore, we scattered in different directions. Many went to the capital. By God's grace some would say, except I cannot believe in God anymore, my wife and I came across a good man with a bullock cart. When he saw our plight"—here he points to their feet, still crusted with dried blood—"he took pity on us and drove us to Ranipur, where Mahen-da took us in."

Mahendra gestures to his wife, who leads the couple away. A commotion breaks out in the courtyard. *Damn Muslims need to be taught a lesson. Better to do it right away, before the ones in Ranipur get any ideas in their heads. Let us drive them out. We do not want any Muslims in Ranipur. Our families are not safe with them here. Let us burn their huts and see how they like that. Better still, let us burn them inside their huts. That is what they did to our Hindu brothers in some of the villages near Noakhali. Why put it off? Tomorrow is a good night, the night of no moon.*

Jamini starts to sweat. Are they really going to commit this carnage? Are they going to massacre people they have known for years, people who have done nothing to deserve this fate? Then she thinks, Perhaps they are right. Perhaps it is better to be attackers than victims.

People are talking about collecting weapons and recruiting their Hindu farmhands and servants to join them. Someone says he can count on his cousins from the next village, they have guns and trained guards.

Then a familiar voice breaks through the commotion. "Respected friends, what are you saying?" Jamini cranes her neck but cannot see the speaker. "The Muslims in Noakhali have done atrocious things, but the Muslims in Ranipur have not. How can we punish them? Wouldn't that make us as bad as the people who attacked our brothers and sisters in East Bengal?"

Amit. Jamini pushes past the auntie in front, not caring when she snaps at her. He stands tall in a simple kurta-pajama, very different from his stylish British outfits. She has not seen him since he and Priya broke their engagement, though she has thought of him many times, wishing she had the courage to pay him a visit.

Mahendra, who has been shouting the loudest, glares at Amit, his eyes bloodshot with rage. "Didn't you see what they did to my cousin? Didn't you hear him talk about the people he saw chopped to pieces in front of his eyes? And my nieces—didn't you hear what happened to those poor, innocent girls and hundreds of others like them? How can you tell us to sit still after that? Are we men or are we eunuchs?" A group of villagers yell in agreement.

"This is a desperate time, Amit," Mahendra continues. "You know me—I've always been a peaceful man. But how can you ask me to sit still after hearing about these atrocities?"

People clamor in assent. A group of men starts moving toward the door. The dark fury on their faces frightens Jamini. Some of them push past Amit, jostling hard against him.

The Amit Jamini knows would have reacted with anger; today he is calm. "Mahendra Kaka, I agree that the horrifying plight of your relatives is enough to make any decent man's blood boil. I am truly sorry for what they have gone through. I only ask that we think carefully before we act. Let us not, in our anger, do something we will regret later. It is easy to start a bonfire, hard to put it out. Wait a few days, please. My father feels the same way. He is the one who sent me here to talk to you."

There are murmurs. People consult with one another, some nod, others scowl. Finally, Mahendra takes a deep breath. "Out of respect to Somnath-babu, we will wait a few days to make a decision. But we will start gathering weapons and alerting friends. That way, we will not be caught off guard like the Hindus of Noakhali. And if we do decide to avenge the thousands of innocents—including my nieces—whose lives have been destroyed by these damned Muslims, we will be ready."

The meeting breaks up, people start dispersing. Bela hot with excitement wants to discuss everything that has happened; she is a gabbler, that girl, she would keep Jamini here all day if she could. But Jamini makes an excuse and slips out to the alley behind the house. She will process the nightmarish events of Noakhali later; right now, there is something else she must do.

As she had hoped, Sultan is tied to a nearby post. She waits, keeping a healthy distance between herself and that bad-tempered brute. He has snapped at her in the past, though he whickers with inordinate pleasure whenever Priya pets him.

When Amit finally appears, Jamini tells him how much she admired his handling of the enraged crowd. "You stopped some terrible things from happening, you saved a lot of lives. And you stayed calm through it all." She means what she is saying; she hopes he hears it in her voice.

She can tell he is pleased. After a moment he asks after her health; he does not mention Priya. O double joy. Jamini longs to engage him in further conversation, but this is not the time. With all her willpower she holds herself back. When he says goodbye, she raises her hand in an elegant, nonchalant farewell.

Amit rides away, sitting tall on that huge and malicious beast, controlling him with the slightest click of his tongue; Jamini watches him intently. It was a crucial moment for Amit this morning, the first time he spoke up in a village assembly—a roiling one at that—and was taken seriously. A day when he stopped terrible violences from being unleashed upon innocent people. He will remember today, she thinks. And he will remember the woman who was there with him, the woman who appreciated his courage and intelligence and applauded his victory.

She says nothing of this to Priya. Why distract her when she is preparing for her journey? It will only open a wound that is not yet healed. Jamini knows this because sometimes at night as she lies next to Bina, she hears her sister in the other room weeping.

Chapter 16

Priya

*B*ecause she is unhappy when she has no right to feel this way, Priya occupies herself with packing. It keeps her busy and grateful, checking off items on the list Somnath has created, fitting them into her steamer trunk. Somnath bought most of the things on the list, and often while she packs, he sits nearby watching her in silence. The breaking of the engagement has shocked him deeply. He begged Amit to reconsider, warned him that he was making the worst mistake of his life. Father and son had a long and bitter argument, the details of which Somnath has not shared with Priya. They did not speak for days. This, too, fills Priya with anguish.

The trunk is made of heavy wood and reinforced with studded leather strips as though Priya is going off to war—and perhaps she is. It has three locks, with three separate keys that she is constantly afraid of misplacing. She fills it with dried fruits, nuts, seasickness pills—and mango and tamarind pickle because the food of the sahibs is reputed to be tasteless. Two of Nabakumar's medical books for good luck. A silver comb-and-brush set with a matching mirror. Coats, sweaters, scarves, gloves, light summer shoes, sturdy winter boots. She tries to imagine snow and fails. Calf-length dresses in sober browns and dark blues stitched for her by Mrs. Avery's seamstress. Mrs. Avery, delighted by Priya's news, has gifted her a box of notepaper smelling of lavender. Priya plans to use the paper to write to Amit, because surely he cannot remain angry with her after she is gone.

Last of all she hides, under her dresses, a patent-leather handbag with a stack of dollars inside. The dollars must have been enormously difficult for Somnath to procure, he must have resorted to expensive, illegal means. More guilt for Priya. Last week Manorama had come into the room as Priya was packing and announced with loud displeasure that one of Somnath's Calcutta businesses was not doing well. Manorama would have said more, but Somnath told her, in a tone sterner than Priya had ever heard him use, to be silent. Priya does not blame Manorama for her anger. She sees Priya as having betrayed Amit, the son she never had. Sometimes when sleep eludes Priya, she wonders if Manorama is right.

The night before she is to leave for Calcutta, Priya stays back at the mansion. She cannot travel to the other end of the world without seeing Amit one last time. Amit comes home very late—in order to avoid her, she is sure. When he walks into his bedroom and sees her, he turns to leave. She runs to grip his arm, she has no pride left, if he pushes her away, so be it. But he stands very still, staring over her shoulder. Only the pulse beating in his temple gives him away.

"I will come back the moment I graduate," she says. "Please, please wait for me."

"How long would you like me to wait?" His tone is more reasonable than she expected. Perhaps Somnath's intercession has had an effect? Hope beats like a hammer in her heart.

"The course takes three years."

His lips twist. "You expect me to wait around for three years, remembering and hungering?"

When he puts it that way, she sees the unreasonableness of her request. "I know it is a huge thing to ask—but please, I love you."

Get over your stubborn pride, she begs him silently, just for once take me into your arms.

His voice is cool and casual, a voice one uses with strangers who do not matter. Somehow it is worse than if he had yelled at her. "I don't doubt that you love me—to the extent you are capable of love. But you love other things more. I am not willing to stand in line for my turn like a beggar waiting for leftovers."

She scrabbles for a response but nothing comes. In the distance Manorama calls Amit to dinner.

"All this time I put Pishi off," he says, "refusing when she wanted to engage a matchmaker, hoping you would change your mind. Thank you for showing me how foolish I have been. Now I can say yes to her with no regrets."

He holds the door open with cold formality. "If you will excuse me, my family is waiting."

The weariness on his face makes him appear years older. This is what Priya has done to him—and must do one more time. She takes from her batua the gold bangles he gave her. She wills her voice not to tremble. "I cannot keep these, considering how things have changed between us."

He speaks tonelessly. "Do not insult the friendship we once had." He waits in silence until she leaves.

As she trudges back in the dark, there is only one thing Priya is thankful for: she was able to hold back her tears until she was outside the gates of the Chowdhury mansion, Amit's home that will now never be hers.

❧

Morning of departure. Priya knows that saying goodbye to her mother will be difficult. She armors herself as best as she can and knocks on

Bina's door. No response. She is not surprised, she expected this. Still, anguish shakes her. Such is the illogic of the human heart. In fear she thinks, What if Ma is not here when I return? By the time I am capable of taking care of her, what if it is too late? Ma, she calls. Ma. No response. She stoops to the doorstep in a resigned pranam and turns to leave.

But Jamini stops her and raps on the door. "Give Priya your blessing, Ma—for your own sake. Should anything happen to her on this journey, you will regret it forever." She must understand Bina best of all, for here is the scrape of metal, the bolt sliding across, and Bina at the threshold, thin and stern as winter. Priya tries vainly to find in her the blushing bride she used to be, the affectionate, smiling mother.

Priya touches her feet and feels on her head a hand fleeting as a bird's wing. She has to be satisfied with that.

Now the final leave-taking. At the mansion Manorama and Amit have absented themselves, but Somnath makes up for it with his enthusiasm and excitement. He has summoned the family priest to do an elaborate good-luck puja for Priya. After the ceremony, incense flowers bells lamps conches blown by the maids heaps of sweets to please the gods, he puts a red sandalwood tika on Priya's forehead. "For victory." He blesses her twice, his eyes damp. "On behalf of your baba, too."

Somnath had planned to travel to Calcutta to see Priya off, his first foray in years. But two days ago he came down with an excruciating attack of gout, and Priya sternly forbade him. So it is only Jamini and Priya who get in the car that Munshiji has sent up from the city. As the car jounces along the uneven road, Priya is racked with a sudden surprising sorrow. Her lifelong wish, for which she has fought so hard, sacrificed so much, is coming true. She should be exhilarated, or at least gratified.

Why then these tears?

❁

They sit in the usual dilapidated booth in the little New Market eatery, three sisters who will not meet again for a long time, if ever. Priya extravagant orders egg parathas. After they eat, she takes out two packets wrapped in old newspaper and pushes them toward her sisters.

"Gold bangles!" Jamini exclaims. "For us? Are you sure? Are they the ones—?"

She knows very well that they are. She was at the engagement when Amit slid them onto Priya's arms. Priya refuses to rise to the bait. "I want the two of you to have them. As a keepsake—or a safeguard in case you ever need the money."

Astonished delight battles with regret on Deepa's face. Finally she says, "Thank you, dear sister, but I cannot take this. How would I explain it to friends? To our colleagues at work? Everyone knows that Raza and I barely make ends meet." She throws open her burkha. "Look at me, still dressed in Salima's old clothes."

"Can't you say it was a wedding gift?"

Deepa shakes her head. "That would just lead to more questions. Who would give me such an expensive gift? If it is from family, why did they not come to our reception? I will have to spin lie upon lie until I am tangled in them." She pushes the bangle back toward Priya. "No. You take it. It will come in handy if you run into an emergency in America. Don't you agree, Jamini?"

Jamini silent stares at Deepa's bangle.

Deepa has noticed. "You should give both bangles to Jamini. They can be part of her dowry, one less thing for Ma to worry about."

The slightest flicker in Jamini's eyes.

"No," Priya says. "I want you to have one of them, Deepa. You can keep it hidden. Jamini, it is a good idea for you, too, to hide yours away."

Jamini juts out a mutinous chin.

Priya thinks, The things we give away are no longer ours to control. At least I am saved from the pain of looking at these.

Deepa leans forward. "Now I have something to tell you both."

"You're pregnant!" Jamini says.

Deepa colors. "No, although I would love that. But Raza says we must put the nation first. I guess he is right. My news is quite different. We are moving to East Bengal, which will soon become part of Pakistan. Raza is very keen on it."

Priya is stunned and furious. The Noakhali massacres are still fresh in her mind, the photographs splotching the newspapers with blood. Surely Deepa has seen them.

"It is too dangerous, Deepa." Jamini grasps her sister's hand. "You must not do it."

Priya says, "Doesn't Raza realize how risky it will be for you?"

"Raza tells me things have calmed down. The Muslim League members in East Bengal have heard of his reputation. They want him to come to the capital. Help them form a proper government. He is very excited. He wants to have a hand in shaping the new nation. Besides, Muslims are not going to be in any danger there. We are more likely to get lynched in Calcutta than in Dacca."

"What do you mean, *we?*" Jamini lowers her voice. "You are not Muslim, Deepa. Have you forgotten?"

Priya finds herself whispering, too. "If anyone finds out that you have been pretending, you will be in grave danger. Raza, too. If you insist on going, maybe you should consider converting for real."

"No one will find out," Deepa says angrily. She ignores Priya's suggestion and turns to Jamini. "Will you tell Ma about the move? We will leave in a couple of months, perhaps sooner. We may never return to India. I must see her before I go. I know she would not want me to come to Ranipur—and she is right, it would be dangerous if someone in the village gossiped, if the League found out. Can you persuade her to come to Calcutta? Please? We could meet in this tea shop—just for an hour, just to say goodbye."

"I will try." But Jamini looks down. Even apart from her anger at

Deepa, Bina will not agree to come to the city that killed her husband. Perhaps deep down Deepa knows it, too. The sisters sit in silence, pondering the changes and challenges that lie ahead, until Deepa sighs and says she must return to work.

❦

Because it is Priya's final night, repentant Shefali has cooked up a feast: pulao, brinjals, cauliflower curry, fish kalia, tomato chutney, payesh. Perhaps also she feels sorry for Priya, because she is going far away to become a doctor, to handle each day with germs and odors and the body fluids of strangers instead of marrying the most eligible bachelor in all of Bengal. Priya eats a little because Shefali has worked so hard. But she is too nervous about her journey, too worried about Deepa, too heartsick for Amit, to enjoy any of it. After dinner, she paces the living room until Jamini turns on the radio to divert her. The news comes on, most of it not good. Different parties are squabbling about which parts of the country will go to Pakistan and which will remain in India when the British leave.

Can you cut up a country as though it were a cake?

Priya is about to ask Jamini to turn off the radio when the announcer says that Sarojini Naidu is in Calcutta today. Tomorrow she will travel to Noakhali to join Gandhi and plan a rehabilitation program for female survivors. Priya feels a stirring, old and deep, a desire to meet this woman who had inspired her father. *Sarojini would tell me if I am doing the right thing.* But it is irrational, impossible, there is no time. Even if there was, where would Priya go searching for her?

The radio is playing a portion of the talk Sarojini gave today to the women of Bethune College. Priya listens avidly. Sarojini uses English with a confident Indian intonation that makes the language her own. "Education is an immeasurable, beautiful, indispensable atmosphere in which we live and move and have our being. Does one man dare to deprive another of his birthright to God's pure air which nourishes his body? How, then, shall a man dare to deprive a human soul of its immemorial inheritance of liberty and life? And yet, my friends, man has so dared in the case of Indian women . . . Therefore, I charge you, restore to your women their ancient rights, for, as I have said, it is we, and not you, who are the real nation-builders."

Excited and inspired, she shakes Jamini, who is busy jotting down the latest New Market transactions in her notebook.

"Did you hear that? Sarojini would support my going to America. She would say I was doing the right thing. After all, she herself studied abroad."

Jamini raises an eyebrow. "I support you, too. That is why I am here. Who are you trying to convince? Yourself?"

Priya, annoyed, wants to argue, but here is Sarojini again: "Remember that woman does not merely keep the hearth fire of your homes burning but she keeps also the beacon fire of national life aflame . . . The power of self-surrender and self-realization had been the typical characteristics of Indian womanhood."

"Sarojini is not quite advocating for women to go off and follow their hearts, is she?" Jamini says dryly. "She is talking about balance and compromise. Didn't Baba mention that she got married before she went to England?"

Priya, stung, reveals the painful secret she has kept to herself. "I wanted that, too, but Amit refused."

She steels herself for one of Jamini's taunts, but her sister turns back to her notebook in silence.

Sleep proves elusive that night. Priya drinks water, visits the bathroom, stares at the garden where Amit once plucked her the most beautiful rose in all the world. Beneath her agitation, the restless bed creaks.

Jamini at the door. Priya steels herself for complaints, but Jamini lies down and holds Priya, nuzzling the top of her head. She used to do this when Priya was a nightmare-tormented child, but Priya had forgotten. Jamini whisper-sings:

Jodi tor dak shune keu na aashe, tobe ekla cholo re.
Ekla cholo, ekla cholo, ekla cholo re.

Though written for a different purpose, the song fits Priya perfectly: *Walk alone, walk alone, walk alone.*

❈

Priya stands on the crowded deck of the SS *Mauritania* along with a hundred passengers who wave to friends and family on the pier. No one for her to wave to. Once she had reached the gangway, she sent Munshiji and Jamini away. The pier was growing crowded, coolies pushing, and Jamini had stumbled twice. But now Priya bereft wishes she had not been so altruistic. Even the thought of her charming little cabin does not console her. She turns her back to the waving families and fixes her blurry gaze on the ship's giant smokestacks. O Amit.

A white man touches her arm, startling her. She will have to get used to such behaviors, which Mrs. Avery has warned her is normal in America. "I think someone is trying to get your attention."

Below, Jamini disheveled, gesturing, pointing, shouting Priya's name. She came back! Around Priya, people unfurl white handkerchiefs, a hundred fluttering doves, a custom she had not known to prepare for. No matter. She waves the end of her sari like a banner. Good luck, be well, don't forget me. Her words are drowned in the blast of the ship's horn. Smooth and powerful, the *Mauritania* picks up speed, making her way down the Hooghly to the limitless ocean. Now sorrow falls away, now the heart quickens, now there is no point looking back.

Bless me, Baba. I am on my way to the greatest adventure of my life.

Part Four

March–November 1947

❖

Here is a country teetering on the verge of independence. Here is a man in a fearful hurry, rushing that country into emancipation without preparation. Here is a stranger hacking the land to pieces. Here is a leader with a gold silk jacket and a rose in his lapel claiming his tryst with destiny. Here is celebration, tricolor flags being raised for the first time. Here are people fleeing. Here are people slaughtered. Here are families scattered and lost. Here are women with their breasts cut off. Here are babies roasted on a spit. Here are death numbers to shake even the most stoic heart. Here is the man harboring the most malignant secret of all.

The country is India. The man in a rush to return to England to further his naval career is Viceroy Mountbatten; he pushes India's independence ahead by ten unsteady months. The hacker is Cyril Radcliffe, barrister; he has never before set foot on this continent. In five weeks he will carve up 175,000 square miles into three pieces. The leader who trysts eloquently with destiny is Nehru; he will be helpless to stop the blood trains gliding in terrible silence to their destinations. The flags raised in beloved jubilation are saffron white green; in their center is the Ashok Chakra, eternal wheel of law. The man with the secret is Jinnah; he has tuberculosis and cancer; the doctors predict he has a year to live. If he had divulged this, one million lives might have been saved.

The year is 1947. It is the best of times, it is the worst of times.

Chapter 17

Deepa

*I*n the narrow bed in the flat above the clinic that was once her father's, she resists the temptation to relax into Raza's sleeping breath his dreaming arms. She has an important task, she must do it before he wakes. Tomorrow will be too late, tomorrow they are leaving for Dacca. From there she may not be able to write to her sisters.

Candle, ink, paper, pen. Deepa takes out a packet hidden behind a stack of books, her sisters' letters. She will read them one last time. Tomorrow, when she cooks, she will burn them. She cannot receive letters from them again, because why would the wife of a Muslim government official in East Bengal be corresponding with Hindu girls from other countries? Even now it is risky.

She rereads Priya's letters first; they hurt less.

The first one describes the voyage to America. What a flair the girl has for description. Deepa is transported with her on the *Mauritania:* a storybook room, a cozy curtained bunk bed, towels hanging from little silver hooks, the dinner menu tucked artfully under a plump pillow.

Is it a ship or a carnival? Books movies dances musical performances even a trip to the towering pyramid at Giza when they stop in Suez. That such things can exist in the world! Deepa wishes she, too, could visit an unknown land. Then she thinks, I am doing that tomorrow.

Three women shared the cabin with Priya. Two of them kept to themselves, but the third, Marianne, was friendly. That turned out to be a good thing, because when they disembarked in New York, Priya discovered that Munshiji's contact, who was to meet her at the docks, was not there. Deepa would have been sick with fear; even the thought of going to East Bengal tomorrow, though she will be with Raza every moment, makes her feel like throwing up.

Marianne's parents drove Priya to Grand Central Station, its huge bustling confusion, and put her on the right train. They even showed her the tallest building in the world, its spire like a giant's needle. A lucky one, Priya, except when she ruins things with her stubbornness. If I had been home, Deepa thinks, I would have guided her better regarding Amit. But then, hasn't she also made a mess of her own relationships?

Priya wrote that she found the Woman's Medical College with its tall brick buildings and stately pillars exciting and nerve-racking. She loved the classes, the procedures were fascinating, she was learning so much. But she was lonely. Sometimes she felt like an exotic animal. Fellow students goggled at her outdated clothes and smirked at her accent. The few who tried to converse soon ran out of things to say. She suspected they made an attempt only out of Christian duty.

Deepa wonders if people in East Bengal will find her hard to understand. Zaahira, who has a cousin in Dacca, says that their intonation is odd. The same words mean different things there. Keep your mouth shut and your ears open, Zaahira has advised her.

Deepa's eyes linger on the last line. *I send you love and wonder when I will see you again.* What Priya really means: *Will I ever see you again?*

Deepa does not know the answer to that.

Jamini's letters are short, sharp as pocketknives; the news in them is always the same. *We are in good health. The quilts are selling well. We have hired another woman to help us. I cannot meet with you when I come to Calcutta because she is always with me. Ma does not like me to travel alone nowadays: she thinks there is too much unrest in the city. I could not get Ma to agree to come to Calcutta. I am sorry. I really tried.*

Deepa cries carefully, silently. Indulgent though he is, Raza grows upset if he sees her weeping for Bina.

Now she must write her own letter. Hide her heartbreak at leaving mother and motherland. Reveal little of who she is and nothing of who she used to be. This way, if traced back, the letter cannot harm Raza.

I am leaving tomorrow. Your brother-in-law is very excited, as are our friends there. He has so many plans, you know how hardworking he is. There will be challenges—which worthwhile endeavor doesn't have them?—but I am prepared. Love will give me strength. Do not worry about me. It will be a grand adventure.

She copies the letter, folds the two sheets carefully. Tomorrow she will give them to Abdullah. He will mail them for her with a fake sender's name.

Exhausted by subterfuge, she slides into bed. Raza sleeping presses his warm face against the side of her neck. O how she loves him.

Why then this churning, this pain as though she is being pulled in two?

❀

They travel through deserted streets to the station. Once Calcutta was a city that never slept: parties, plays, vivacious wedding processions, music mehfils that lasted until dawn. But since the riots, people are reluctant to venture out after dark. Their train will travel all night, reach Dacca tomorrow. Deepa has never traveled such a distance.

The coolie places their luggage in an empty third-class compartment. The League had offered them more expensive tickets, but Raza said it was inappropriate, the country required the funds for more important things. Deepa does not mind. She chooses a window seat and waits in childlike excitement for the train to start.

Just before departure, two tall, muscular men enter the compartment. Raza introduces them to a startled Deepa. Sharif, the younger one, has joined the League recently. Hard-faced Mamoon has come from Dacca to escort them back. Deepa catches the glint of a pistol at his waist before his coat covers it up. She offers them a silent adab from behind her burkha; one of its benefits is that she is not expected to make conversation.

Two other travelers are at the compartment door. "No space here," Mamoon says, blocking their path. The travelers, protesting, point to the empty seats. Mamoon lets his coat fall open. They see the glint of metal and back away fast. He locks the door, the click echoes through the night. To hide her disquiet, Deepa stares out the window at the inky shapes—huts trees haystacks—rushing past them. While the men talk in low voices, she tries to figure out where West Bengal ends and East Bengal begins, but she cannot. It is one land, after all, though men have decreed otherwise. The train's rhythm lulls her, her head drops onto Raza's shoulder, she sleeps.

She wakes in the small hours to find that her veil has slipped from her face. The train has seduced Raza into sleep, Sharif also. Only Mamoon sits straight-spined, burning with intensity. In the dim compartment light he is staring at her. What is it in his eyes that makes her blush uneasily? She turns to the window, pulling the cover over her face.

❖

The League has sent a large, boxy car, along with a chauffeur in a military uniform, to drive them home. Deepa is disconcerted when Mamoon and Sharif also get in, crowding next to the driver. She had hoped for privacy, a chance to ask Raza questions. Tired and queasy from the long journey, she is not impressed by her first glimpse of Dacca. The roads seem narrower, the buildings shabbier, compared with Calcutta. Disobedient tears rise to her eyes. Recently it seems she is always crying.

Their neighborhood is more opulent than she had hoped. A guard salutes crisply, the car glides down a driveway of flowering vines, the two-story mansion stands elegantly bordered by coconut palms. But Raza is not pleased. "This house is too lavish. The League should have arranged for something smaller."

Mamoon grins his feral grin. "No worries, Raza-bhai. It didn't cost us even one paisa. The family that lived here—yes, they were Hindus—wisely decided to move to Calcutta. They left in a great hurry, taking almost nothing, so the house is fully furnished." He turns to Deepa. "Anything else you want, Aliya Begum, let me know. I'll make sure you get it."

Deepa nods. But even if she needs something crucial, she would not ask Mamoon. He makes her uneasy—and besides, she has Raza. He will get her whatever she requires. For a moment her mind shifts to the family that had lived in this beautiful house, how distressed they must have been to leave it. Then she pushes the thought away. She has enough things already to sadden her.

Focus instead on the airy bedroom to which a maid leads her. In the tamarind tree by the window, birds call to each other. Deepa enjoys a long bath, dons fresh clothes. On the way to the dining room, she passes three extra bedrooms, perfect for visiting family members—except that none of her family will visit her.

Entering the dining room, she is taken aback to find that the two men are still there. She pulls the end of her sari over her face and turns to fetch her burkha.

Raza tries to stop her. "I will be working closely with Mamoon and Sharif. Think of them as family. No need to be so formal—"

But she will not listen, she leaves.

Behind her Raza is apologizing: strict small-town upbringing, serious about purdah.

And Mamoon, vibrant with approval: "It is good to see a woman observing the rules of modesty."

When Deepa returns shielded by her burkha, she sees that the cook, an older woman named Nadia, has gone to great trouble to prepare a grand luncheon: biriyani, dal, fried brinjals, cauliflower and peas curry, mustard fish. Ravenous, she asks for a large helping of everything. The mustard fish tastes just like Bina's; she has to blink away tears.

Mamoon is filling Raza in on the situation in the city. "Quite a few Hindus are deciding to leave for Calcutta. Good riddance, I say. It is helping properties open up for our party members. Even a lowly worker like me has been assigned a nice little two-story house of my own. Once in a while, a Hindu proves to be stubborn. In those cases, we offer him certain incentives to leave—unofficially, of course."

His rasping laugh roils Deepa's stomach; she no longer feels like eating. The people who lived in this house, what kinds of incentives were they given? How had they felt, fleeing for their lives? Were they in Calcutta now? Were they dead?

Here comes Nadia again, beaming, with her masterpiece, which she ladles generously onto plates. To Deepa's dismay it is beef curry. She tells Nadia that she is too full, but the cook is adamant. "You have not had bara gosht until you have tasted my curry," she insists in her heavy East Bengal accent. She places a large chunk of meat on Deepa's plate. Deepa watches the brown gravy spread across the plate, glistening with fat. Bile rises in her throat. She must rush to the bathroom—luckily one is close by. She barely reaches it before vomiting up everything she had eaten. She stays in there, too embarrassed to come out. Raza knocks on the bathroom door and asks if she is alright. I am fine, she says, could everyone please go about their business.

But he keeps knocking until finally she must open the door—what else can she do?—and step out. O mortification. Everyone is standing there staring. She cannot read the others' expressions, but she can see that Raza is thunderstruck.

Nadia runs up with a glass of sweet lemon water, her glance full of knowing. "Drink at least a few sips, it'll keep the nausea down. My dear Bibijaan, you should have told me. The first time is often the worst in these matters. No worries, from tomorrow I will fix your food special, only what you feel like eating."

That is how Deepa learns she is pregnant.

Chapter 18

Priya

All winter her tiny attic room, the cheapest in the cheap board-inghouse where she lives, was freezing; this Philadelphia June morning, it is already too hot. When she returns from college, it will be sweltering. Buttoning her sturdy collared dress, she wills herself to not sweat. Her classmates are airy in their light prints, but she has only the same outfits summer and winter. Priya would like a dress with tiny puff sleeves, maybe one of the flared skirts that all the girls are crazy about, but everything here is more expensive than Somnath and she had accounted for.

It is not important, she tells herself. Except for college clinic hospital, she goes nowhere. At first her classmates invited her to cinemas and dance halls, ice-cream saloons. Church, too; some of them had the notion of saving her soul. They tried to introduce her to men from neighboring colleges so she could go on group dates. But Priya declined. She knows she has gained a reputation for being stern and bookish. No one sees that she is lonely and homesick and sometimes afraid. Thank God for her friend Marianne in New York, who calls her faithfully on the rooming house phone every Saturday morning, cheering Priya up with her latest escapades, scolding her for working too hard, urging her to live a little. If it were not for Marianne, Priya would have forgotten how to laugh.

Soon after she arrived at the Woman's Medical College, the dean gave her a laminated article about Anandibai Joshee. She was one of their first international graduates; they were proud of shaping her success. *We hope Dr. Joshee's life story will inspire you.* But it only depressed Priya. Anandibai had many challenges, she was prone to long bouts of illness, but she had one great advantage. Her husband, Gopalrao, wanted her to succeed. He supported her every step of the way and waited patiently in India for her return.

And I? I lost the man I love by coming here.

Priya had hoped that, after he cooled down, Amit would forgive her. That he would understand. Though postage was expensive, she wrote him long weekly letters about how much she missed him; she described her days in detail, hoping it would keep them connected. Six months passed, the lavender notepaper was long gone; she had not received a single reply. Does he even read her letters? She remembers the fury with which he threw his engagement ring into the muddy riverbank. She should stop writing; clearly it was futile; she should at least hold on to the shreds of her self-respect. Then she remembers his eyes when she told him she was coming to America. That betrayed look. Love and guilt swoop down upon her with their twin raking beaks and again she writes.

Priya hurries to the kitchen where the boarders at breakfast wish her good morning. The women here are good-natured and down-to-earth. They work in offices, stores, the post office. Evenings, they invite her to listen to *Amos 'n' Andy* with them in the parlor. But the jokes baffle her. Why are the white actors pretending to be black? She prefers the fast-paced *Shadow*, with its mysterious hero and heroine who solve the oddest crimes. But she cannot afford time for frivolities. The exams are coming, and she still has work to make up from the semester she missed.

Salt porridge again for breakfast. Mrs. Kelly the landlady, a thrifty widow from Ireland, is fond of porridge because it is cheap and filling. To Priya it tastes like glue, but it is either that or go hungry. Dinner is stew. Priya does not inquire too closely into its ingredients. But Mrs. Kelly is not ungenerous: Sundays she gives them a boiled egg each, on special holidays she makes pancakes, a treat since sugar and butter are still in short supply. Perhaps she feels sorry for Priya because no gentlemen come calling for her. For a little extra money, she packs her a sandwich and an apple so that she will not have to buy lunch.

All day Priya rushes from lecture to lecture, with clinic and laboratory work tucked in between. Early on she dreaded anatomy lab, the cadaver naked and peeled open, the roiling odor of formaldehyde. The first time the stench had been too much. She rushed to the toilets to vomit out her breakfast. Her classmates, adepts by then, eyed her with condescension or pity. But Dr. Manchester, the young professor in charge, gave her cotton wool soaked in cologne to stuff in her nostrils and said he had the same problem when he started. He remains a caring mentor, the only professor who asks after her family. Priya admires all her professors, especially the women, but Dr. Manchester, who is teaching obstetrics now, is her favorite.

Today a group of them go to the Woman's Hospital to observe Dr. Manchester deliver babies. There is a special exhilaration, Priya thinks, in helping infants take their first breath, in placing them in their mother's arms. She senses that Dr. Manchester still feels this way although he has done it a thousand times. When Priya becomes a physician, she knows she will care for many kinds of patients, but delivering babies is what she will love the most.

The first case is easy; the second is a tricky one. The mother, in labor for hours, is small and malnourished, one of the hospital's charity cases. She lies half unconscious, eyes closed. Dr. Manchester examines her and announces that he will have to perform a cesarean. Would any of the students like to assist him? It is clear that the assistant's role will be minor; he is doing this only to give her some hands-on experience. An attending nurse stands by to help in case of complications. Still, the students are nervous; even Priya's seniors hang back.

Priya does not know what comes over her. Is it the memory of a lantern-lit hut where she once helped save a woman's life? She says she will try. If Dr. Manchester is surprised—she is only a first-year, and on the quiet side—he does not express it. She is nervous as they scrub and don their masks, then calmness rises in her, she follows instructions exactly. She hands him instruments, recites the steps for the procedure when he asks, helps him suture the incision. Finishing, he commends her on a job well done, and her classmates stare at her with new, reluctant respect.

Washing up afterward, he asks how she knew what to do. Is there an extra warmth in his voice? She finds herself telling him about helping her father in the village, about the riots that put an end to his life and her training. If Dr. Manchester notices her tearing up, he gives no indication. He ushers the group on to the next patient, firing questions at her classmates, giving her the chance to recover. She is grateful for that kindness.

During their Saturday call, she tells Marianne about Dr. Manchester. Marianne, intrigued, declares that he sounds most attractive. She asks a hundred questions. Finally she says, I think he is interested in you. Priya laughs. I think you have an overactive imagination, she says.

❈

On the table where Mrs. Kelly sets out the mail, a thick packet with Indian stamps, Somnath's dear handwriting. Priya itches with impatience, but Mrs. Kelly runs a tight ship, as she often likes to remind her boarders. So first Priya must eat dinner and help clear the dishes, then she must take a bath because it is her bath night, she gets only two each week. Finally she reaches her stifling room and raises her garret window. O blessed night air. She slits open the package. She knows she should study for tomorrow's quiz first. Once she reads the letters she will be too distracted. But she cannot bear to wait any longer for news of home.

Inside the package she finds envelopes from Somnath and Jamini, who sends her letters through Somnath because postage to America is expensive. There is also a stack of newspapers because Priya had complained that American news paid little attention to India. Now more than ever, with independence fast approaching, Priya appreciates Somnath's thoughtful generosity—especially as she knows from Jamini's letters that the estate is not doing well. Somnath's best Muslim tenant-farmers have left for East Bengal; large stretches of land are lying uncultivated.

Before she turns to the letters, Priya shakes out the package. Once again, nothing from Amit.

Dearest child,

I hope you are safe and well and the horrendous winter weather has abated. I greatly enjoy your amusing descriptions of your classmates and your boardinghouse. I am sorry about the bland American food you are forced to endure. I have instructed Munshiji to send more pickles. Your activities in the clinic and hospital are fascinating. I am glad you are learning so much. I read your letters aloud at dinner, and though Manorama and Amit pretend disinterest, I see them listening intently.

My health is stable, though gout has become more faithful a companion than I would like. Manorama has vetoed sweets from my diet quite completely. I think she is taking out on me her frustration because Amit has not agreed to any of the highly eligible matches she has found for him. I have my suspicions as to why he is so reluctant!

I have handed over the care of the estate and the Calcutta businesses to Amit, who is a wonderful support to me and a hard worker. How that boy has changed and matured. I am sad to see, though, that he rarely smiles. He is deeply involved in village politics and tries to keep the Hindus calm—increasingly difficult as more refugees arrive in the village. He tries to involve the Muslim community, too, but with little success. I am sad to report that tensions are rising, now that it is clear that the country is to be divided. Along with Punjab, Bengal will bear the brunt of it. We have hired more guards, and Amit carries a pistol when he goes on his rounds.

Your father is often on my mind. Nabo would have been delighted to see his lifelong dream of an independent motherland coming true. I pray the transition will occur smoothly, that we have all learned a lesson from the horrifying Calcutta riots which so tragically claimed his life.

A tumult of emotions in Priya as she reads: homesickness amusement affection concern. She considers Amit with his new gravity, his gun, his refusal to marry. O why is that man so stubborn, why will he not write?

The letter continues.

Jamini comes over almost every day to help Manorama because two of our maids have left. At first Manorama was reluctant, but your sister has quite won her over. Jamini often stays late. We send her home with a guard—that will tell you how the village has changed. If a guard is not available, Amit escorts her back.

I should not write this—I know you need to be in America and I should help you to be strong, to succeed in your dream—but I miss you dearly and wish you were here.

He has scratched out a line, but holding it up to the lightbulb, Priya can read it. *I have a bad feeling—*

Priya's chest constricts. What does Somnath mean? Is he worried about the village? The country? Or Jamini and Amit? She imagines Jamini on Sultan, Amit's arm around her to hold her steady. She remembers the night in Calcutta when her sister had called out Amit's name in her sleep. Now she is with him every day and Priya half a world away.

Priya should not blame Jamini. She knows this. The rift between Amit and Priya is Priya's own doing. But when was anger ever corralled by logic?

Too agitated to read Jamini's letter, Priya turns to the newspapers. But they are unsettling in their contradictions. The *Amrita Bazar Patrika* lauds Nehru and Vallabhbhai Patel; the *Star of India* favors the Muslim League's demands; *The Statesman* praises British efforts to facilitate independence. Things are happening at breakneck speed; Prime Minister Attlee and the new viceroy, Mountbatten, have accelerated the transfer of power from June 1948 to August 1947. What do they fear? The Congress has endorsed Nehru's acceptance of the British Plan of Partition, Bengal and Punjab to be divided between the two nations. Bengal has voted: western Bengal will remain with India, eastern Bengal will go to newly minted Pakistan. Turmoil everywhere as people rush to the "right" side of the border, though the border itself has not been fixed. In distress, Priya imagines the chaos, remembers the terrors of Noakhali. Humankind would be better off, she thinks, if there were no religions.

When she gathers up the papers, a blank envelope falls to the floor. She stares, she forgets to breathe. But the letter is from Abdullah, who must have mailed it to Somnath. As with Deepa's letters, which have now stopped coming, there is no greeting, no signature. Priya used to scoff at Abdullah's excess of caution; now she wonders if he is right. The note is terse: Raza and Aliya are settled in Dacca; they are doing well; because of Raza's medical expertise the new government has put Raza in charge of the Dacca Municipal Corporation; Aliya is expecting a baby.

Priya reads that last half-line over and over. How magical that she will have a niece or nephew, even if on the other side of the globe. She is delighted for Deepa, too; the last time they met, she had sensed that her sister was ready for a child. And how is Bina feeling, for surely someone must have informed her about her coming grandchild? Perhaps this will finally repair the rift between mother and daughter.

Then, darker thoughts: What if there are complications? What if Deepa dies in childbirth like thousands still do in India? Even with a healthy baby, Deepa who is not married, not Muslim but forced to bring up her child in the faith, would grow more tangled in deceit.

A distant clock strikes one. There is a quiz tomorrow Priya has not had time to study for. If she is to not fail miserably, she must rest.

But how can she sleep without reading Jamini's letter?

Dear sister,

Although I miss you as always, perhaps it is good that you are away. Things are tense here. We do not know from day to day what may happen.

I stopped going to New Market after a few violent incidents occurred on the train. Ma is increasingly nervous and barely lets me out of her sight. We have been living on our savings for almost two months. No one in the village wants to buy embroidered quilts right now. Everyone is hoarding what little money they have.

I hope you are well in America and enjoying great success. You deserve it.

At another time Priya would have worried about Ma and Jamini; today she is too angry. This is what Jamini always does, exaggerating her troubles to gain people's sympathies. Well, she is not getting Priya's anymore. And why has she hidden her visits to Amit's home from Priya? Surely that indicates an ulterior motive.

Priya crushes the letter and throws it in the wastebasket. She makes herself lie down, though she would rather pace. It is a long time before she is calm enough to sleep.

Chapter 19

Jamini

ugust 14. All across Ranipur, excitement like a tidal wave. Even pragmatic, suspicious Jamini is carried along on it— how can she resist? Tonight will bring the moment so many, including her father, had longed for fought for died for. From Calcutta Som- nath has ordered loudspeakers, floor fans, a more powerful radio— and sweets from Bhim Chandra Nag's famously expensive shop, an indulgence surely justified on this once-in-a-lifetime occasion. Many important families will join him this evening to celebrate their free- dom from centuries of British oppression and listen to the country's brand-new prime minister. Nehru is good with words, he studied at Harrow and Trinity College. Let us see how the pandit uses the colo- nizer's language against them, Somnath says.

Jamini is going to be there. She, too, has been invited.

No. Jamini has her faults, but she does not believe in lying to herself. She was asked to help after she cleverly pointed out to Manorama how complicated the evening would be: welcome the guests, seat them in order of importance, make sure the servants serve the refreshments on time and in the right order without stealing, oversee the cleanup. Can you blame her? A girl like her—not as beautiful as Deepa, not as smart as Priya—has to look out for herself.

As Jamini had hoped, when Somnath heard, he said it would be too late for her to go back home. *Let the girl spend the night here.* Always kind and proper, he added, *Let us invite Bina, too.* But Jamini knew her mother would not come. Manorama put Jamini in the smallest room, though bigger bedrooms were lying empty. Jamini pushed away anger and focused on elation. She would spend the evening with Amit. She would sleep under the same roof as him, something Priya had never done.

❋

Early evening she says goodbye to Bina. She is uneasy about leaving her alone all night but not enough to give up this special opportunity. Bina is not happy about Jamini being away, but she does not forbid her. Jamini had been prepared to argue, but Bina only asks her to take down Nabakumar's framed photograph from the wall and place it next to her bed. She seems calm enough. Or perhaps Jamini chooses not to look too closely. She reminds Bina to eat the dinner she has made for her, to listen to the evening's proceedings on the transistor radio Jamini has borrowed from Amit. She is not sure Bina will do either. She tells her to keep the door locked. When she hears the bolt click, she hurries to the Chowdhury mansion.

Guests congregate on the lamp-decorated, carpet-covered upstairs veranda, women on one side, men on the other. Thank God Amit installed electricity a few months ago; the floor fans are robustly battling humidity and mosquitoes. Their droning adds to the excited chatter, the patriotic songs on the shiny new radio. Loudspeakers have been placed on the edge of the balcony; Somnath wants any

villagers who stop outside to feel they, too, are a part of this momentous occasion.

Jamini notices that the evening's guests are all Hindu, although
Somnath sent invitations to several prominent Muslims, too. Ah well.
Muslims and Hindus in Ranipur rarely socialize. Why should tonight
be different?

Jamini scans the veranda for Amit but does not see him. Manorama
is busy greeting guests but not too busy to give her a look, so Jamini
makes herself useful by ordering the maid to serve tea. She takes
around a platter of rosewater-flavored sandesh. The women, dressed up
as though it were a wedding, are not unfriendly to her but not friendly
either. Everyone knows that Priya and Amit have broken up, that
Bina's quilt business is doing badly. Jamini is glad she decided to wear
her best sari, the yellow silk that Amit had gifted her at his engagement. On her right hand is the gold bangle she took from its hiding
place; she is annoyed to find she still thinks of it as Priya's. She flashes
it discreetly as she hands out sweets and smiles without explaining
when people inquire where she got such a lovely piece of jewelry. She
wonders what she will say if Amit asks her about it.

As though she conjured him with that thought, Amit strides in.
How he has changed in the past months, his face a man's now, harder,
more resolute. Jamini walks toward him, but he is busy telling Somnath
that many villagers have gathered on the street outside the mansion.

"Good, good," Somnath says. "I am happy to see them caring about
such things. Nabo would have liked that." He wipes his eyes, he has
been emotional all day, Amit puts a consoling hand on his shoulder.
Jamini's eyes well up, too, partly for her father and partly at Amit's
tenderness. *Pir Baba, may Amit one day turn his caring toward me.*

But this is not the time to dream. Somnath commends Amit for
having thought of the firecrackers that will be set off in celebration afterward. He asks Jamini to announce to the crowd outside that sweets
will be distributed at midnight. Amit offers to go downstairs in her

stead, but she raises her hand to dissuade him. It is true that the stairs, worn smooth with age, give her leg some trouble. But she does not want Amit to think she is an invalid.

Amit has noticed the bangle. Jamini sees the surprise, the flicker of fury, before he forces his face into expressionlessness. Fear leaps in her chest. Has she gone too far?

"I will explain," she whispers. "After the guests leave." She takes a deep burning breath. All or nothing, Jamini. "I will be in the down-stairs bedroom next to the kitchen."

Amit turns away. She cannot tell what he is thinking.

❀

A little before midnight the radio plays "Bande Mataram." The an-nouncer reminds listeners that this patriotic song, written by Bankim Chandra and sung by Tagore at the 1896 session of the Indian Con-gress, was immediately banned by the British. But everyone learned the song; freedom fighters chose it as their special anthem. Jamini re-members Nabakumar humming it as he went about his chores. He must have sung it on the Salt March, perhaps even as he was being struck down. Now finally it is on the radio. People wipe their tears, even Jamini, who is not sentimental. She joins in the rousing chorus. The words vibrate through the mansion and flow into the street, where the crowd, too, is singing.

Bande Mataram,
Bande Mataram,
Salutations to the motherland.

They stop only when the announcer asks for silence to honor the martyrs who died to bring them this precious gift.

Nehru's voice comes on, deep and grainy, filled with optimism and the gravity of the moment. Jamini's English is not as good as Priya's, but she understands enough for a shiver to go through her.

"Long years ago we made a tryst with destiny, and now the time comes when we shall redeem our pledge . . . when the soul of a nation, long suppressed, finds utterance . . . To the people of India, whose representatives we are, we make an appeal to join us with faith and confidence in this great adventure. This is no time for petty and destructive criticism, no time for ill will or blaming others. We have to build the noble mansion of free India where all her children may dwell."

A translator repeats the speech in Bengali; cheers break out from the street below. The announcer adds that Gandhi has chosen to be not in Delhi celebrating but in Calcutta with the Bengali people, fasting and praying for a nonviolent transfer of power, may his hope come true. More cheering, firecrackers bursting, food and drinks served. Gandhi's favorite song by Tagore, "Ekla Cholo Re," comes on the radio. Jamini hums it as she goes downstairs to make sure that the two guards have opened the gate and are handing singaras and jilipis to the crowd outside. Yes, all is going as planned. She starts up the stairs, hungry for another glimpse of Amit even if he is upset with her.

But there is a commotion. In the hazy light of the torches set outside, she sees jostling. A group of passing revelers have had an altercation with the crowd at the gate. Their lungis and skullcaps reveal them to be Muslims. Voices and fists are raised, people are shoved, someone shouts, *Why don't you go to your own country.* And suddenly a full-fledged fight is going on, people shoved into the compound and thrown to the ground, fists smashed into faces. Jamini shouts to the gatekeepers to close the gates, but the press of the crowd is too much. She shouts for the other guards, but they do not hear her, they are on the roof setting off fireworks. She hurries upstairs to alert the Chowdhurys, cursing her leg for slowing her down.

Then she hears a terrible, booming sound. It takes her a moment to decipher. A gunshot. Amit is on the edge of the balcony, pistol in hand. As Jamini stares, he fires again. He aims well above the heads of the crowd, but it is enough to shock them into stopping. He shouts at the troublemakers to go home before he is forced to hurt anyone. The guards on the roof rush down, they help their companions push the gates shut, the crowd disperses grumbling. But the festive mood is ruined. The guests stare down in distaste at the entrance: trampled flowers, ground littered with food, an overturned cauldron of tea.

"Stupid, illiterate villagers!" Bela's father, Mahendra, grumbles. "Can't stop their bickering even for an occasion like this."

A young man says, "It is not the fault of Somnath-babu's tenants. They were listening peacefully until those Muslim hooligans came and started the fight."

"Why are they even here?" someone says. "Hasn't Jinnah snatched two big chunks of our motherland for people like them? Why don't they leave for Pakistan?"

"Maybe we should persuade them to go," someone else adds. Several people nod enthusiastically.

Amit frowns. "Educated men like you should not be saying these things. Didn't you just hear the prime minister calling for togetherness? Didn't he entreat us not to be communal in our thinking?"

The men mutter among themselves, they do not seem convinced. Jamini tries to defuse the situation; she calls for more sweets, more tea; but even Bhim Nag cannot restore the jubilant mood. People begin to leave.

Later Somnath says, "What an unfortunate end to the evening."

Manorama clicks her tongue angrily. "All the efforts we made to plan, all the food we bought. Ruined." Jamini knows what she is thinking: *Expenses we can ill afford.* "I do not understand what all this fighting is about. Haven't Hindus and Muslims been living side by side in Ranipur for generations? It is the fault of the politicians—they have them riled up."

"Hopefully it will die down soon," Somnath says. He looks at Amit for confirmation, but he is staring out over the dark fields.

Speakers and fans disconnected, carpets rolled up, the floor mopped, the driveway swept clean of waste, the radio repacked in its box because Amit says it should be returned to the store. Jamini oversees everything, chiding the servants superbly. She hopes Manorama is taking note. But Manorama has retired, yawning and inadequately appreciative. Never mind. Jamini, too, retires, calling out a loud good night. Her bedroom is charming, even though it is the smallest, the least ornate. Its windows open onto a banana grove. The leaves whisper in the dark August wind, a secret, an invitation.

Jamini leaves the door unlocked. She sits on her mahogany bed—yes, it is hers tonight—and runs her hands over carvings in the shape of lotuses. She does not change out of her silk sari. She unbraids her hair and lets it fall down her back. Bina calls it her best feature. She will tell Amit the truth about how Priya left the bangle behind, why she did not want to take it with her. When one lacks better choices, it is smart to stay with what really happened.

Jamini waits. The grandfather clock strikes two, three, four A.M. At some point she falls asleep with her head against the bedpost, waking in the morning with a crumpled sari, a stiff neck, and mortification at her stupidity. She leaves without saying goodbye to anyone.

❀

Disappointment and shame are no strangers to Jamini. She has wrestled with them ever since she was old enough to recognize the look in people's eyes as they observed her unsteady approach, pity mingled with relief that they had been spared such misfortune. But last night has humiliated her in a different way. Foolish to believe that she could entice Amit into coming to her bedroom. Foolish to suppose that she could fill the emptiness her shining sister left inside him. Until now Amit has treated Jamini with affection and respect. She fears she has lost that.

Back home, she replaces the gold bangle in its hiding place, stuffs the sari into a trunk. *I will never wear them again.* She tells Bina she is unwell and takes to bed, covering herself head to foot to forestall interrogation.

After two days, Bina is worried. Jamini has never been one to lie around even when she is sick. Bina touches her forehead; she has no fever. She must suspect something, but she asks no questions. For the first time since Nabakumar's death, she ventures to the market to buy ingredients for Jamini's favorite dishes: fried pumpkin, shrimp with coconut milk—food they do not have the means for. *Eat, eat.* Jamini chews obediently, but she cannot swallow. Bina turns on the borrowed transistor so they can enjoy the Independence Day celebrations. The Indian tricolor flag has been raised above Red Fort, in front of a crowd of thousands. Gandhi has made Hindu and Muslim leaders promise that they will work together for peace. Nehru's new cabinet contains people of many religions. What place is there for her, Jamini thinks, a girl with a limp and a head filled with romantic folly, in this new India?

In the evening, a knock. Her heart, unlearned as always, thrashes like a caught bird. Yesterday Somnath had sent a servant to ask if all was well with Jamini. Who might he have sent today? But it is only their neighbors, Leela's Ma and her daughter. Leela's Ma is frightened because her husband went to Calcutta last week and has not returned. Do Bina and Jamini know that there was trouble in the main bazaar today? Muslim fishermen were boycotted, their wares left rotting. Muslim women were barred from entering Hindu shops; people refused to sell them food.

"Who knows what will happen next?" She clutches Leela to her chest. "As soon as Leela's father gets back, I will make him take me to my parents. They have a big joint family, my brothers and their wives all living in the same compound. I will feel a lot safer there. If you like, you can come with us."

After Leela's Ma goes home, Bina sits silently, forehead furrowed. She will never leave this house filled with memories of Nabakumar, but Jamini can see she is afraid. Jamini should be afraid, too, but she is only numb. That night in bed Bina puts her arm around Jamini, a rare gesture. For protection? For comfort? Once Jamini would have turned and held her. Now she lies stiff as wood.

❀

Past midnight Jamini is startled awake by a rapping, an urgent male voice at the door. Groggily she registers other sounds: clanging, yells, women screaming. The sliver of sky outside their window glows dull red. *Jamini Apa, get up quickly, it's Hamid, open the door, no time for delay.* Ignore him, Bina whispers, but something in his tone makes Jamini pull the door open. For a moment, she does not recognize the man standing there, hair in disarray, face streaked with soot, fear-shot eyes.

"You must get away from your house, Apa," Hamid says. "Find a place to hide." Words jumbling in hurry, he tells them that earlier this evening, Hindus came to his neighborhood and set the huts on fire. People barely got out, Hamid lost most of his belongings, several of his friends were badly burned. A child was trampled to death. The attackers demolished the Pir's dargah, too—the Pir who loved and blessed all. Some of the fishermen managed to run to the village to the south which had a large Muslim population. They returned to Ranipur with an armed mob, and now Hindu houses were burning. The mob was moving in this direction.

"I must go," Hamid says. "If they find out I came here, they'll kill me. But I had to. Daktar-babu saved my wife and child. I couldn't just—" Midsentence, he melts into darkness.

The air vibrates with shouts, the torches blur into a sheet of fire. Jamini's brain whirls, she must warn the neighbors, but where is the time? Bina, who has followed her to the door, clutches her arm tightly. *Baba's photo my quilts my silk threads.* Jamini must drag her past the shal trees to the small pond filled with waterweeds. The buildings at the end of the street begin to blaze. Bina struggles, her flailing fist strikes Jamini's eye, for a moment the world goes starry and then black. Jamini shakes her head to clear it and forces Bina into the muddy water until they are submerged to their chins. She turns Bina's head away from the houses, this way she will not see what happens next, and arranges the weeds over their heads. She instructs her to duck deeper if the mob advances in this direction. The trees and the pond are a little way from the houses, but nothing, Jamini is learning, can be counted on tonight.

The women on their street are screaming. She recognizes the voices even though she does not want to. Shouts, guttural grunts, clang of metal on metal. The men are fighting back. Bina is shivering hard, cold or wet or shock. Jamini takes her mother's fingers and pushes them into her ears.

She knows she should not, it will do no good, but logic is drowned in a wave of loss. She must look at their house one last time.

Two figures, a woman and a child, on the porch. Any moment the mob will see them.

The woman beats on the door, terrified, until it swings open. It is Leela's Ma, calling their names. *Help, help, where are you?* Furious dismay fills Jamini. What did the woman think they could do for her? She finds herself struggling out of the mud and hobbling toward them, waving, calling. Futile, but she cannot seem to stop herself. She will never be able to reach Leela and her mother in time and bring them back to the pond. The best she can hope for is to pull them into the shadow of the shal trees. Behind her, Bina is screaming. *Come back, daughter.*

Idiot girl, Jamini thinks. Now you have endangered everyone.

Leela's Ma sees Jamini gesturing. She picks up Leela and starts running toward the shal grove. The yelling mob swarms the street. Jamini is sure they have been seen, but the mob is distracted by a line of men armed with scythes and axes. The three of them reach the grove without being detected. Leela is crying. Her mother claps her hand over the girl's mouth. The melee moves closer. The men with scythes fall back, there are too few of them. Jamini's house is on fire, the house Nabakumar had worked so hard to build. The roof blazes. The doorpost. A woman stumbles out of a flaming house, her hair alight. A neighbor swings a sickle at an attacker. Leela stares horrified at the spurting blood until her mother covers her eyes. A young woman runs toward the shal trees. Two men break off from the mob and follow her, yelling, waving torches. They see Jamini's trio and yell louder. Jamini tells Leela's Ma to go, hurry now; she points her away from the pond where she hopes Bina has had the sense to remain. Jamini, too, runs, but already she is falling behind. Thorny branches tear at her arms, clutch at her sari. Terror drums in her chest. One of the men is very close. Looking back—a mistake—she sees his eyes glitter in the light of his torch. His bared teeth are drawn back in a grin. Jamini's foot catches on a tree root. She falls, and he is on her.

She gouges at his eyes, screaming, but he is too strong. His fist makes her head ring. He straddles her, using his knees to pin her arms, yanking at her blouse until the old cloth tears. His pants are down, his sex gorged and monstrous. A shape looms behind him. O God, is it another man? The shape brings a brick down on the man's head. But he twists at the last moment—did Jamini's widened eyes alert him?—and the brick in Bina's hand hits his shoulder instead. Cursing, he slams Bina's head against a tree. Again, again. She slumps to the ground. He turns back to Jamini, but she has pushed herself off the ground and grabbed the torch. She swings it with all her fury, but he is too quick. She misses him; he lunges for it; she thrusts again, panting, and this time rams it into his chest. He screams his rage, grabs the handle. She holds on to it with everything she has, but he wrenches it away. Now he is the one thrusting it at her, backing her into a copse. He is no longer interested in raping her; he plans to burn her alive.

The torch jabs at her belly. Sharp, scalding pain, even through the sari that drips mud. It sears her forehead. Her hair is wet, or else it, too, would catch fire. Her cry makes him laugh, an excited panting sound. She had not thought people could take so much pleasure in another's pain. He is about to thrust again when they hear gunshots.

Jamini's assailant stares past her, swearing, then drops the torch and disappears into the trees. Turning, she sees horsemen. They are shooting into the air, trying to get the mob to disperse, fighting back only when threatened. Jamini recognizes one of the horses, black coat shining in firelight as he wheels. Sultan, with Amit on his back. Amit shouting instructions, rifle raised, as he gallops into the thick of the fight. Jamini finds herself holding her breath, gabbling a prayer. The mob tries to use their torches to make the horses panic, but after one of them is shot, the rest break and run.

Jamini tries to wake Bina, but she does not move. She is afraid to drag her injured body along the ground. Reluctantly, she leaves her and goes for help. The horsemen have gathered the villagers. Together, they fill buckets from the ponds to douse the flames. For most of the huts it is too late, but Jamini's house, built of brick, still stands. The men throw water on its burning doors and windows. Once the fire is reduced to smoldering, Amit peers in, calling for Jamini and Bina. Is that regret in his voice? Jamini stands in the shadow of the trees, her words trapped in her throat. Something makes him turn and look. The shock on his face is like a slap. *God, Jamini, what did they do to you?*

She backs away, arms crossed over her chest, her shame. But he takes off his shirt and puts it on her. The pity in his fingers burns her more than the torch did. She turns toward the trees, pointing to where she left Bina. The sudden movement makes her head spin. She crumples and in the blackness feels his arms come around her.

❀

The rattling motion hurts her all over; her skin screams in agony. She realizes she is lying on a seat in the Chowdhurys' carriage. Bina lies across from her. She reaches out and touches her mother's hand. When Bina moans, Jamini is thankful because it means she is alive. She struggles to sit up, but her body disobeys. Lie still, says a voice—is it Leela's Ma?—we will be at the big house soon, they will have a doctor there. Jamini says—or does she only imagine saying it before she sinks back into the pain?—I don't want just any doctor. I want my sister. Priya will know how to take care of me.

Someone opens the carriage door. They have reached the mansion. The veranda is full of people who have lost their homes. Some cry, some sit silent with their heads heavy in their hands, some have formed an angry knot in a corner. Amit gives instructions; two servants carry Bina up the stairs. Jamini tries to sit up, grimacing.

"Stop," Amit says. "You mustn't strain yourself until we can get a doctor to look at your injuries." He lifts her as though she were a child, careful not to touch the burns. "I'm putting you and Bina Kaki in the room next to mine." The servants have put Bina in the large four-poster. A smaller bed has been placed near the window. Amit lays Jamini on it and smooths her mud-streaked hair. "I am so sorry that I didn't get there in time to prevent this from happening to you and Kaki. I failed in my promise to Nabakumar Kaka."

Jamini wants to tell him, *You did not fail, you saved us both.* She wants to say, *I will love you always for that, but also just for being yourself. Stay by me a few minutes, hold my hand.* But it is too much effort to shape the words. After a moment Amit covers her with a bedsheet, checks on Bina's breathing, calls a maid to watch over them, and goes back downstairs.

❀

When Jamini was seven years old, she cut her foot on a piece of glass. It hurt hugely, and she was terrified of being stitched up. But Baba gave her a numbing shot, and by the time he sutured the foot, she felt calm and distant from all her troubles. Many times since, she has longed for that calmness. Now, strangely, it has returned. Though her burns still throb and will leave scars peppered across her stomach, the thought does not trouble her. The events of the night of the fire—including her assault—seem like scenes from a film, something that happened to someone else. While changing clothes, Jamini examines her body without embarrassment or sorrow. In the beginning she was ashamed of how it had been touched against her will. Now she sees that it was not her fault—just like her limp. She no longer feels the need to be apologetic about either of them.

❦

Once she is stronger, Jamini asks the doctor to teach her to dress wounds, and when he does, she takes care of her burns and the lacerations on Bina's back. She helps him with his other patients, too, the injured ones staying downstairs until their homes are rebuilt. For the first time she understands Priya's obsession with medicine. There is a godlike satisfaction in reducing pain, in banishing fevers, in helping a body stand up and walk again.

In the midst of all activities Jamini keeps a cautious eye on Bina, who is taking a worrisome amount of time to heal. She shelters her mother—and herself, too—from the news, from the chastened voices of radio commentators and the headlines screaming of rape and killings and torture spreading like an infection across the country even as politicians make lofty speeches and enact new laws. She focuses on the moment. Bina has no appetite, she complains of back pain and migraines, she does not want to leave the bed. Jamini cajoles and scolds until she sits up and eats a few mouthfuls of easy-to-digest soojir payesh, until she walks down the corridor to the toilet. The doctor fears a kidney may be damaged, but Jamini suspects that the injuries are more subtle. Bina's sleep is fitful; she often wakes Jamini with her cries. Jamini tries to make her talk about the night of the fire, but she refuses. If Jamini persists, Bina pulls the bedcover over her head and acts like she cannot hear. It scares Jamini. This is how Bina was after Baba died. Jamini does not think she could bear it if her mother relapsed again.

There is only one thing that Bina responds to. When Jamini tells her, *You saved my life,* the smallest of smiles appears on her lips.

Manorama and Somnath are even less successful with Bina. When Manorama asks if Bina is feeling better, she stares vacantly. When Somnath tells her, *You are going to live here from now on, this is your home,* she does not say yes or no. She brightens only when Amit stops by, and so he makes time for her in spite of his busy schedule—he is helping rebuild destroyed homes for both Hindus and Muslims in Ranipur. He sits on her bed, holding her hands; they talk to each other in low, confidential tones. Jamini would love to know what they are discussing, but if she comes into the room, Bina gestures for her to leave.

Aggrieved by this unfairness, Jamini retreats to the roof. Only the maids come up here to hang the laundry, so she is safe. Among the flapping white widow's saris and bedsheets, she sings the songs her father used to love.

O amar desher mati, tomar pare thekai matha.
O soil of my motherland, I lay my head upon you.

Utho go Bharat Lakkhi.
Arise, goddess of India.

And always, finally, the last one she sang for him, "Aji Bangla Desher Hridoy Hote."

O Mother, when did you emerge from the heart of Bengal,
O beautiful, O splendid,
I cannot take my eyes from you. O Mother . . .

It is the only time she weeps for her father, the only time she allows herself to think how different her life might have been if he were alive.

❧

Once Jamini is stronger, she makes her slow way to her house to see if anything is salvageable. Their clothes are scorched heaps and so are the quilts Bina and she spent so many joyful days creating. Amit's transistor is a twisted lump of metal and melted plastic. Nabakumar's photo is ash; when his face fades in her memory, there will be nothing to bring it back. The gold bangle is safe behind the brick, so are the two gold chains, hidden under the bed in a small metal box. Miraculously, Bina's silk threads, stored in the steel trunk, are unharmed. Jamini brings them back and sets them out on the balcony to air out the smoke-smell. She tries to get Bina started on a new quilt, but her mother has lost all interest in stitching.

Death, even if it touches us in passing, transforms. Jamini feels it has led her to accept that Amit does not love her. Angry though he might be with Priya, his heart will always be hers. Despite that, Jamini loves him because she does not know how to stop. He continues his kindnesses, asking after her health, commending her for helping the doctor, bringing her a sprig of night-blooming jasmine. At an earlier time, she would have read into these gestures what she longed for; now she is grateful and resigned.

In the brief hours of Jamini's leisure, she tries something she has never done before. She writes down the traumatic events of the night of the fire. Addressed to no one, it is not a letter—unless perhaps a letter to herself. She writes even though she lacks the artistic skill the subject deserves, the rare and powerful metaphors. She writes without recrimination or self-pity, though sometimes her body begins to shake and she has to close her eyes and take deep breaths. Then she sends it to Priya—not to guilt her but because she wants her to know, after all these years of hide-and-seek, who Jamini really is.

She sends her everything except the part about Amit. What she feels for him. What she knows he will never feel for her and why. That part belongs to Jamini, only to her.

Chapter 20

Deepa

ooking back at the last few months, Deepa is surprised at how much she has grown to love her life in East Bengal. Her house is comfortable but not opulent—that would have made her uneasy; her bedroom looks out on a mango grove filled with birdcalls; her servants adore her because she is kind. Also she praises them often, gives them baksheesh, and seldom interferes in the running of the household. Everyone is excited about the baby who is coming. Her personal maid, Pari, spoils her with back massages and foot rubs. A doting Nadia fixes whatever she wants to eat, scouring the market for hours for karela and neem leaves because Deepa has developed a taste for bitter things. It is not easy; supplies are often disrupted, and the maids whisper that the best things are being sent away to Pakistan.

When the car is not needed for official business, Raza sends it home. Arshad, the grizzled old chauffeur whom Deepa won over when she addressed him as Chacha, suggests shyly that Aliya Begum might like to go for a drive, fresh air is good at this time. The maids are eager to chaperone her, the car fills with women and laughter. Deepa discovers Dacca to be a charming city; a village girl at heart, she finds that she prefers its slower pace to the frantic cacophony of Calcutta. She strolls around Dacca University with its stately buildings and domed turrets; she feeds pigeons by the lake next to the majestic Hussaini Dalan. Once she visits the War Memorial in Victoria Park, where sepoys who took part in the First Independence War had been hanged, but it makes her sad. She does not go back. Sadness is bad for the baby; she feels it is her duty to avoid it.

That is why she tries hard not to worry about her sisters, her mother. When the newscaster announces the latest details about the bloodbaths occurring along the borders of the two countries, she tells herself that sleepy little Ranipur is surely secure and turns the knob to a station that plays music. She has grown fond of the energetic, patriotic songs of Kazi Nazrul, who is more popular here than Tagore. She has picked up several of them. Now that she is away from Jamini's restrictions, she sings all the time.

Raza, who overhears her when he comes home unexpectedly one afternoon, is astonished. "I did not know you could sing so beautifully," he says. "You should consider performing on the radio. I hear they are looking for artistes." Out of the question, Deepa tells him, with the baby coming. Still, the compliment makes her happy.

When he is tired and dispirited, which nowadays is more often than Deepa would like, Raza asks her to sing his favorite Nazrul Geeti, "Chal Chal Chal." She is glad to oblige, to bring a smile to his face. She fears he works too hard, cares too much. She sings:

Chal chal chal
Urdha gagane baje madol
nimne utala dharani tal
arun prater tarun dal
chal re chal re chal.

March forward,
shatter the night,
O youth of the new dawn,
march forward.

She feels her voice hitting the high notes perfectly. She says to herself in astonishment, Why, I really am becoming a good singer.

❋

Deepa's time with Raza shrinks each day. He is now involved with the East Bengal Legislative Assembly and meets regularly with the cabinet. Khwaja Nazimuddin, the chief minister, thinks well of him and has placed him high up in the Health Ministry. Part of Raza's job is to travel to hospitals around East Bengal and make sure they are following health regulations, which most often they are not. It is frustrating because the directors, who are all older than him, do not take his orders seriously unless he threatens to report them. Deepa warns him to be careful. She fears he is making enemies, this husband of hers straight as an arrow.

"I wish you would not go to all those remote locations," she says.

"Don't worry," he says. "I travel in an armed truck accompanied by guards."

But that, too, is troubling—that the League believes he should need such protection.

One thing comforts Deepa: Sharif has become Raza's assistant. He is with him all day in the office; when Raza goes out of town, he accompanies him. There is a puppylike innocence about Sharif. He follows Raza around with an adulation Deepa finds charming. Like Raza, he wants to make things better for his countrymen and is willing to strive hard for it. He often comes home with Raza and labors with him late into the night. On such occasions, Deepa invites Sharif to have dinner. He calls her Apa. Indeed, around him she feels like an older sister. Is that perhaps a reason for her fondness? At the table, cajoling him to eat more, she dispenses with her burkha.

Fortunately she has not encountered Mamoon in the last few months. She had told Raza that something about the man made her uncomfortable. Raza shook his head at her pregnant-woman fancies; but since that time he has invited him only when he has organized official all-male dinners that Deepa is not expected to attend.

Deepa kept track of Mamoon, though, the way one might a dangerous animal. Ever since he came back from Calcutta, people said, he was changed, a driven man. He was rising fast in the army, he was promoted to the rank of captain, he was invited to give a report at the Legislative Assembly, he was developing a reputation for dealing with troublemakers. His unit was often summoned when college students gathered for a protest or when fights broke out between Muslims and the small contingent of Hindus who had stubbornly hung on to their ancestral properties.

Raza says, "You have to give the man his due. He is not afraid of anything. On a mission, he is always in the forefront. His men hero-worship him. He is a crack shot, too. Not many have those skills. No wonder the chief minister has chosen Mamoon's unit to provide security when he appears in public."

They are in bed, where they can converse without being overheard, so Deepa says, "The real reason is that Mamoon knows how to flatter the right people." She adds, "It is a skill you would do well to learn." She is only half joking. It frightens her, the way Raza speaks out against corruption. Sharif has told her that recently at the Legislative Assembly Raza questioned parts of Mamoon's report. Mamoon responded politely, but Sharif could tell that he was furious.

"Now, now, Deepa," Raza says in his mild way. He still calls her Deepa when they are alone because he knows she likes it. "Sleep now, it is late." He kisses her forehead and turns off the light. But

Deepa senses that something about Mamoon makes him uncomfortable, too.

❋

Today Raza has a rare day off, so Nadia packs a picnic lunch with luchis, potato curry, and sweet curd, and they leave the city behind. Arshad finds them a deserted stretch by a river and retreats to allow them privacy. They spend a leisurely afternoon eating and watching kingfishers swooping down to the water. She leans her head against his shoulder as he speaks of what he hopes this new country will offer their child. They have already decided on names, choosing ones common to both Hindus and Muslims: Kamal for a boy, Sameera if it is a girl.

Afterward Raza asks for assistance with a speech. A new part of his job is to persuade the poor and illiterate in the various cities he visits to come to hospitals and get vaccinated, but he has not been having much success. Deepa is delighted; she loves her easy lifestyle, but sometimes she feels her brain is rotting from disuse. She suggests that he give his speeches not in the maidans or government halls but at factories, docks, bazaars, mosques, and slums. "Describe in graphic detail what happens to people who get typhoid and cholera. Bring along doctors and nurses who can vaccinate people on the spot. Send some doctors to the schools, too, to get the children vaccinated."

Good ideas, Raza admits. "But the poorest children most in need of medical care don't even go to school."

Deepa is struck by an idea. "What if I go with you to the slums and talk to the women? Maybe I could persuade them to get themselves and their children vaccinated."

Raza refuses. "I'm not taking you on the road. What if there is a complication? What if you get sick?" But finally she sweet-talks him into letting her accompany him to one of the poorer neighborhoods in Dacca.

❀

Raza is hosting an important dinner. In addition to regular guests, he is excited to include a young student leader, Mujibur Rahman, who is studying law at Dacca University. Raza likes Mujib, because they are both passionate about improving the lives of the poor. He feels Mujib has a bright future; already he is organizing a Muslim Student League. Raza has a request for Deepa. Mujib moved recently from Calcutta and loves the songs of Tagore, but the radio stations here rarely play them. Mujib has asked if Deepa would kindly sing a Rabindra Sangeet or two that evening.

Deepa is reluctant; finally Raza persuades her. Just one song, from behind a curtain.

"How did Mujib find out that I sing?" Deepa asks suspiciously. "Who could have told him?" Raza shrugs. He does not know, does not think it is important. But it troubles Deepa.

The night of the dinner, a gauze curtain is hung in the living room; from behind it Deepa, the veil of her burkha thrown back, sings. She is pleased with her choice, a piece her father loved; it is patriotic and poetic but, unlike many Tagore compositions, does not mention God, which might be problematic in this milieu.

Amar Sonar Bangla ami tomay bhalobashi
Chirodin tomar akash tomar batash
Amar prane bajay banshi
Amar Sonar Bangla

O my golden Bengal, I love you.
Your sky, your breezes, forever
they are a music to my soul.
My golden Bengal.

The guests applaud. *Kya baat, a golden song in a golden voice.* Through the gauze she watches Mujib, tall, thin, bespectacled, wearing a mustache so he will look older, so people will take his ideas seriously. His face is wet with tears, his eyes unfocused; he does not speak. The song has transported him elsewhere. A true tribute, Deepa thinks. The other person who is mesmerized is Mamoon. He sits so still, a genie might have turned him to stone. He stares at the curtain with narrowed eyes as though he can see through it, as though he can look into Deepa's very being. Was he the one who informed Mujib about her talent, who engineered this evening? Deepa disquieted bids the company a quick goodbye and leaves the room. For a long time that night, she cannot sleep.

❀

They choose Korail Basti, the largest slum in Dacca, for Deepa's first foray. Pari's aunt, who lives there, has many friends. Pari says she will get them to come and listen to Aliya Begum. Though Raza has warned her, the basti stuns Deepa. Miles of shanties crammed against one another, roofs patched with palm leaves or tin. Narrow alleys strewn with garbage, bordered by feces, stinking of rot. Naked swollen-bellied children run after them, begging for a paisa. Men in ragged lungis squat on porches, scowling and spitting. The stench of rot and piss rises all around Deepa. She fears she will throw up. She grips Pari's hand tightly, allows herself to be pulled along. She cannot give up, everyone is depending on her, an entire procession follows her: Raza, Sharif, two nurses borrowed from Mitford Hospital, four guards carrying medical supplies, sweets, and nightsticks.

They enter a relatively prosperous neighborhood, dwellings of brick and mud, painted doors. Pari knocks on a blue door; a middle-aged woman in a worn but clean sari welcomes them. Inside, a group of women watches them warily. Some carry children on their hips. Several seem ready to bolt. Deepa asks the men to wait outside; she removes her burkha; she eats a mouthful of the puffed rice the hostess offers her.

The women relax. They begin to ask her questions: Is this her first pregnancy? When is the baby due? From there she is able to move on to topics of health. She explains the dangers of pox, typhoid, and cholera; she says she will vaccinate her child as soon as possible; she shows them the small vaccine scars on her own arm. *It hurts for a minute but protects forever.* Pari and her aunt volunteer to be inoculated; others follow. Then they go to fetch their friends, their older children. When they return, some of their menfolk come with them, and Raza vaccinates them out on the street. People gather to look. More agree to take shots. Afterward, sweets are handed out. Deepa's heart twists as she sees the children smiling as they bite into their treats.

"Please send them to school," she tells the mothers. "The government is offering free education. They will learn to read and write, get good jobs. Don't you want that?"

Some of the women nod, but others say that they cannot afford it. The older children are already working to bring in money, and every paisa helps. The younger ones watch the babies so the mothers can go to work. Deepa sees the truth of what Raza says: there are no easy solutions. To bring change, the leaders must work selflessly, tirelessly, for a long time.

More people arrive on Pari's aunt's street as news travels. Deepa is exhausted. Pari finds her a stool and asks if they should leave. But she does not want to ruin the momentum. They vaccinate people until they run out of supplies. Raza whispers that this is beyond his wildest dreams. Deepa promises the women that they will return. *We will vaccinate all of Korail! We will have sweets for every child who comes, sandesh, jilipis rasagollahs!* Driving home in a cloud of euphoria, she understands for the first time why Priya was so determined to be a doctor.

It does not work out as Deepa plans. The rest of the vaccinating party will return to Korail, but Deepa starts having pains and is put on strict bed rest by her doctor. Raza phones to check on her every few hours, at home he brings his work to the bedroom so he can sit by her, he berates himself for taking her to Korail, for letting her get overtired. He kisses her hands and says she is the best helpmate.

Baby Sameera arrives four weeks early, but she is healthy enough, with a strong pair of lungs that she uses to full effect. Deepa's first thought is one of gratitude. Not only because she is normal and healthy, but also because she is not a boy. Otherwise her child would have had, forever, the mark of his father's religion cut into him. She has heard on the radio how Hindu mobs have been forcing men to lower their pants so they can decide who should be spared and who chopped to pieces. She suspects that Muslim mobs are doing the same thing.

Now the entire household revolves around Sameera. The maids clamor to hold her. Arshad drives to the store multiple times a day for baby necessities. A stern Nadia, her loyalties shifted quite completely, bullies Deepa into swallowing endless glasses of barley water and bowls of mashed papaya so she will produce the best breast milk. Raza takes off three whole days—something he has never done before—and spends most of them gazing besottedly at his daughter. At night they lie with Sameera tucked carefully between them and discuss their dreams for her future. They have sent two letters to Dr. Abdullah announcing their good news, with a cautiously worded request to let Deepa's family know. Raza waits eagerly for his uncle's blessings, but no replies arrive. The mail service between India and East Bengal has many problems. Raza thinks the letters may be lost. "We will write again." He kisses Sameera. "Meanwhile, we have our hands full with this little one."

Can pain wrench our hearts in the midst of greatest joy? That is how it is with Deepa. As she smiles at her husband and daughter, she thinks, How delighted Ma would have been to hold her first grandchild. How—because of the choices I made—she will never do so.

Chapter 21

Priya

$\mathcal{T}$he days speed up as the new semester starts; the evenings refuse to pass. Priya's studies grow easier, leaving her more time to worry. All August, she paces her room in the evenings until the tenant below complains. With whom in this country can she share her excitement, agitation, guilt, loneliness? Marianne is sympathetic, but she has always lived in an independent land. She does not really understand.

India balances on the verge of independence, then August 15 arrives, then it is gone. Priya scours the newspapers in the college library and finds a few unsatisfying paragraphs tucked between discussions of gambling laws, government inquiries into rising food prices, and an unprecedented heat wave. *The New York Times* states, "Ceremonies at New Delhi and Karachi Mark Independence for 400,000,000 Persons—Death Toll in Communal Fighting Reaches 153." A pity, she thinks, that people should die at this dream-come-true time. Still, 153 is not so bad.

India's independence should inspire her own, Priya tells herself. As her countrymen hold their heads high with self-respect, so will she. She will no longer go knocking at the door that has been slammed shut in her face. She stops writing to Amit. A decisive step like that should make her feel better. Instead all day there is a dull pain in her chest.

Dr. Manchester is not teaching any of Priya's classes this semester. She finds herself missing the care with which he pointed out the intricacies of a disease, the many ways it camouflaged itself in the body. She appreciated that he was never easy on her. He challenged her to think beyond the obvious, expressed his disappointment when she did not. Inquiring at the department office, she learns that he does not teach the upper-level courses; his own flourishing practice keeps him too busy. She is surprised by the sharpness of her disappointment.

But then she walks out of Pediatrics, her last lecture for the day, and there he is in the corridor. He says, "Someone told me you were looking for me. Did you have questions?" He suggests discussing them over a meal because he is famished. Now that she is not his student, such things are permissible. They walk to his car, sleek and chocolate colored, gleaming in the last of the sun. Amazingly, the top folds back. She had not imagined that such a car might belong to this man with his simple dark clothes, his earnest mustache, his diligent focus on the task at hand. He grins boyishly, pleased to have surprised her. The sweet, moist wind tugs playfully at her hair as they drive.

She is afraid he will take her to a fancy restaurant where she will feel out of place in her plain dress and boxy shoes. Additionally, it will be too expensive when she offers to pay her half, as she must because this is not a date, she would never go out on a date, because . . . There her thoughts stutter to a standstill.

Does he guess her hesitation? He stops outside a simple, squat diner with a crowded parking lot, saying, "Charley makes the best Philly cheesesteaks and chicken pasta." They join a long line of waiting customers. But then a plump, mustachioed man in an apron—Charley himself—sees Dr. Manchester and ushers them to an inner room, saying, No, Doctor, you don't stand in line in my diner, telling Priya how he delivered Charley's daughter and saved her life, too, because she was blue and not breathing when she came into the world. Now, Charley, Dr. Manchester says, flushing with embarrassment, which Priya thinks is rather charming.

Priya does not know what most of the menu items mean, so Dr. Manchester asks if he might choose for them both. He must know about Indians; he skips the beef and pork and orders cannelloni stuffed with chicken and mushrooms. It is the best meal Priya has had since she came to America. The pasta, drizzled with a creamy sauce, is a world apart from the clumpy spaghetti Mrs. Kelly dollops out twice a week. The morsels of chicken melt in her mouth. Daringly she sips the white wine Dr. Manchester has ordered for them and feels she is floating. Dr. Manchester asks her to call him Arthur. He has lived in this city all his life, though he did travel in Europe before the war. He thinks it very brave that she ventured across the world on her own. His father, like Priya's, was a doctor and inspired him to become one, too. Priya finds herself telling him about her family, the village, her lifelong dream of becoming a physician, and finally, though she had not intended it, the horrifying night of her father's death. It is the first time she has spoken about it. She breaks down more than once, but Arthur hands her a stack of napkins and waits calmly for her to continue. When she is done, she feels divested of an immense burden she had not known she was carrying. When he pays for dinner she does not protest, it no longer seems important. Has she not already accepted a far greater gift from him?

But now it is late and they must hurry because Mrs. Kelly is a martinet when it comes to curfew; she has been known to lock out boarders if they are not back in time. That would not do, Arthur says, that would ruin this perfect evening. He drives too fast along the emptying streets, gliding through stop signs and even once a red light, both of them laughing like truant children and him claiming he has never done such an illegal thing in his life, it must be Priya's witchy influence. There is just enough time when he drops her off for her to say thank you and good night and yes, it was beautiful, I would love to do it again.

She slips into the boardinghouse hoping to avoid people, but here is Mrs. Kelly at the entrance, arms crossed, feet tapping, impatient to lock up. She gives Priya a knowing look, though not a disapproving one. Mrs. Kelly likes her young ladies to make profitable alliances, it enhances her reputation, and she has noticed the gleaming chocolate convertible. All she says is that there is a packet of letters for Priya on the mail table.

Priya picks up the packet, which is heftier than usual, with an odd reluctance. For the first time she does not long to immerse herself in news from home. It is always wrenching, in some way or other, and does she not deserve one evening free of responsibility and worry, heartache and guilt? I will read it tomorrow. Tonight I will sit on the windowsill and look at the sky and think about my evening, the one perfect laced-with-tears-and-laughter evening I have had since I came to this country.

But then, because she is who she is, she opens the packet.

❊

She begins with Somnath. He is the safest.

Dearest girl,
First let me assure you that your mother and sister are secure in my
house, and here they will remain from now on. How blind I was, not
to sense what was coming. I failed your father, and you, too. Had I not
promised to take care of them, had I not promised you need not worry?
Thank God Amit got to them in time.

The letters lurch, she cannot connect the words: *fire night Hindus attack Muslims houses many ash many homeless Amit gun rescue Jamini burns Bina injured depression.* Can this really have happened in peaceful Ranipur? To her mother and sister? She drops the letter, spreads out the newspapers to double-check. Calcutta Bombay Delhi. Somnath must have had Munshiji special-order the papers. The headlines contradict each other. "India's Millions Rejoice." "Scenes of Splendor in the Capital." "Bengal and Punjab Border Award Announced." "Border Award Condemned." "Political Freedom for One-Fifth of Human Race." "Are You Leaving for Pakistan?" "Free India Will Ring Out Colonial Imperialism." "Killings Continue in Lahore." "No Foothold for Foreign Powers in Asia." "Rail Journey Between Delhi and Lahore 'Dangerous.'" "Wild Scenes of Jubilation in Delhi." "Horrors of Partition." "Fires Blaze All Day Long." "Warning to Passengers." "Deadly Attack on Passenger Trains." "Death Toll Rises." "Murder and Arson Reach New Peak." "Gandhi Begins Fast as Calcutta Burns."

No, she says. No. But denial cannot erase truth. *Baba, is this what you fought for, longed for, sang about?*

Finally, all that is left is Jamini's letter. She cannot delay it any longer. Except it is not a letter, she is not sure what it is, poem or confession, rulebook, catalog of loss. It will transform her understanding of her sister, keep her awake all night. Through the weeks to come, it will flash in her brain like a migraine attack.

Never seen such hatred in a man's eyes, his grinning teeth. How it went through me, the thwack of Ma's head against the tree trunk. I swung the burning torch with all my might. I would have killed him gladly. How the sky glowers against a village in flames. We are refugees in our own land. They eye me, pity and horror, and thank God it was not them. House: gone. Ma's quilts: gone. Baba's photo: gone. Deepa: gone. Priya: gone. Absurd hopes of love: gone. Gone also: belief in human intelligence, benevolence of the universe, India's shining future. Count only upon yourself. Be ashamed of nothing anyone can do to you.

❀

She dives into work through the next weeks, takes on extra duties, transcribing lecture notes, helping prepare the labs, assisting in the clinic after classes. She rushes out of her last class the moment it ends, she does not want to be found, she burrows into the far corner of the library. She cannot stand to be in her room, the light is too stark there, no place to hide. She pores over books until the building closes and the librarian shoos her out. Nothing she studies penetrates the clammy fog that fills her skull. At night she thrashes, her frantic imaginings will not let her sleep. Somnath and Jamini have not responded to the panicked notes she sent the next day and again the next week, paying extra for express delivery. To Jamini: *I am distressed and anxious beyond measure, let me know how you and Ma are doing.* To Somnath: *I want to come home, perhaps I can be of help there, but it will be very expensive, and I will miss many classes, tell me what should I do.* Is her mother getting worse? Why did Jamini mention nothing of Amit, how he saved her life? Why does Amit not write? Is such a huge calamity not reason enough to forgive her? She does not recognize the man Somnath wrote about, a man who frightens away a mob, rescues women, rebuilds villages, handles his father's affairs. He is fine, he is admirable, but he is not her Amit. She loses weight, there are purple bruises under her eyes. At the boardinghouse she pushes away her dinner until Mrs. Kelly doses her with hyssop to make sure she is not coming down with some strange foreign disease.

Then Arthur waylays her outside the lecture hall before she can escape and insists that they go on a drive. Beside a quiet turn of the Wissahickon, under a canopy of white oak, he unpacks a hamper: bread, fruit, a great wheel of cheese, blackberry preserves bottled by his housekeeper. *I know this is a hard time for you.* He has scoured the newspapers, he has learned of the turmoil in her homeland. He waits patiently until she eats. One bite, two, three. The preserves are delicious, she cannot stop, she eats an entire hunk of cheese. She begins to talk.

When all the words have poured from her, and the tears, Arthur says she should not go back to India so suddenly. What her family has gone through is terrible, but they are safe for the moment. What can Priya do for them right now? On the other hand, if she goes away midsemester, she will have to make up the work. She may fail the exams, may have to repeat the courses. She has come here for a purpose, her uncle has spent a great deal of money, the admissions committee has trusted her with a valuable seat, taking it away from another candidate. At the least she should wait and make a decision after exams. He stops there, but she sees the rest in his eyes. *I am here for you, you are not alone, let me take your hand.*

She allows herself to be persuaded. It makes sense, his advice. To go back home now would be to destroy the dream for which she gave up love. She allows herself to fall into a welcome rhythm with Arthur. He picks her up after classes and brings her to his home, where she is most properly chaperoned by Mrs. Thackeray, the housekeeper who has worked for the Manchester family since Arthur's birth. Priya studies at one end of the maple dining table while Arthur reads his medical journals at the other. Mrs. Thackeray serves them dinner: hearty corn chowder, roast chicken. One night she brings out for dessert a delicious latticed apple pie. When she retires to the kitchen, Arthur whispers that the housekeeper bakes this only for people to whom she has taken a special liking. A bashful smile flickers over Priya's face.

That evening Arthur kisses her before he drops her at the boardinghouse. It is a gentlemanly kiss, but with an undercurrent of passion held back only because he does not want to frighten her away. Look forward, Priya. Her heart beats hard as she kisses him back.

❀

Another letter has arrived for Priya, an unusually slim envelope. The writing on it is Somnath's, but when she tears it open, she sees with a lurching heart that the writer is her mother. It is the first letter she has ever written to Priya.

> *Dear Daughter Priya,*
>
> *I know you have learned our horrifying news from Somnath, so I will not repeat it. I have still not recovered fully from my injuries and do not know if I ever shall.*
>
> *But amid all this horror is one piece of good news. Jamini is to be married to Amit. It will be a quiet ceremony held in a month's time.*
>
> *I know you will be unable to come because of your studies, and indeed you should not interrupt them. I only wanted to let you know.*
>
> *Send good thoughts to your sister, she has suffered much. But for her I would be dead today.*
>
> *I wish you all success and happiness.*

On the back of the sheet, a hasty scribble from Somnath:

> *I do not know how this happened. Amit refuses to discuss it. I fear he is making a grave mistake.*
>
> *But the first mistake was mine, to encourage you to go so far away, to create a rift between you two. I meant well, I wanted to fulfill your dream, through you I thought Nabakumar's passion would live on.*
>
> *Now I see that meaning well counts for nothing. Only what happens in the end matters.*
>
> *I cannot advise you in this, nor can I request you to return. You must do what you feel is right. Know that whatever you decide to do, you will always be my dear daughter, and I will always support you.*

She stays home the next day and the next, missing class, something she had not done even when she was ill. She tells Mrs. Kelly she has the worst migraine. She thinks and paces, paces and thinks. On one side her past, on the other her future. They grasp at her with avid fingers, they pull in opposite directions, they are tearing her in two. In the evening Mrs. Kelly pants her way up the stairs and raps on her door. A Dr. Manchester has called twice each day; this last time he said that if Priya was not better by tomorrow, he was going to come and check on her.

Mrs. Kelly prides herself on being a plain speaker. Are you in trouble? she asks. Are you in the family way?

If she were not so distressed, Priya would laugh. She manages to tell Mrs. Kelly that she need not fear for the reputation of her boarding-house. Only after Mrs. Kelly leaves does she acknowledge to herself the depth of the trouble she is in, although it is a different kind. She returns Arthur's affections, yes, but in the core of her being it is Amit she still loves. She must see him one last time before he becomes someone else's.

No, not *someone else's*. Jamini's.

If Amit had agreed to a marriage arranged by his aunt, Priya would have wept, she would have been heartbroken, but she would have accepted it. Jamini, however? To think of Amit marrying Jamini, who has always coveted him, feels wrong in a different, deeper way.

That is why she must go to India, must look into Amit's eyes, must ensure he is doing this for the right reasons.

Early the next morning, she goes to Arthur's house. Unfair to ask his help with this, but who else does she have? When he sees her face, he takes her by the hand and leads her to his study. He phones the college and cancels his classes for the day: something she has never known him to do. She feels deeply grateful, abominably guilty.

All night Priya has rehearsed her words, but now as she speaks she cannot stop the tears. She is sure her garbled story will make no sense to Arthur: a sister's sudden marriage, a mother's grave illness, an uncle's graver distress, a best friend she must speak to one last time though she cannot explain why. But he is a doctor, used to deciphering pauses that say what words cannot, to translating the accents of pain.

He understands. Perhaps especially he understands *best friend*. He tries hard to dissuade Priya, fails.

But he is a large-hearted man; though disappointed, he does not hold a grudge against her for choosing her past over her future. That same day he argues eloquently on her behalf to the faculty committee, procuring emergency permission. The committee is not happy. This is the trouble with women from foreign cultures, they say. Too emotional, too entangled in family. They grant Priya a leave of six weeks, four for travel there and back, two to take care of family needs. The letter Arthur hands to her states, *If you are not back on time for your semester-end exams, we will admit a woman from our considerable waiting list in your place.*

Tickets purchased on the next ocean liner to Calcutta, for which she must wait an entire interminable week. A telegram to Somnath. Arthur insists on driving Priya to the station. He had wanted to accompany her to New York, put her on the ship, but she said no. Waving away the porter, he lifts her luggage onto the train: just a small case, she has left everything else in his house. His eyes are the color of cinnamon bark, color of loss. How long, she wonders with a pang, before she sees him again? Before boarding, she clasps his hands. "Thank you. I don't deserve this kindness, this more-than-kindness. When I come back I will be free of ties and obligations, free to make decisions. But I cannot ask you to put your life on hold."

He turns over her palms, he kisses them the way his father might have done, courting his mother. He says simply, "For you, I will wait."

At New York, a teary Marianne wrings her hands, blunt with distress. "You're making a gigantic mistake, leaving behind a wonderful man who loves you, who is eager to help you in every way. Why are you going to India at all? Except for your uncle, no one wants you there—and even he would not want you to jeopardize your career like this."

This is all true; Priya is too honest not to admit it. There is nothing for her to do except hold her friend close and ask Marianne to wish her good luck.

One ship, then a second one, walking the decks morning and evening while the days inch ahead. But could it be that only Priya's days are inching along, that in India they are flying, wedding preparations being made, things changing shape, never to go back to what they were again? At last the Calcutta docks loom, faithful Munshiji waits. This time so much is different, even beleaguered Priya feels a small, fierce joy on seeing it. The officials are Indian: customs, police, army, port supervisors; they all hold their heads higher, their eyes shine brighter, they are working in their own country, for their own Bharat. Yes, in places the hate-fires are still burning, but they will put them out, and meanwhile there is a wind, wind of independence, blowing away centuries of fog, revealing blue sky.

She must swallow her impatience, her anxiety; she must stay in Somnath's Calcutta home for the night because it is not safe to travel in the dark. She asks Munshiji to find out when, in the next few weeks, ships will depart for America. Efficient man that he is, he has thought of this already, he hands her a schedule. She tucks it into her purse without looking. A small hope glimmers inside her, perhaps it is a superstition. If I do not read it, I will not need it.

To distract her, Munshiji hands her the newspaper. She opens it wide and discovers an unsought gift: Sarojini Naidu has been chosen as the new governor of Uttar Pradesh. Though gouged by the years, she is still majestic in her massive chair. She was ill but is better now; she tells her countrymen not to worry: "I am not ready to die because it requires infinitely more courage to live." The words buzz inside Priya. Yes, yes. She has given up on her dream of meeting Sarojini, but she is thankful for her message, she will take it to heart. She phones Dr. Abdullah hoping for news of Deepa, but he tells her that he has heard nothing from Aliya or Raza, not a single letter, that is how young people are nowadays. He speaks curtly, but she can hear the heartache and worry behind his words because Raza is the son he never had. But why should he worry? Is it not true that in East Bengal the Muslim League is king?

Finally the village, beloved and hard on the heart. It is Durga Puja season, and as though to mock Priya everything is blooming: marigold hibiscus jasmine, the maddening sweetness of honeysuckle. Clouds like white cotton candy dot the unworried sky. Bamboo pandals are being constructed for the goddess, but cautiously, young men of the neighborhood taking turns as guards. She asks Somnath's driver to loop the carriage past their ruined home. It is as desolate as she had feared, roofless, with burned doorposts and windows. The charred bricks scrape at her insides.

At the mansion Somnath, unshaven uncombed hollow-cheeked, clings to Priya when she touches his feet; she can feel the brittleness of his bones, the weight of his hope. He says, Thank you for coming, daughter, now that you are here surely all will be well; but she has little hope of it. Bina is sleeping, her face is bone and shadow, her eyes dart wildly under their lids. Priya cannot bear to wake her. Amit is away managing estate work, rebuilding damaged homes. Everything has fallen behind because last week he had to go to Calcutta to make inquiries; they will need to sell the shipping business, it is not doing well. Somnath sighs. The boy drives himself too hard, I worry, he is never home before dark.

Manorama welcomes Priya with cautious affection. It is late in the day, but she has saved lunch for her. She is happy but also worried. Is it about the mayhem Priya might cause? Priya puts away the thought and focuses on the meal, food of childhood on her tongue after many deprived months: pui shaag with its succulent stalks, mourala fish cooked in mustard. She eats even the bones. Manorama watches with satisfaction, wipes her eyes when she thinks Priya is not watching. No one can find Jamini. Maybe she is delivering food to the homeless, maybe she is bandaging wounds—such a helpful girl, always thinking of others.

Afterward, Priya sits on her mother's bed, rubbing her feet until—
she can tell by the uneven rhythm of her breath—Bina wakens. But
it is a while before she opens her eyes and even more time before she
beckons Priya close, touches her cheek with a thin hand. Whispers, I
am glad you came, I thought I would not see you again. They remain
like that, without further conversation, until Bina says, "You must not
blame him. He is marrying Jamini because I told him to."

Priya is a statue, not blinking, not breathing.

Bina says, "Every day after he brought us here, Amit would come
and sit with me. I was miserable all the time, skin scraped raw, pain
pulsing in my head, my back. It hurt to walk, to eat, to go to the toilet.
I had lost everything. Even the sari I wore belonged to Manorama. And
my poor Jamini, everyone looked at her like she was soiled goods. I
wanted only to die. He held my hand, talked to me. I refused to respond. He kept saying he was sorry he had not been able to keep his
promise to your baba. Had not been able to reach us in time. Had not
been able to prevent or protect. He begged me to stay in this home the
rest of my life. I will make sure you want for nothing, he said. I said no,
my daughter and I do not want charity, we want to go back to our own
house, to live there or to die. But he would not give up.

"One day I said, There is one thing you can do if you truly want
to help, if you want us to remain here. Anything, he said. I told him,
Marry Jamini. No one will marry her now, after the attack. No one
cares that it happened because she was trying to save our neighbors.

"I said, Deepa and Priya have left, flown where they wanted. They
are living the lives they chose. But Jamini chose me, and now her future
is ruined. I said, If you do this, I will consider your promise fulfilled. I
will stay in your house once it is Jamini's, too. For three days, Amit did
not speak to me. On the fourth he came to my bedside and said, I will
do what you want."

❀

In the evening Priya goes down to the river. She has not seen Jamini yet. Perhaps they are hiding from each other. The fishing boats return home beneath sunset hues so beautiful she could weep. She is angry with everyone, then with no one, then with herself. Then for thinking that this was her own fault for wanting too much. No matter how her story ends, she refuses to believe that a woman cannot have the joys of home and also a place in the world.

The sky gives up its brightness, the mosquitoes whine in her ears, Priya waits in the half-dark. What is she waiting for? Lights from the house reflect on the water, the small waves kiss the shore and dissolve. And he comes as she had hoped and feared, because this was where things were broken, and if anything can be mended, it will be here. She turns to him and is startled by how much older he looks, and harder. The playfulness has gone out of his face, and in its place, as she had read in a book of Bible stories Nabakumar had bought for her long ago, is the knowledge of good and evil.

She makes herself smile, she starts to say something light and teasing and meaningless. Did you think you could get away without inviting me to your wedding? But he moves more rapidly than she had expected, he is holding her so tight she cannot breathe; she does not want to breathe, not if it means he will have to let her go. He is kissing her, he is crying her name, he is saying *why*. Does he mean why did she leave? Does he mean why did she come back now? No, he is saying why was he so stubborn, why did he not reply to her letters like he longed to. And then like a punishment her letters stopped coming. Perhaps this is a dream, because on his finger is the engagement ring he had thrown in the mud of the Sarasi River. He sees her looking and gives a rueful smile. The next morning I went down to the river with the servants. We searched the bank for hours until we found it. I kept it in the almirah until you left for America and then I wore it. He is saying, I cannot lose you again, Pia my love, I will go with you to America if that is what you want, we will find a suitable husband for

Jamini, Baba has given the Calcutta house to me and I will sell it; with a large enough dowry anything is possible.

Hush, she says, her mouth against his chest. Hush.

They sit on a fallen tree trunk, fingers intertwined, whispering love words. He wants to imagine their life together, but she only wants this moment, her head on his shoulder, his lips in her hair, an old song looping through her mind, *Amaar poran jaha chay, tumi tai, tumi tai go. My heart's desire, it is you, it is you.* An old song by Tagore, one of Baba's favorites that he used to ask Jamini to sing.

Now the memory comes back fully, Jamini singing the song at Priya's engagement, glancing from under her lashes at Amit because she could not help it.

And as though the memory has pulled her from air, Jamini stands on the brick path, shadowed by fronds so that Priya cannot read her expression. How long has she been watching? In the lightest of tones she says, "Ah, here you are, you two. Pishi sent me to find you. Dinner is getting cold."

But that night she comes into Priya's room and says, Why did you come back? You had everything you wanted in America. Says, I had given up on love, but then Amit chose me. Says, If he should leave me for you, I do not think I can bear it. She says some other things. Priya cannot tear her eyes away from her sister. She had expected hatred on Jamini's face. Fury. Instead, Jamini looks surprised. As though she had not expected to say these hurtful things, as though she cannot stop herself. As though her lips have taken on a life of their own.

Long after Jamini is gone, Priya lies awake—maybe it is the time difference with America, maybe it is guilt. She hears in her head what her sister said, over and over, like a refrain. Not only the words but the fear also, the sadness that Priya has brought to her from across the world.

Chapter 22

Deepa

*W*inter is not so different in East Bengal; the seasons know no borders. Woolen shawls are taken out of trunks, quilts are sunned, none of them as good as Bina's. Pari massages Deepa and Sameera with warm mustard oil, Nadia fries sweet potato pithas and soaks them in syrup. Home at day's end, Raza warms his hands at the stove set up in the living room. Deepa brings him hot milk with isabgul; Sameera throws around her arms gurgling in excitement, impatient to be picked up. Raza smiles, the day's troubles falling from his face. In bed after lovemaking, he holds Deepa close. My life is complete. Then he sighs. If only there was less infighting in the League, less corruption, less kowtowing to Pakistan.

"Jinnah is planning to make Urdu the official language of East Bengal. Many of us disagree. We have told him we cannot give up Bengali. Our mother tongue is who we are. But he refuses to listen. The League might split in two—"

Deepa stiffens. "What will you do then?"

"I will go with Mujib. He has a vision. He wants to involve the students, like we did with the League in India, before independence. You cannot breathe a word of this . . ."

Deepa nods, but a cold metal coil heavies her stomach. Peace, that is all she wants, a quiet life with her husband and daughter. Is that too much to ask?

✿

Someone calls from Dacca Radio. They need artistes, especially women. They have heard of Deepa's talent, could she sing some Nazrul Geeti for them once a week, they have Urdu singers for the other days. Deepa is nervous, but Raza encourages her: Sing our Bangla songs, he says. She starts going into the station, taking Pari along as chaperone. Once she gets over her nervousness, Deepa begins to enjoy the excitement. She imagines her voice inspiring listeners, bringing solace. When she needs to expand her repertoire, Raza finds her a teacher proficient in Nazrul Geeti, an old man with a quavery voice but a keen, strict ear. She is amazed to discover that Nazrul wrote almost four thousand songs, also poems and plays; he was an intrepid freedom fighter, jailed in Alipore because of his inflammatory writings; she is sad to learn of his illness, both mental and physical. She widens her range, learns folk songs and ghazals; she is asked to come in twice a week, three times; fan letters begin to pile up at the station.

Fame has its drawbacks. An invitation arrives from the Bengali Muslims in the League: Suhrawardy, ex–prime minister of Bengal, is visiting, there will be a celebration, could she perform? The thought of singing in front of a live audience, even from behind a screen like the other Muslim women, terrifies Deepa. The mention of Suhrawardy conjures up the terrible night of the Calcutta riots, which he failed to contain: fire and blood, her father's dying eyes. But Raza holds her close and says she cannot refuse, it will send the wrong message, already he is eyed askance for criticizing League policies. Besides, she just might enjoy it.

"Never," she says, mutinous. "Every moment would be torture." But she gives in. How can she not, if it will help her husband? For the event, Raza buys her a beautiful silk burkha, blue like midnight.

She is astonished to discover that a live cheering audience is like an electric charge.

"You were marvelous," he tells her later.

"I loved it," she confesses.

He smiles; he is a wise husband, he does not say, *I know you better than you know yourself.*

❀

Raza must go on an inspection tour, this time to Chittagong in the south, almost a day's journey. There is rumor of an outbreak of cholera. It must be stopped before it spreads. Deepa does not like the idea. "Why must you be the one to always do these dangerous things?" she asks.

He kisses her forehead. "There is nothing to worry about. I am vaccinated, and it will take a week at most. I promise I will only eat fresh-cooked foods, only drink boiled water." When Deepa continues to look unhappy, he adds, "When I come back, I will ask for a different assignment, something that does not require travel." He cajoles her until she gives him a goodbye hug.

It is silly to fret, Raza is careful and efficient. So Deepa allows herself to be pulled into her many responsibilities. There are new songs to practice for the radio station, where now she has programs thrice a week; Sameera has developed a hacking cough, the doctor must be summoned, a mustard poultice applied; Nadia's niece is getting married up in Mymensingh, she needs a week of leave, but who will handle the kitchen? She thinks nothing of it when the army truck pulls in a day early. Raza is famed for his efficiency, for cutting through red tape.

But Raza does not swing down from the truck and lope toward her calling, Aliya Begum, I'm starving, tell Nadia to fix me hot-hot rice with kheshari dal and onions. And where is that baby? Pari, bring her to me right away, let me see how she's grown. Ah, there's nothing like being home!

Instead it is Sharif, stricken-eyed, stumbling with a bloody bandage around his arm, saying, Apa, I have bad news, saying, Hai Allah, why couldn't I have been the one? And that is how Deepa learns that on a narrow highway at night a group of rebel Hindus armed with guns had ambushed the truck, and the covered body that the guards are carrying from it now is her husband's.

She flings herself onto Raza, surely he cannot be dead, someone has made a mistake, his face is calm as always, his cheek supple when she kisses it—only his eyes will not open. But when they remove the sheet, all is soaked red, like the bandages around her father's chest in the Calcutta clinic. Pari and Nadia have to pull her off the body, they have to drag her to the other room; she is shouting *no*, she slaps Pari hard, leaving a blotch on her cheek. The girl blinks away tears, says nothing. Someone calls the doctor, he forces her to take a sedative. Until she passes out, she can hear Sameera in the next room. Usually she is a quiet baby, but today she screams until she is out of breath.

By the time Deepa wakes, the men from the mosque have arrived. They are all business, they have much to do and only a little time within which to fit it all. They must wash the body, they must wrap it in a white kafan, they must take it to the mosque for the burial service. They ignore Deepa and speak instead to Sharif, instructing him to keep her out of the way. As though she were a child or feeble-minded. When she insists on asking questions, they grow stern. They tell her she needs to leave them alone so they can concentrate on their job. No, they cannot give her more time with the dead, that would be haram. See, the hearse is here already. They carry the body out. No, she may not go with them, women are not allowed.

"You can't keep me away from my husband," she shouts, "I will not let you. I will send a message to the chief minister himself, he knows me." But Sharif holds her back, Apa-jaan, calm yourself. Still she calls his name, Raza Raza Raza. She throws herself onto the rough gravel of the driveway in front of the vehicle. Someone gives a gruff order, she feels hands on her, Nadia and Pari pulling her out of the way so that the hearse can leave. She watches its squat blackness recede down the driveway, disappearing around the bend. She realizes she will never see Raza again. With sudden strength she flings Pari and Nadia aside and bangs her head against the ground. Blood splotches her face until Sharif, terrified, calls the guards at the gate to carry her to the bedroom and sends again for the doctor.

❀

In a week's time there is a resplendent memorial service: high honors, guns firing salutes, troops chanting "Tarana-e-Pakistan," Mujib wiping his eyes, Suhrawardy himself giving the eulogy: an honest man, a true patriot, our comrade cut down in his prime, what a pity. She must hear of it later from Sharif because the widow cannot be there, it is not the custom. The widow must wait at home, stiff and speechless in her black burkha.

A week passes, or is it two? It is hard to tell time from inside the mist that swathes her thickly, making it hard to breathe. Then suddenly one day officials from the League pay her a visit, apologetic but firm. They will need to take the car and driver, they are needed elsewhere. The phone line will have to be disconnected. They will let her keep the house for now, though she would do well to start looking for another place. Another place? she echoes stupidly. But where can I go with the baby, what shall I do? The thought of having to find a new house, of packing, of leaving behind the home that holds the last lingering traces of the attar Raza liked to use, dizzies her with distress.

Just then a car pulls up into the driveway. Mamoon steps out, dressed in mourning white. Deepa's heart sinks. O that this man should witness her humiliation. But when Mamoon realizes what is going on, he chides the League officers sternly. Is this any way to behave toward the begum sahiba, the widow of a shaheed, so soon after she has been struck by such an enormous tragedy? Do you have no decency? He sends them away shamefaced, then turns to Deepa. "Begum, I am devastated by this tragedy and by this insensitive behavior on the League's part. I will speak to the right people and make sure you are allowed to remain in this house as long as you wish."

When Deepa stammers her thanks, he shrugs them away. "No, no, it is the least I can do for Raza-bhai, who died for our country's sake."

After he leaves, the servants whisper about how he arrived at the right time, like a farishta sent by Allah Himself. How helpful he was, how modest, how correct in his condolences. Even Nadia nods her approval and says that at this dreadful time, it would not hurt Aliya Begum to have a few friends in high places.

Mamoon comes back to check on Deepa's welfare the next week and each week after. His behavior is impeccable. He stays only a few minutes. He does not seem to mind that she always makes sure to keep Pari in the room with her. He promises Deepa that she and Sameera will be taken care of, he has heard the League has a fund for tragic situations like hers, he will make sure to put in her name for it. He sends his personal guards to patrol her grounds so no intruders will try to sneak in, knowing she is a widow alone. He places his car and driver at her disposal so she may visit the mosque in comfort to offer alms for the peace of Raza's soul. He gets her the pension she is entitled to as the widow of a state employee who died in the line of duty. It is not much, but he makes up for that by sending fresh fruits, live chickens, a sack of kalijira rice for Nadia to fashion a decent biriyani. He hires an armed gatekeeper to make sure Deepa is not harassed by unwelcome visitors. After a month of such innocuous visits, Deepa allows herself to relax.

She admits to Pari that she was wrong about Mamoon. His intentions are clearly altruistic. His championship has made her life much easier, he must know that; but not once has he asked anything of her.

Then late one night Pari smuggles Sharif into the house through the servants' entrance, Sharif dressed like a servant himself, head and face covered in a cheap shawl. He tells Deepa that he has been trying to see her, but the gatekeeper will not grant him entry.

"I did not want to distress you further at this time," he says, "but I found out something disturbing and feel I cannot keep it from you. It is not definite that the men who shot Raza were Hindus. I went back to Chittagong in secret to investigate, but I could not find any information about insurgent groups in that area. Also, how was it they knew just when Raza-bhai's truck would be coming around a narrow bend? How was it that every one of the attackers escaped, no injured or dead left behind for identification?"

She is dizzy with rage, grief, and, most of all, fear. She remembers the night on the train when she awoke to view the naked desire on Mamoon's face. The time when, singing behind the curtain, she saw his avid attention. When she can speak, she says, "Who do you think might have been involved?" When Sharif replies reluctantly that he cannot be sure, she says, "Could it be Mamoon?"

He looks troubled. "Not directly. He has watertight alibis. But he might have encouraged certain factions who were already unhappy with Raza-bhai—just like he was. He has definitely made it hard for Raza-bhai's friends to be in touch with you. I myself am being watched. I do not know if I can manage to come to see you again. Be careful, Apa."

❖

Often when Mamoon comes by, Deepa sends Pari to tell him she is not well, she is lying down. But today she steels herself to meet him. She asks after his health, offers refreshments, thanks him for his continued kindnesses. Then she tells him that she wants to visit India. Just for a few days. "It will ease my sorrow if I can see my family in Burdwan and my cousin Salima in Calcutta. I would like to spend a little time with Abdullah Chacha, too, he was like a father to Raza." It is hard for her to say her husband's name without choking up. "Please help me."

Mamoon's face lengthens in sympathy. If he is pretending, he is adept beyond Deepa's powers of detection. He says he would love to help her, but the government has decided she cannot be allowed to go to India. She knows too much, all the plans and secrets that Raza shared with her. They trust her, of course, but what if she is kidnapped? What if she is tortured for information?

"But Raza didn't tell me anything," she cries. She cannot stop her sobs, although she is ashamed for breaking down like this in front of Mamoon. Thank God for the burkha, which allows her to retain the tiniest shred of dignity.

Mamoon looks distressed. He tells her he believes her. But greater powers have decided that these precautions must be taken. "However," he says when he takes his leave, "I will ask around and see if there is any way around this."

Returning the following week, he tells her, "There is one way. After the mourning period ends, four months the mullahs say, you could remarry. If your new husband is trusted by the government, if he is powerful enough and willing to accompany you, they would allow you to go to India." There is no doubt as to who he means. For a moment, his gentlemanly facade falls away and he stares at her like a hawk watching its prey.

Deepa fears she will explode with anger disgust hate, but she thinks of Sameera upstairs in her cradle, Sameera who does not know that her father is gone and only her mother left standing between her and chaos. She draws on acting skills she did not know she possessed. "I am truly grateful for your kind counsel, Mamoon Sahab. It is too soon for me to think of such things, but I will hold your advice in my heart."

After he leaves, she weeps in helpless fury, and Pari holds her and weeps with her. When Deepa has wept enough—but no, it is not enough, it is only postponed until she has the luxury of more tears—she wipes her eyes and starts making plans.

❧

Next morning, Pari visits her aunt in the Korail slums. Her aunt looks in on a friend who lives in the next patti. The friend's cousin, a feisty woman but discreet enough when necessary, works for Sharif. And thus a letter addressed to Dr. Abdullah makes its way to Sharif, who will hold on to it until he finds someone he can bribe to take it across the border.

Abdullah Chacha,

I know you have always thought of me as a trouble-bringer, and perhaps you are right. But I write to you today because I have no one else to turn to. I write on behalf of Raza's daughter, fatherless Sameera, who deserves your help even if I do not.

Yes, Raza is gone, shot to death under suspicious circumstances. Raza who loved his country, who only wanted the best for the people of East Bengal.

I am a prisoner in my home, prevented from visiting you in India and even from writing to you. Worse, I am under pressure to marry the man who I fear may be responsible for my husband's death.

I do not know if I will be able to write again. Many people are endangering themselves to get this letter to you. Please let my family know of my situation.

I want to come home.

If you—or they—can help, send word secretly to Sharif Ali at the address below.

Aliya

Part Five

November 1947–February 1948

❖

Here is a newborn nation, shaping itself. Here is a man who per-
suades princes by any means necessary. Here is a call to citizens to
raise their voices. Here is war already, and refugee camps. Here is a
bullet, an old man falling. Here are his last words, which lodge in
the country's heart.

Infant India's first cabinet is formed of Hindus, Muslims, Sikhs,
Christians, Parsis. Sardar Patel convinces more than five hundred
princely states to join hands to support the government. The Consti-
tution gifts every Indian the right to vote. Pakistan's militia crosses
the border at Muzaffarabad, Maharaja Hari Singh asks India for
help, the First Kashmir War begins. In Delhi, half a million ref-
ugees flood the camps: Kingsway, Humayun's Tomb, Purana Qila.
Assassin Godse's bullet finds Gandhi's chest. Darkness descends, an
age ends. The year is 1948. The month is January. Everything has
changed.

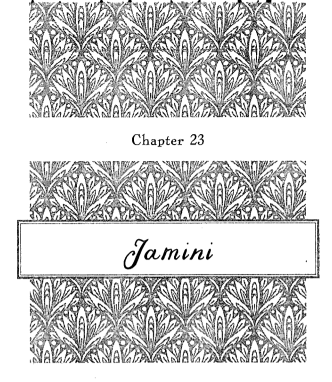

Chapter 23

Jamini

*M*orning of Jamini's marriage, the moment she has dreamed
of for years. Like many longed-for events it has arrived
differently clothed, carrying complexities she never imagined. She
wants to trace it back to where everything started, but things get
murky. Better to begin with the night she went to Priya's bedroom and
said, I cannot live without Amit, not after he promised to marry me,
to be mine. Am I a plaything to be picked up and dropped at will? If
he goes back on his word because you decided to reenter his life, I will
kill myself. Her voice was mild. I am not threatening you, I am only
informing, so that later you cannot say, Had I known this I would have
acted differently.

She paused, but Priya said nothing. The old Priya would have rushed
in, argued, raged; she would have insisted that Jamini was in the wrong,
that Jamini was being selfish. Jamini would have known how to fight
her and win. This Priya only looked at her with wide-seeing eyes, and
after a while there was nothing for Jamini to do but leave the room.

That night she lay in bed and considered the threat she had thrust at Priya like a sword, *I will kill myself.* She turned it around and around in her mind, observing it from all angles. It did not look so frightening. Perhaps she would do it, perhaps not. I will decide tomorrow, she thought. But in the small hours before sunrise, Priya came to Jamini and Bina's bedroom. She woke Bina and said, I have decided to return to America. There is a ship in seven days. In the dark Jamini could not see her expression.

Jamini wanted to say thank you. She wanted to say, I wish you luck, may you find success, may you find love or at least solace with the professor you have mentioned in your letters. But though she meant all of this, she knew the words would sound insincere, would sound like a taunt. She said nothing.

By the time the rest of the household awoke, Priya had left for Calcutta.

❁

Soon after, Amit came to Jamini, his face like he had been in the desert without water for a long time. He said, What did you say to Priya to make her leave? Jamini did not answer. In truth she did not know which of the many words she had hurled at her sister had pierced her.

He said, Release me from my promise. She said, I will not, I cannot, it is my life-breath you are asking for. But you can break the promise yourself, I will not stop you. He said, You know I cannot do that. It is entwined with that other, older promise, the one I made to your dying father. But know this: if you hold me to the word I gave before I knew myself, I will marry you but hate you always. She said, I will take that chance.

Then Amit called Manorama and said, Make ready for the wedding. I want it over as soon as possible.

Manorama, astonished and distressed, asked, Why the hurry? She protested that there were no auspicious days so soon. Amit replied he did not care for foolish superstitions, in any case there was nothing auspicious about this marriage. Manorama went to Somnath and said, Stop your son from ruining his life like this. But Priya must have spoken to Somnath before she left. He only said, his face expressionless, Amit is a grown man, he must choose his path, and sent to Calcutta for wedding necessities.

Jamini knew the reason for the rush. Amit was chaining himself to her to stop from running to her sister, Priya who had left him again but for a different reason this time. Perhaps she told him, as they kissed one last time, to follow the path of honor.

A voice inside her said, Don't do this, Jamini, no good can come of this. It was the voice from the night of the fire. But another voice rose up, older darker louder. *I did not ask for this marriage. It came to me. Now it is my right. I will not give it up.*

❈

In the room that is and also is not hers, Jamini is getting dressed for the ceremony. Bina is helping her. They work in silence because every word is a risk, a crevasse for falling into. Bina's hands are hesitant. Is she wondering if she has made a mistake, if in helping one daughter she has mortally wounded the other? Jamini has put on a red Benarasi, a silk so thickly worked in gold thread that it weighs her down. Bina fixes her jewelry: earrings, nose ring, seven-layer necklace, bracelets, armlets, anklets, waistband—all belonging to Amit's mother or Manorama because Jamini has almost nothing of her own. She does not wear Priya's bangle. She will not do that to Amit.

In the courtyard they exchange garlands, they go around the fire, they throw puffed rice, they repeat the mantras after an old priest who falters as he chants. Jamini thinks, In all his years the man has probably never seen a wedding like this. No laughter, no songs, no decorations, no guests, no marriage games, only the autumn sun shining in bright mockery. No joking and applause when the curtain between bride and groom is removed for shubho drishti, for them to look into each other's eyes. A single maid to blow the conch; two widows and one bent old man to offer blessings. Jamini wonders what the priest makes of the expressions on the faces of the young couple: the bridegroom grim, the bride—but what is the look on her face? Is it abashed, is it guilty, is it nervous? Does it give away the secret hope she is hiding? The priest scowls as he watches the tall, handsome man walking too quickly around the fire, the woman straining to keep up in her exquisite Benarasi, the cost of which could have fed his family for a month. He refuses the simple wedding lunch; he takes his fees and leaves quickly, disapproval oozing from his footsteps. Jamini must make an effort to suppress the hysterical laughter spiraling in her throat. She thinks, He believes Amit got me pregnant. Why else would a man like him marry a woman like me?

❧

In the marriage bed, which Jamini has strewn with flowers herself because there are no friends, no sisters, to do it for her, she speaks to Amit's back as he lies as far from her as possible. As my spousal right, I ask you for three nights of sex, I will not call it lovemaking. After that I will consider your promise fulfilled. I will not trouble you further with my presence, I will sleep in the small bedroom downstairs, if you prefer, or I will live in the Calcutta house. I will not question anything you do. If you decide to go away, I will take care of your family.

But secretly she thinks, Perhaps Fortune, who has turned her back on me in so many ways, will favor me this once. Perhaps now that his shrine has been rebuilt, by Pir Baba's blessing there will be a child, and who knows what a child can transform. She pushes the thought from her quickly to ward off ill luck, and when Amit says, Very well, and takes her roughly, angrily, she bites her tongue to keep from crying.

One night. Two. Perhaps on the third he feels pity, because at heart he is a kind man. Perhaps it is because he knows his responsibility is almost done. He knows she will never again experience bodily pleasure because that is the lot of a good woman in traditional families like theirs. He is gentler, he kisses her mouth, her breasts, he moves in a way that pleasures her so she clings to him gasping. When they are done, he turns from her, but not cruelly; he tells her she can stay the night. She lies without sleeping, thighs clenched together because she has overheard village women say this increases the chance of pregnancy. Torn clouds flit over the moon. Jamini measures the rhythm of Amit's breath, the shape of his shoulder, the line of his hip. The glint of the ruby ring on his finger. She memorizes it all so she can remember it in the lonely nights to come.

Chapter 24

Priya

*H*er ticket is bought, her single bag packed, a telegram sent to Arthur, who telegrams back in delight. He will come to New York, he cannot wait to see her; he has collected notes from her classmates for the classes she has missed, she will have no problems passing her exams. *Dearest Priya, my heart has been empty without you.* She feels at once grateful and guilty.

Still three interminable days remain for her ship to leave. Thoughts of Amit rage inside her like a wildfire. They rode on Sultan south along the Sarasi River until the villages fell away and there were only bamboo forests with jackals howling even at noon. They sat by the water silently, holding hands. They did not need words to understand what was in each other's minds. When the sun sank behind the bamboo trees they kissed once, then again, then a hundred times. She gave her body to him, and he gave her his. What better occasion could they have saved themselves for?

No. That is what she wishes she had done.

In reality Priya had departed without seeing him. O coward heart, she had been afraid he would make her change her mind. She had only left him a brief letter. *I can live with lost love but not with the guilt that would poison that love forever, for us both.*

Another day creeps by. Impossible to sit still, though the dahlias in the garden are blooming like diminutive suns and Shefali fries the fluffiest luchis for her. Perhaps Amit and Jamini are getting married now. Priya knows Amit like her own self: having made up his mind, he would not wait. They are exchanging garlands, they are feeding sweets to each other. Priya can smell the marigolds in the garlands, the sandalwood paste on their foreheads, the tuberoses of the marriage bed. She shuts herself in the bathroom and runs the faucet full force so Shefali will not hear her weep.

There is a new maid in the house, a Punjabi girl with enormous, scared eyes who hangs her head low as she mops the floor. Priya tries to take an interest in her—for her own sake more than the girl's—but the maid does not answer when spoken to. When she goes to the bathroom to refill her bucket, Shefali whispers that her name is Banno, she is the gate guard's niece, the rest of her family died on a train from Lahore, chopped to pieces. God knows how she escaped, how she found her way to Calcutta. Ah, the cost of independence. Shefali sighs. My own family has suffered, my sister's only son was beaten up so badly in the 1946 riots, even now he can walk only with the help of a cane.

Priya stares at Shefali. So many secrets nested inside us all, even the people to whom we give little thought. Now she understands the housekeeper's antipathy toward Raza.

But Shefali has moved on with Banno's story. For two months the girl did not speak, she would only crouch in corners. The gate guard was at his wit's end. Finally Shefali wrote to Somnath, who told her to hire the girl, allow her to stay in the house. For weeks Shefali let the girl sleep beside her in her bed because otherwise she woke up screaming at night. But she is better now, eating her food, even smiling once in a while. Thank God for the resilience of the young. She looks at Priya as though to say, *Soon you will feel better, too.* Or does she mean *See how lucky you are.*

Priya observes the girl who is mopping the room a second time in careful, rhythmic swipes, because Shefali may be sympathetic, but she does not tolerate a dirty floor. Banno's neck is thin as a stalk, her lips so tightly pressed that they have disappeared. A noise outside that might be a bus backfiring makes the girl startle and shudder. Priya wants to gather her close, protect her from the world's cruelty. Unwillingly she admits her own privileges, safeties she took for granted.

Still the day is intolerable, sticky as molasses. What would Amit be doing now? Is he checking on a distant field, is he balancing the estate books, has he come home to eat the lunch that Jamini is serving him, *Have another fried brinjal, another fish, just one more sweet, I know you like sweets. Here is some paan to redden your lips, and I will take one, too. Shall we rest together on the four-poster bed until the afternoon cools?* To distract herself she phones Abdullah; maybe he will have news of Deepa by now. When no one picks up, she decides to visit him in the clinic, although that will create its own pain.

❈

Reaching the clinic, she is shocked at how run-down it looks, paint peeling, signboard hanging awry, the patients outside poorer looking than before. Her heart twists, thinking of her father, how proud he had been of this place. Inside, Abdullah looks older than he should, he moves slowly and responds testily to Priya's greeting. He calls in a querulous voice to the harried Salima to bring the iodine tincture, make sure the lancets are sterilized, give out a bottle of fever medicine. And why is that child running around the waiting area, bumping into people? He motions for Priya to take a seat, but she washes up and starts helping Salima, who whispers thanks. Priya wants to tell her that she is the one who is grateful, that as she stitches up cuts, examines crusty eyes, and listens to wheezing chests, the tightness in her own chest eases a little.

Once the current patients are taken care of, Abdullah tells Salima to lock the door and motions to the surprised Priya to join him in the inner room. He takes a smudged, crumpled letter from his medical bag and hands it to her. "A truck driver from East Bengal dropped this off yesterday. It is too much for me. I do not know what to do, who to ask for help." His voice is distressed, his hands shake. "My health has not been good since your father's death; the clinic, too, has been a struggle. I cut myself off from the League soon after that terrible night because some of the leaders told me I should not treat Hindus here. In retaliation, they made sure I lost my Muslim sponsors. I was planning to mail the letter to Somnath. But it would be quicker and surer if you take it to him."

From the looped handwriting Priya knows that the letter is from Deepa. When she reads it she has to sit down. For a moment she thinks it is too much for her, too. She will give the letter to the ever-capable Munshiji. He will rush it to Amit, who will know the best way to handle this problem. And why shouldn't she take that path? Hasn't Amit insisted over and over that Nabakumar asked him—not Priya—to take care of his family? And didn't he promise to do that? Isn't that why he promised to marry Jamini? Priya has a life to lead: oceans to cross, examinations to pass, a good man waiting for her, his uncomplicated heart filled with trust and tenderness.

She finds herself saying, "Don't worry, Abdullah Chacha. Today itself I will take the letter to Ranipur. I will do everything I can to help Deepa."

At the house there is a flurry of things to be taken care of: tickets canceled, telegrams sent to Arthur and to the college committee in which she begs for understanding, for a few additional weeks. *There is another family emergency. My other sister's life is in danger. I promise I will work day and night to make up the work when I return.* Fear squeezes her chest as she sends them off. What if the committee refuses because she is unreliable? What if Arthur decides she is too much trouble?

But Deepa is in danger, Deepa and Sameera, her niece whom she cannot imagine but loves already, and what can be more important than that?

❀

It is evening by the time she reaches the beloved mansion that she had expected to never see again. No one is expecting to see her either. She imagines what each person's reaction will be. Somnath: joy because he loves her, pure and simple; Manorama: consternation because she does not know what this will do to her Amit; Bina: anxiety because here is Priya again roiling up matters; Jamini: anger shining, keen and justified. Amit: but here imagination fails her and sorrow takes over, and in her chest a pain twists so sharply it makes her gasp.

Priya needs to conserve what little energy she has, she does not want to start with fending off incredulity and rage, offering excuses and explanations. She tiptoes up the steps intending to bypass Amit's room—Amit and Jamini's now. But here is Jamini with her arms full of clothing. Why is she removing her saris from Amit's almirah, where is she taking them? And on Jamini's face not rage but a fear so profound that Priya wants to weep. How has it come to this between the two of them?

She says, harsher than she intended, "I have not come to cause trouble. This is not about you or me. Deepa is in danger. Deepa and her baby. They need our help. I am going to Somnath Kaku's room. You bring Ma and Pishi so that I can explain it all at once."

❀

But the story cannot be told all at once, it has to be paused and re-traced and told again and again to Bina, who cannot seem to compre-hend. My Deepa widowed in East Bengal with a baby? My Deepa not allowed to come home to me? The last of the sunlight seeps from the sky; Amit returns, he stares at Priya with astonishment, incredulity, a leaping joy. He is about to stride across the room to her, but she shakes her head and hands him the letter because danger is more urgent than love. He reads the letter, reads it again. Then Bina, who has been rock-ing and weeping, lifts her swollen face to him and says, "I have used up all my coin with you, you owe me less than nothing. Still, I must ask for your help."

"You need not ask," Amit says. "With my life I will help Deepa. But I must figure out the best way."

They sit on the veranda, where in happier days chess was played and the voice of Nehru promised the people of India an awakening into life and freedom. They discuss the problem deep into the night; even meticulous Manorama forgets to serve dinner. Finally an agreement: a connection must be made with Sharif, a plan created together. But who will take the message? Who can pass unsuspected, unnoticed, across the border? The men who have remained in Ranipur or Cal-cutta, the ones whom the Chowdhurys can trust, are all Hindus. They would be detected. Priya's brain spins uselessly. It is Jamini, branded by the night of fire, who comes up with a name that makes Amit say, in surprise and admiration, Yes, you are right.

❧

A message is sent to Hamid the fisherman: the Chowdhurys have a guest, they would like some fresh ilish though it is not the season, could he help. Hamid comes, the pink-and-silver fish still thrashing in the handi he carries on his head. He thanks Amit for rebuilding the homes in the fisher village, including his. When they tell him the purpose for which they have called him, he thinks for a while, brow furrowed. Finally he says it might be done. Fishermen on both sides of the border work the same rivers, they are still on good terms, often telling each other where new shoals have appeared. In the delta, one stream connects with another. He and his cousins have rowed their boat from the Sarasi to the Ichamati to fish on the East Bengal side, on the Betna and Kobadak Rivers. Before Partition they once went as far as the Padma, what a great waterway that was, with surging currents. He could ask around; if he gets the message to the border, someone might agree to take it from there to Dacca if Amit-babu is willing to pay enough.

In a week's time a letter makes its way to Sharif: *We would like to help Aliya and her daughter return to Abdullah Chacha in Calcutta. Tell us what to do.* In two weeks an answer comes back. Priya had worried that Sharif would be suspicious that a Hindu family wanted to help Aliya return to India, but he says nothing of it. Possibly he thinks Aliya is a convert. Possibly there are other women like her in East Bengal, turned Muslim for one reason or another.

Sharif speaks of Aliya Apa with respect and of baby Sameera with affection, but the news he sends is troubling. An army captain, a powerful and dangerous man, has expressed interest in marrying Aliya once her mourning period is over. This man keeps her under close surveillance in her home in Dacca; his guards accompany her to the few places she is allowed to go. She will be hard to get to and harder to spirit away. Even Sharif has been unable to see her in several weeks; they communicate secretly through a network of servants, but that, too, has recently failed. *I am trying hard to get in touch with Apa. Perhaps we can come up with a plan. Be patient. I will write again as soon as I have news.*

❁

One week passes without a letter. Two. A purgatory of waiting. Beneath Somnath's jokes and teasing, his loud rivalry at chess, Priya feels anxiety pulsing like a carbuncle. He worries because there is no news, he worries more about what Amit will do once the news arrives. Priya cannot bear his distress; she makes an excuse to leave the room. Daily, dutifully, she listens to the news, because many momentous events are beginning to take shape: the Constitution penned, voting rights granted, the princely states starting to integrate into one great country. It all seems unreal to her. Her personal troubles, paltry though she knows them to be, overshadow the greatest national gains. Deepa waits in East Bengal, Arthur in America. Each day another set of missed classes at the Woman's Medical College. And here is Priya, hobbled and useless.

Baba, I am failing you.

In the kitchen, Jamini's displeasure deters Priya from helping. She visits the village clinic that was once her father's to see if she can be of use, but the new doctor is uneasy with her presence. Nothing to do except go on aimless walks that end inevitably on the blackened porch of her home, to wait there until evening forces her back to the mansion. Priya has promised herself that she will avoid Amit; wordlessly he has understood and submitted himself to this sentence. She asks Somnath for permission to eat her night meal by herself in her room, but this he cannot bear; he has the maid bring food for the two of them to the veranda. For the first time, the Chowdhury family splits up at dinnertime. This affliction, too, Priya has brought upon them.

Chapter 25

Deepa

$\mathcal{E}$ach week she looks into her daughter's trustful smiling face and says to herself, I cannot give up. Still, the shroud of despair tightens. Sharif's maidservant, the one who brought his letters to Pari's aunt, has gone missing. No one knows her whereabouts. Has she been imprisoned? Has she been tortured? Has she perhaps given them away? Fear chokes Deepa's throat. She finds it difficult to sing and this alarms her more, for singing is her livelihood, her respite, her safety. The studio of Radio Dacca is a place Mamoon cannot forbid her to go, nor can he accompany her there without raising eyebrows. Her job brings her money—not too much, but she draws upon the skills she had learned after Nabakumar's death and manages to cover household expenses. More important: as long as people continue to love her songs, as long as they send in hundreds of requests and letters and gifts each week, she cannot be disappeared, not without inquiry. She sings and sings, she is learning new songs each day, songs to inspire the youth, especially the college students who under Mujibur Rahman are becoming a force. *Amra shakti amra bol, amra chhatra dol. We are power, we are strength, we the students.* But also she sings love songs: *Tomarei ami chahiachhi priyo. You are the only one I have wanted, beloved.* The love songs are the most popular. At first she is taken aback; then she thinks, But of course. In a country still bleeding from its many wounds, what is a better poultice than the promise of everlasting passion?

When Deepa has almost given up hope of hearing from Sharif, Pari brings a letter. The maidservant had not been arrested after all. She had run off with a man only to discover that he cared more for her purse than her person, at which point she boxed his ears roundly, expounded at length on his genealogical connection to pigs, and returned to Korail and her job. Deepa opens the letter and discovers inside it another one, stained, crumpled, torn in places as though it had been carried around in a waistband. It is from Amit, he tells her not to be afraid, promises he will bring her home. Beneath his handwriting there are others, her sisters sending love, and at the very bottom, Bina. *Daughter I am waiting to see you and my grandchild.* O wondrous life, typhoons followed by rainbows. Deepa weeps, she laughs, she kisses Sameera a hundred times, making her giggle; she whirls Pari around the room until they are both breathless. That evening at Radio Dacca, in thankfulness she sings, though it is not the season, *O mon Romjaner oi rojar sheshe elo khushir Eid. O my heart, Ramadan has ended and joyful Eid is here.* Listeners hearing the fervor in her voice wipe their eyes and say, Mashallah, that Aliya Begum, truly she is devoted, it is always Eid in her heart.

❈

That evening when Mamoon arrives, Deepa sits across from him in the drawing room and motions for Pari to leave. She pours his tea herself, adding the two spoons of sugar he likes. Then, for the first time, she lifts her veil. He stares at her, a pulse beats in his temple, but she can see from his eyes that he is suspicious also. He will be a difficult man to trick. Fortunately, the lies she has to tell today are small ones.

"Mamoon Sahab, I would like to ask your advice. I want to do something for our troops, those brave men, many of them separated from their families, risking their lives daily so we can sleep unworried at night. Would it be appropriate for me to sing something inspiring for them, for free of course, and from behind a curtain?"

He considers, frowning. She holds her breath. Finally he says he sees no harm in this, it is a generous thought. True, the soldiers live a hard life and experience few pleasures. They will appreciate the event, especially if she chooses the right kinds of songs. He can arrange for a small concert at the Kurmitola Cantonment, north of the city. She lowers her eyes, allows her lashes to flutter, thanks him prettily. A bitter amusement rises in her. She has not forgotten feminine guile, though it has been a long time since she employed it. With Raza there had been no need; he loved her as she was, with all her faults.

Don't think of Raza now.

At the door she injects a tremor of uncertainty into her voice. "Maybe once I create a list of songs I could ask you to take a look? If it is not too much trouble?"

"Nothing you ask for could ever be a trouble to me, Aliya," he says with a bow.

Her insides clench at the familiarity of his address. She forces herself to relax. She stands at the door waving as he gets into his car, she watches him angle his head so he can keep looking at her as the car moves away. She curbs her fierce smile until the car has passed the gate and turned onto the street.

❀

The concert is a success. The audience is made up of men from Pakistan as well as East Bengal. Both the Bengali and the Urdu speakers are taken by Aliya Begum's sweet voice, her modest demeanor as she greets them from behind a curtain and thanks them for their service to their country. Already they know her heart-wrenching story, Mamoon has made sure of it: her husband a shaheed tragically cut down in the flower of youth, leaving her alone with an infant daughter; and yet she has not asked for even one paisa for this evening. The program is a winning mix of Nazrul Geeti and Rabindra Sangeet, patriotic and upbeat, with a few ghazals of love and loneliness Deepa has learned specifically for the men who had to leave their sweethearts behind in Pakistan. There are so many encore requests that the event continues longer than expected. When at the end she sings "Chand Roshan Chamakta Sitara Rahe," the song that had aired on Radio Pakistan after Jinnah's independence address, the applause shakes the hall.

Thus she begins to sing for the troops—first those posted around Dacca, then slowly farther: Narayanganj, Mymensingh, Comilla where she has to stay overnight so she takes Pari and Sameera with her because the baby is still nursing. To her dismay, Mamoon comes along, too. The arrangements are most proper: he stays in the officers' quarters and she with a devout widow in town. Still, she feels like a bird who attempted flight only to discover her wings clipped. *Patience, Deepa.* She asks if she might visit one of the historic masjids in the area, she loves masjids and dargahs, especially old ones, she would love to get blessings for Sameera. Hasn't Allah shown her how short life can be, how fragile? She will make a dua for Mamoon Sahab also. Mamoon assents—how can he do otherwise when she makes such a pious request, and so charmingly, too? He is only sorry that he cannot accompany her, he must attend a meeting. He sends her in a military jeep with two armed guards to make sure she is treated with due respect. In the jeep she lets out her pent-up breath and clasps Pari's hand. *A small victory.*

❧

Back in Dacca, Deepa and Sharif continue to craft their plan. She will choose to perform her concerts only in towns with famous dargahs and ancient masjids. She will visit each of these holy sites until Mamoon gets used to her idiosyncrasy. If he accompanies her to them, she will spend hours praying until he tires of it and allows her to go alone.

When Mamoon becomes accustomed to her routine, when he allows her to travel on her own, she will plan a visit to one of the towns near the Indian border, maybe Khulna, maybe Jessore. The Ichamati River runs along the border there. Once the concert is confirmed, Sharif will get word to Amit. Amit has already procured a small motorboat, he and Hamid have learned to maneuver it. They will use it to cross into East Bengal at the right time.

Sharif has secretly met with Deepa's old driver, Arshad, who currently works for a major in Dacca. Arshad promises to be at the masjid with a vehicle so that Aliya Begum can get to the river quickly. "You just let me know when. My employer has a jeep, I will bring it. I don't care if I lose my job. I have been wanting to retire to the village anyway." Bashfully he asks if he might have a photograph of Sameera-jaan, she must be so big already.

So much love on one side, Deepa thinks, so much undeserved generosity. And on the other, wrenching hands, devouring eyes, the whine of bullets boring into chests like poisonous metal bees. How to teach Sameera to live in a world that holds such contradictions? That evening she sings lines from a new favorite, Rajanikanta Sen:

Ami dekhi nai kichhu bujhi nai kichhu,
dao he dekhaye bujhaye.

I have seen nothing, understood nothing,
Lord, help me see, make me understand.

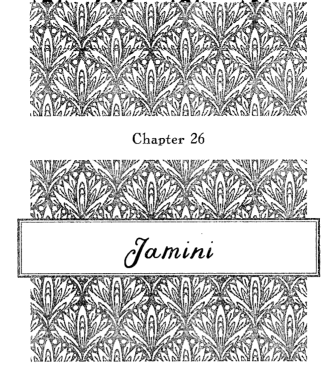

Chapter 26

Jamini

*I*s there a torture greater than seeing your beloved's avid eyes search a room as he enters, then rest in disappointment on your face? If so, Jamini does not know it. She longs to blame Priya, but how can she when Priya is doing all she can to stay away from Amit. She wants to blame Amit, but how can she when he has told her to continue sleeping in her marital bed—torturous though it is for her—so that she will not be shamed in front of her sister. She longs to blame Bina, Manorama, even Somnath who goes through the hours in a daze, who rubs his chest surreptitiously when he thinks no one is watching. But she is too intelligent to fool herself. There remains no one then to blame for her misery but herself; acknowledging this makes her doubly miserable.

❀

Just as the light fades from the evening sky, deliverance arrives in the form of a letter. It has taken a week to arrive, via three different fishermen; in the interim, its crumpled news has grown even more urgent. They gather around the dining table—all of them huddled together after days of purposeful separation—while Somnath reads to them in his quavering voice. A day from now, Deepa is going to Satkhira, a town close to the border, to perform for the battalion in that area. There is a good chance that she will travel by herself. Governor-General Jinnah is expected to visit East Bengal soon; officials in Dacca are in the throes of frantic planning. Mamoon, who was recently promoted to major, is heavily involved. A week ago at dinner, which he now takes regularly with Deepa, much to her dismay, he confided that he has heard rumors. A Medal of Excellence might be awarded to him on this occasion because of the fine work he has done discovering and destroying rebel cells. Deepa murmured that she could not think of anyone more deserving.

Deepa writes: By fortunate coincidence, not far from the town of Satkhira there is an ancient mosque, the Tetulia Shahi Masjid. She plans to visit it the day of her performance with Pari and Sameera, for Maghrib prayers in the early evening. But they will slip out from the back door of the women's area before the prayers begin. Sharif and Arshad will be waiting nearby with a vehicle. They will rush her to the banks of the Ichamati River and signal Amit, who needs to arrive there by then. They can be on their way back to India, God willing, before anyone realizes what is happening. *Brother Amit,* the letter ends, *I am depending on you.*

Before Somnath finishes reading, Amit is up. He pulls open a drawer and unfolds a map that he has kept in readiness for this moment, an older map that shows both Bengals, undivided. His nostrils flare, his eyes shine, his breath comes fast. The wait, Jamini sees, has been as much a torment for him as for her, though for different reasons. He jabs at the map, his voice vibrates with new energy. "Deepa will be here in Satkhira in one day's time. Hamid and I—ah, I must send word to him right away—we will need to start early tomorrow if we are to make it in time."

Hamid had not hesitated when Amit requested he take him to East Bengal. He had only said to Somnath, Babu, should something happen to me, take care of my wife and child.

Amit continues: "We will have to go against the current up the Sarasi to one of the small rivers that connects to the Ichamati, and then we must come southward again. In case there are border patrols, we will have to stop and hide." He turns to Manorama. "Pishi, can you get some food ready for us, just puffed rice and jaggery, so it won't spoil. And water, too—this close to the ocean, the rivers will be brackish. Pack enough for four people. It looks like Deepa's maidservant will be coming with her."

"Pack enough for five people, Pishi," Priya says.

"No," Amit says. "It's too dangerous."

Priya stands face-to-face with him. She is shorter than Amit, but in her determination, Jamini thinks, she looms as tall. "And that is why you need someone with medical training."

Amit throws up his hands. "I don't have time to argue. Come if you must." Under his exasperation Jamini hears a perilous joy.

She does not stand up. With her impaired leg, she is no match for their heroic postures. But her voice, though quiet, is iron. "Sorry to increase your work, Pishi. Make that six."

All eyes are on her, accusing. She knows their thoughts. *You will only slow us down.* But it is not the truth, it is only the prejudice she has been subjected to, again and again. "For God's sake," she says. "We'll be waiting in a boat, not running a footrace. And if we are looking for a signal, surely another pair of eyes will help."

Now Amit: "Why do you want to come?"

Because I don't want the two of you to go off on your adventure, leaving me behind. But that sounds too much like the hurt cry of an uninvited child, so instead she says something that is, in its way, as true. "Because I am your wife. My place is by your side." She bites her tongue to keep in the next words. *Hers is not.*

"Very well." Amit's shoulders slump. They have exhausted him, the sisters, even before the journey has begun. Jamini is sorry for that. Meekly she follows him with a waterproof canvas bag into which he throws necessities: medicines, money, extra clothing, a flashlight, binoculars, his gun. There is one other thing they might need, Jamini thinks, especially if the plan goes awry, but they do not have it in the house. No matter. I will send word to Hamid and he will bring it to-morrow.

❧

Stepping into the boat at dawn, Jamini is terrified. She does not trust the river's fluidity, its constant restlessness. Its rambunctious nudging against the prow makes her keenly conscious of a fact she has been careful not to bring up: she cannot swim. She scrambles to lower herself onto the hard wooden plank, takes care to remain as far from the edge as possible. But once Hamid starts the motor and the boat cuts spear-straight through the waves, she is entranced. She slides over to the side and trails her hand through the silky, silty water. Floating ducks, swooping swallows, the silver arcs of leaping fish. For a while a school of dolphins follows them, mesmerizing her with their intelligent gaze. Everything on the river has its rhythm, nothing can be hurried. Hamid and Amit converse in murmurs, take turns to guide the boat. Priya frowns at the horizon, thinking faraway thoughts. The boat is more spacious than Jamini had thought. She lies down on a plank and adjusts under her head the bundle that Hamid had given her that morning. She closes her eyes to feel the winter sun more fully on her face. She sleeps.

By the time she sits up, groggily rubbing her face, they have reached the far shore of the Ichamati. Behind them, on the other side, the Indian sky is scarlet with sunset. Clever Hamid has tied the boat under an overhang of mangroves and vines, it is barely visible from land. He has forayed abroad and cautiously questioned a local peasant. Amit's map has guided them well; they are not too far from the Tetulia Mosque, he has glimpsed its narrow spires. All that remains now is to wait for the signal.

Half the adventure is over, and Jamini has missed it. Why did you not wake me? she asks querulously. I tried, Priya says, but Jamini does not believe she tried very hard. Priya unrepentant hands Jamini a portion of puffed rice, a bottle to drink from. The others have already had their share. Just a few sips, Priya warns. They have to save water for Deepa and Sameera; also, it is embarrassing to have to urinate in the open field.

Now Jamini watches the night with intense eyes, determined to be of use. Only stars and fireflies, and in the bamboo groves the foxes howling. Help me, Pir Baba. And look, the darkness is broken by a slash of light, inland and to the left. She clutches Amit's arm; surely such a gesture is warranted at this time. Amit waves the flashlight. A jeep makes its bumpy way to them; Jamini is terrified that someone will hear the engine, which seems to reverberate across earth and sky. But the vehicle reaches them undetected, looming blackly. Light-headed with excitement and relief, she whispers, Sister, whispers, Niece.

But no Deepa descends from the vehicle, no maid with a baby on her hip. Instead, two men stumble toward them: the younger's shoulders are slumped, the older wrings his hands. In distressed bursts they explain their failure. Aliya Begum came to Satkhira this evening for prayers, just as planned. From behind the trees they saw her get down from the jeep, who could miss that royal-blue burkha. Pari the maid followed her, carrying Sameera. Sharif and Arshad were about to signal when a man stepped out behind Aliya. Mamoon in his major's cap, gun at his hip. A jeepload of soldiers pulled up next to him.

"There was nothing we could do," Sharif says. "I cannot guess what made Mamoon change his mind. It must have happened at the last moment; Apa would have sent me word otherwise." He sits slumped on the ground, he is disheartened demoralized; they all are.

Finally Amit says, "Let us not give up. Let us start planning again."

Sharif shakes his head. "It will be a problem. The Satkhira military camp is the closest to the border. A recent makeshift addition, it has no compound walls. The other cantonments, which are bigger, are inland or to the north, and they are more heavily guarded."

"It would take us a long time to bring Aliya Begum from any of them to the river—if we could get her out at all," Arshad says. Gloomily, he adds, "We may not even have a car. After tonight's escapade, my employer is sure to fire me."

Amit sighs. "A real pity, this setback. It looks like there's nothing to do but return to Ranipur and wait to hear from you."

Priya grips his arm. "No! We cannot just go back, leaving my sister behind. We cannot!"

"We have no choice, Pia," Amit says sadly. *Pia.* Intimate diminutive word, exploding inside Jamini's ear like shrapnel. She watches him putting his hand over her sister's. She makes her decision.

Sharif agrees reluctantly with Amit. Arshad sniffs the wind. "Best you folks start back across the river right away. Safer at night. Also, rain is coming. Khuda hafiz."

Hamid is loosening the ropes. Priya sobs. The two men walk back to the jeep slowly. What is the point of hurrying anymore?

"Wait." Clutching her bundle, Jamini limps after them.

"Jamini," Amit calls. "Jamini, what are you doing?"

She ignores him. In a low voice, she tells the two men the idea that came to her last night, the just-in-case plan if all else failed. Desperate, foolhardy, but perhaps possible.

Sharif's eyebrows draw together. "Are you sure?"

She nods. "Completely."

The men consult for a moment. Then Sharif shrugs. What better option do they have? Besides, Jamini is the one who will be in most danger.

Arshad shouts to Hamid in a regional dialect that Jamini finds hard to follow. He points south. It sounds like he is telling Hamid to take the boat to a cove shaped like a half-moon, it will be closer to the camp. If the jeep does not get there within two hours, that will mean they have been caught. Hamid must leave for Ranipur because soldiers from the camp might come searching for collaborators. Additionally, the tide here is strong. Once it starts going out, he will be pulled to the ocean. It will take forever for his small boat to make it back—if it can do that at all. Hamid nods, sober-faced. Men may be persuaded, he knows, but nature is implacable.

Amit frowns. "What are you planning, brothers? What?"

No answer. The men have heeded Jamini's request to say nothing of her scheme. The jeep revs, backs away. From the rear seat Jamini, who climbed on while the rest of them were distracted by discussion, leans out to wave at Amit and Priya with a jauntiness she does not feel.

Goodbye, sister. Husband, goodbye.

Chapter 27

Deepa

*I*n the makeshift greenroom in the Satkhira military camp, Deepa uses all her willpower to stay focused on what she must do this evening. She breastfeeds Sameera and hands her to Pari, who will wait in the greenroom. In front of Deepa stretches a covered corridor along which she will walk in a few minutes to the curtained-off stage. She adjusts her blue burkha, she goes over the song list she has written down for the evening. Her heart is so desolate and hopeless, she does not know how she will muster the energy to perform. Her mind keeps skittering back to all the things that went wrong.

A week ago, through Pari's aunt, Deepa had sold the little jewelry she possessed: a slender chain, a pair of earrings, Priya's bangle. Yesterday she handed some of the money to Nadia, who cried until her face was swollen. Deepa kept some money for Arshad. But when she tried to give the rest to Pari, the girl pushed out a stubborn lip. Wherever you are going, I am going with you. Deepa felt a lightness flowering in her chest because she had come to love the girl, to depend upon her like the sisters who were no longer within her reach. But she said to Pari, "My family back in India is Hindu."

She steeled herself—for what she did not know. But Pari shrugged and said she cared nothing for religions. She brought out a small suitcase—a large one would rouse suspicion—and helped Deepa pack.

When Mamoon came for dinner that night, Deepa tried to be extra gracious. It was, after all, the last time she would have to do this. She put on her attentive face as he droned on about official news, she gave him a solicitous second helping of goat curry. He cracked the bone with his teeth and sucked out the marrow.

Then he said, "Governor-General Jinnah has sent word. After his visit to Dacca next month, when he returns to Pakistan, he wants me to go with him. He is building up the Pakistani army and wants me to help. He is making me a lieutenant colonel."

Deepa began to congratulate him, but Mamoon went on in a rush. "I want to marry you and take you with me. Sameera, too, of course. We will live in the capital, Karachi. I hear it is a lovely city, on the ocean. Would you like that, jaan?"

The request in his eyes. That made her more uncomfortable than if he had ordered her outright.

Through the pounding in her skull she said, "But the period of mourning—"

He clasped her hands. "Don't worry. I have asked for special permission from the imam at Tara Masjid, he is the most respected man in all of Dacca. For the good of the country he has granted it. We can have the nikah in two weeks."

Two weeks. She left her hands in his, tried not to stiffen. It did not matter, she would be gone tomorrow. Look happy, Deepa, look grateful. But he must have noticed something that gave her away, an alarm in her glance, a trembling of her lip. He slapped his hand on the table, announcing a sudden decision. He would join her tomorrow in Satkhira.

"I have not been spending enough time with you, jaan. I am sorry for that. It will be good to go to the masjid there together, to ask for Allah's blessing on our union. It is a pretty place. Perhaps we will take an extra day and go boating on the river."

"But your work—?"

"My superiors will not mind. They all know about my upcoming promotion. Besides, it will give me an opportunity to check on our border security, tighten it up. That is especially important now because of our governor-general's visit."

All night she could not sleep. Unfortunate, foolish girl. Why could you not camouflage your feelings better? You've ruined everything. It was too late to warn Sharif and Arshad. They had gone ahead to scout the area, to figure out the shortest path to the river. At the Tetulia Mosque, her heart plunged and twisted when she glimpsed them peering helplessly from behind a hedge of oleanders. All the planning, the danger, the sacrifices—for nothing.

Someone rings a bell. It is time to begin the performance. Her body is heavy, her feet stumble as she makes her way to the stage. Her throat feels swollen as though she is coming down with a disease. And she is: the disease of despair. On the other side of the curtain she glimpses the important officials in the front row, Mamoon seated among them adazzle with pride. He has already announced their upcoming nikah to his colleagues. The tent is a simple one, flat on top, the side flaps rolled down and secured because the night is cold. Loudspeakers are set up both inside and outside; this way the townspeople, too, can listen to the renowned Aliya Begum from Dacca. Deepa begins with something different, Dwijendralal's "Dhana Dhanye Pushpe Bhara," a favorite of Gandhi who, she had read recently, wished to travel in Pakistan without a military escort, hoping by this act to reduce hatred between Hindus and Muslims. Poor man, she thought, he will most likely be killed.

Emon desh ti kothao khuje pabe nako tumi
Sakal desher rani she je amar janmabhumi.

You will never find a land like this, no matter where you search.
Queen of all countries, land of my birth.

But this is not the land of her birth, is it? It is the land she is trying to escape.

The last verse, now:

O Ma tomar charan duti bakkhe amar dhori
Amar ei deshetei janma jeno ei deshetei mori.

O Mother, I hold your feet close to my heart.
May I die here, in the land where I was born.

The men in the audience are touched. A few wipe their eyes. Even Mamoon takes out his handkerchief. There is no shame in weeping for love of the motherland. Her own voice quavers with tears. She knows what they are thinking. Ah, patriotic Aliya Begum. No one would ever guess the irony twisting in her like a skewer. She will probably die—like Gandhi—in Pakistan, a country that in her imagination is filled with jagged mountains, salt flats, ice-gray skies. Unless she dies right here in East Bengal while trying to return to her true home. If it was not for Sameera, she would gladly choose that fate.

The song has ended; lost in her thoughts, she has not started another. Mamoon peers at the curtain, concerned. In a minute he will come to the wings to check if all is well. It is his right, now that he considers her his betrothed. To forestall him she quickly begins the next piece.

Jokhon prothom dhoreche koli
Amar mallika bone
Tomar laagia tokhoni bandhu
bedhechinu anjali.

When the first buds formed
in my jasmine garden,
dearest friend,
I gathered them for you alone.

Where did this song come from? It was not on her list. The first time she sang it was after her wedding reception, that stiff, stressful evening of falsehood, of pretending to be married to Raza. When they returned to their flat above the clinic, she had fallen onto Raza's narrow bachelor's bed, exhausted and terrified, hiding her face in his pillow, thinking, What have I done, what have I dragged him into? But he turned her to face him, he removed the pins from her hair and buried his face in her curls. He kissed away her anxiety, saying, No matter what happens I cannot regret this. Later he said her body smelled like fresh-picked jasmine; he would never again smell jasmine without remembering this night. It was then that she had sung this song.

Through the curtain she can feel Mamoon's gaze, his intense alarming elation. He thinks I am singing this song for him, but Raza my love, I can only ever sing it for you.

Ekhono boner gaan bondhu
hoy ni to abosaan
Tabu ekhoni jaabe ki choli.

The song of the forest has not yet ended,
dearest friend,
why are you leaving so soon?

The applause when the song fades away is muted, deep, people re-calling their first loves, the lost ones, the ones whose absences sear the deepest.

She shakes off memory. She must stay in the present. She looks through her list for something cheerful to invigorate the evening. That, after all, is what the audience came for. But there is a movement at the corner of her eye, Pari beckoning urgently. Why is Sameera not with her? Deepa's breath snags. Could Mamoon have taken her? But no, he is sitting in the front row, smiling politely at some remark another officer has just made. She makes a quick announcement—apology headache aspirin five minutes—runs down the covered corridor, flings aside the curtain. There is a woman in the room dressed in a cheap black burkha. She holds Sameera, cooing to her. Sameera, who does not like strangers, who shrieks her displeasure if they come too close, is listening intently.

The woman is veiled, but Deepa recognizes her voice.

"Jamini?" she gasps. How is this possible?

Jamini kisses her niece, hands her back to Pari, shrugs off her burkha. "Quick, put this on and give me yours. I will take your place onstage. Go out from the back of the tent with Sameera and your maid as soon as I start singing. Stay in the shadows. Arshad and Sharif are waiting at the edge of the compound with a jeep. They will take you to the boat."

"This is a crazy plan, it will never work," Deepa says. But already with shaking fingers she is exchanging her silk burkha for the old black one, which gives off a fishy odor.

"Sorry about the smell—it belongs to Hamid's wife, Fatima," Jamini says. "Of course the plan will work. It is a perfect plan. I came up with it myself. We are about the same build, and no one will notice a limp under a flowing burkha, not for a few steps. The only problem is they might wonder how my voice got so much better so suddenly!"

Deepa does not laugh at the joke. "What about you? What will you do when the concert is over?"

"Don't worry, there is a plan for me as well, a good one." Jamini gives Deepa a hug and a push. Clad in the blue silk burkha, which fits her perfectly, she starts for the corridor. "Go on, get my niece out of here. That is the most important thing."

Deepa is filled with uneasy questions for which there is no time; any minute Mamoon might decide to come to the greenroom to investigate. She holds out her list of songs. "You will need this."

Jamini taps her forehead. "I have my own list right here."

"Wait, the song I always end with, 'Chand Roshan Chamakta Sitara Rahe,' you don't know that."

But already Jamini has disappeared into the corridor.

❧

Furtive footsteps as they undo a tent-fastener behind the greenroom and slip out from the back. Deepa's heart thunders so loud, it is a wonder it does not give them away. She and Pari crouch behind a large elephant-ear plant. Jamini's voice is close enough to Deepa's; no one in the audience seems to have noticed anything amiss. An armed guard is patrolling the compound, but when he goes to the other side of the tent, the women sprint across the courtyard. Finally, Alhamdulillah, they reach the jeep. Sharif jumps down to take Sameera from Deepa. The women scramble into the vehicle. Tears are shed, hands clasped, hurried words of thanks whispered. Then they are hurtling through the night. Once the road turns and they can no longer see the camp, Deepa allows herself a sigh of relief. Perhaps Jamini was right, perhaps this crazy plan will work after all.

The jeep eats up the road; through a gap in the growing clouds, a moment's moonlight silvers the countryside; the song pours from the loudspeakers. They can hear, even from a distance, the words of the song Jamini has chosen:

Boli go Sajani jeyo na jeyo na
Mor katha tare bolo na bolo na
Sukhe se royeche sukhe se·thakuk
Mor tore taare diyo no bedona.

The song is perfectly sung, but Deepa, who knows it well, can tell
that the lines are curiously out of order.

Dear friend, do not tell him about my love
May he not suffer for my sake
Let him be joyful
Let him be joyful forever.

And that is how Deepa comes to understand the other half of the
plan and the message she is meant to convey to the rest of the rescue
party. Jamini uncherished has decided to sacrifice herself for the welfare of her sisters, for the happiness of the man she loves.

Chapter 28

Priya

The wind gusts, it has grown stronger, they must leave very soon. Amit and Hamid are busy discussing a worrisome gathering of storm clouds to the west, so Priya is the first to see the headlights. She runs out from the coconut grove where they have been hiding, shouting, waving the flashlight. Then she is holding Deepa tight, welcoming Pari, kissing Sameera over and over. Amit hugs the baby, even Hamid puts out a shy hand to touch her curls. Sameera squirms; she protests vociferously against this overabundance of affection from strangers. The three women are laughing crying talking all at once. Amit pumps Sharif's arm, *Amazing, amazing.* Sharif grins like someone handed him the moon. It is all Arshad's doing, he says modestly. He drove like a fiend. Grizzled Arshad murmurs, Allahu Akbar, and wipes his eyes. He asks if he can hold the baby before they drive off. If he drives through the night, he might make it back before his employer gets too upset with him.

Once again Priya is the first to notice. "Where is Jamini?"

The hard task of explaining falls to Deepa. "But for Sameera, I would never have let her do this," she ends guiltily.

Astonishment, sorrow, remorse; self-blame by both Priya and Amit that could continue all night—no, all their lives. Except there is no time. The wind whines more loudly. The storm is coming.

Amit says, "Brothers, I know it is asking too much of you, but I have to go back to the camp. I must try to get Jamini away. You know what will happen to her when they realize what she has done."

A long moment. Then Arshad shrugs. "Anyway I am an old man. What do I have to look forward to except cataracts and rheumatism?"

And Sharif: "What, Arshad Chacha, just because you have seen a few more summers, you think you are braver and smarter? I am coming with you. Someone will have to strategize."

United, the three men turn on Priya when she strides up to the jeep, her medical bag hanging from her shoulder. She carries the two burkhas that Deepa and Pari were wearing. No, no, no, too dangerous.

"Tell me," she says, her voice eminently reasonable, "how exactly do you plan to get into that tent and bring Jamini out without alerting the assembly?" She lifts a triumphant eyebrow at their silence and climbs in.

❈

Inside the tent, Jamini leads the audience in a rousing patriotic song: *Bolo jai, bolo jai, bolo jai, muktir jai bolo bhai. Proclaim victory, brothers, proclaim freedom's victory.* The men clap and stamp their feet. It is late, the concert will end soon, only a couple more songs. Priya, covered by Fatima's burkha, knows she has only a few minutes to get to the back entrance of the tent, which Deepa has described to her. She glides silently from shadow to shadow, the way she did, holding her sisters' hands, on that heart-pounding night an age ago, Calcutta blood-soaked and burning around them. But no, she is startled to realize, it has been only a year and a half since her life was changed forever by Direct Action Day.

Behind a stand of bamboo the men remain with the jeep turned around, poised for escape. They have grudgingly agreed that, should anyone happen to spy them, two burkha-clad women on their own will attract less suspicion.

Lift up the tent flap, sidle into the greenroom, then through the passage to the stage wings. The hardest part is to attract Jamini's attention. But finally, when the song ends, she sees Priya dressed in Fatima's burkha. Priya can sense her sister's dismay. Does she think Pari and Deepa have come back to get her? That her sacrifice has been for nothing? Priya beckons. Jamini announces that she needs a few moments of rest so she can perform her final song with proper energy. She thanks the audience for their indulgence and walks with small, ladylike steps so no one will see her limp.

In the greenroom, Priya does not try to argue with Jamini, who is saying in a fierce whisper, You should not have come, don't you see? I did this for Amit, I know he will never care for me, I wanted him to be happy with you, as usual you have ruined everything. In silence she pulls Aliya Begum's royal-blue burkha off the struggling Jamini, who hisses and hits out at Priya: Let go of me, let me go back onstage. Stop it, Priya hisses back. You are endangering us all, including Amit, who is waiting in the jeep.

His name is like a spell. It stills Jamini.

Priya lets the silk garment fall to the floor in a heap; she buttons Pari's simple cotton burkha under her sister's chin; she pulls her unprotesting into the night. Jamini lurches, she has been on her feet all evening, but once she is outside the tent, she moves as quickly as she can. Perhaps she realizes she has no other options. Perhaps it is because she knows Amit has come to fetch her. They pass a guard, whisper, Salaam alaikum. He gives them the uninterested glance one reserves for servants. A last compound for them to traverse. Priya points: See the jeep, waiting behind the bamboo?

But an outcry rises from the tent. Did Mamoon, concerned by his Aliya's absence, go to check on her, did he find the blue burkha spilled on the floor and raise an alarm? Priya is furious at her stupidity. O why did I not think to hide it behind a chair, why did I not bring it back with me? Someone shouts into the night: Stop or I'll shoot. Priya hisses at Jamini to move faster. A bullet whines by her ear. Jamini sobs and stumbles, now she is down on the gravel. Priya tugs hard at her, but she can see they will not make it. Soldiers are swarming from the tent like fire ants.

Then another pair of arms pulls Jamini up and carries her. Amit.

Run, run. Arshad has seen them. He starts the jeep. More bullets, a sharp cry from Jamini, but they have made it to the vehicle. Sharif pulls them up into the back seat. Arshad is driving without headlights, he speeds around a bend and pulls off the road, perhaps this way they can evade the vehicles that follow, thank God it is cloudy, perhaps they can disappear among the trees. O clever Arshad. The truck that was chasing after them thunders down the road. Arshad waits calmly, though Priya is clenched with fear. Questions fill her mouth; she bites her lip hard to keep them in. What if another truck appears around the bend? What if the soldiers see them? Finally Arshad starts the jeep again. Now he is driving too fast, weaving through the trees, try-ing to make up for lost time, trying to get to the river before the tide turns. Priya clutches the seat in front; she prays they will not land in a ditch. Jamini moans, she shows Priya where a bullet has grazed her arm, which is now splotched with blood. Priya pulls out the bag with the bandages, wraps the arm by feel. That should do for now, it's not so bad; once we're on the boat I will look at it again. Arshad cries, Subha-nallah, I think we have lost them for good.

Then Amit slumps over on the seat.

Even in the gloom Priya can see the sticky wetness of his back. There is a lot of blood. It must be a major wound. Her hands begin to shake. Is that moan coming from her, or is it Jamini? She tries to find the bullet's entry point but she cannot detect it in this godforsaken darkness. Her fingers slip in the blood, she cries for light, Arshad holds up a flashlight. She tears Amit's soaked shirt off him. The wound is worse than she thought. He is losing a lot of blood. She presses all the bandages she has into it, tries to figure out if the bullet has hit a lung. But her medical expertise has dissolved into the gloom around them, leaving only terror behind. Jamini sobs, an ugly, raking sound. It takes all of Priya's self-control not to snap at her. Amit is still bleeding, though less now. She tears strips off her sari and ties them around his chest, she makes him lie on the seat and presses her hand hard against the wound. My love, my love, hold on.

He whispers her name. If he can speak, surely there is hope. Please, please. She prays all the way to the boat, though she is not sure whom she is petitioning.

❦

They are on the night river now, the waves hitting hard against the prow, the motor straining as the boat pushes against tide and wind. Grim Hamid focuses his full attention on the river; he grips the tiller as tight as he can. Still, it is difficult to keep the boat from being pulled out to the ocean. He mutters a dua to Bon Bibi, goddess of the swamps. Pari, who has never been on the water, crouches in terror on the floor of the lurching boat, holding Sameera tight. Sameera, fed and changed, is in a good mood; she likes the rocking motion, once in a while she crows. She looks around her with curiosity, then grabs her toes. Recently she has discovered her feet and is fascinated by them. How lucky she is, Priya thinks. She will remember none of this.

Stricken-eyed Deepa stares out over the water's choppy darkness.

When Deepa had seen Amit being carried from the jeep, she threw herself down, beating her head against the ground. I did this, I am cursed, I destroy everyone who comes close to me. I should never have asked you for help. Her voice rose, shaking and out of control. Priya had to slap her hard to get her to stop, had to say, in a voice of iron, Pull yourself together. We cannot afford you getting hysterical, on top of everything else.

Now Deepa looks back toward Dacca where Raza is buried, where she will never return to keep vigil at his grave. Before she got on the boat she had wept, her arms tight around Sharif and Arshad. She had given them all the money she had. But how can you repay people who risked their lives for you, who would now have to disappear into the Korail slums for years because Mamoon was a vengeful man.

The men had laid Amit down on the plank for Priya to examine. She saw that the bullet had passed through him. He was bleeding from his chest as well as his back, the damage worse than Priya had thought earlier. In the dark without medical instruments, there was not much she could do for him. She had no more gauze to press into his wounds; wearing only the burkha, she took off her sari, what was left of it. She tore it into strips and bandaged him as best as she could. When Jamini, who had not said a word, handed her sari to Priya, Priya tore that up, too. Amit groaned in pain until she could not bear it and gave him a morphine injection, though she knew it was dangerous when he had lost so much blood.

Now he lies quiet, his hand in Priya's, fading in and out of consciousness. His pulse is erratic, his heartbeat too high. It bothers Priya to see his feet dangling crookedly off the edge of the plank, though that is silly, is it not, when he has far greater problems. Priya kisses his face, his eyes. Nabakumar had told her once that the sound of loved voices helped patients stay alive, so she talks to Amit. When she cannot think of what to say, she describes the night: winds rising, distant thunder, a black log floating by that might be a crocodile. Jamini sits on the floor of the boat rubbing his feet, pale, silent, dry-eyed. In the jeep she had asked Amit, Why did you do this? And Amit, smiling through his pain, said, Because you are my wife.

The morphine is fading. Amit opens his eyes, moans. He wants water. In America Priya had learned that you should not give water to a patient in this condition, it might induce vomiting. But it seems too cruel. She holds the bottle to his lips, though he only has the strength for one mouthful. He beckons her closer.

"I misunderstood," he whispers. "We both did."

"What do you mean?"

He pauses to gather strength. "Remember what Nabo Kaka said that night?"

"Yes," she says, flinching at that memory, another man she had loved, dying. "He said, *Take care of.*"

"We thought he meant *take care of my family*. I thought he said it to me—"

"And I was sure he was talking to me. I am sorry I fought with you about it." How adamantly Priya had stood in the way of her own happiness—and Amit's as well. If she had another chance, she thinks, she would do it differently. But chance is a slippery customer, and she can feel Amit's hands growing cold.

Amit's breath shallows; he gasps between words. "But Kaka didn't mean that. He meant *take care of each other.*" He includes them all in his smile: Jamini and Deepa, intent and breathless; Sameera, who has fallen asleep; Pari, crying out as the boat shudders; Hamid, gripping the tiller with all his might. A night bird flies over the boat, calling mournfully.

How could Priya have missed, all the while, this immense precise truth? *Take care of each other.* Abashed, she says, "You are right."

His face is distorted with pain. Still, he raises an eyebrow. "Never thought I would hear you say that."

No point anymore in having him suffer. She gives him another dose of morphine. She gives him her mouth to kiss. She lays her head on his torn chest. His voice is fading. "Where are we now, Pia?"

She puts her arms around him. She says, "You are with me. We are home."

❀

Again the Sarasi River, again the burning ghats, again the priest chanting. But this time the muddy bank is full of mourners, though Somnath submerged in sorrow had not informed anyone. Perhaps they heard from Hamid this story of love and rescue, heroism and tragedy. At least for today, Hindu and Muslim stand soberly side by side.

They had been waiting up all night, Somnath and Manorama and Bina. Hamid had hardly docked the boat behind the Chowdhury gardens when they were on their way down the uneven path beside the banana grove, lanterns bobbing. When they saw what was in the boat, Manorama's wail cut the mist to pieces. "My lovely my brave my golden boy. You killed him, you ill-luck girls. O God that he had never become tangled with you."

Bina sank to the ground, but Somnath's voice was adamantine. "For shame, Manorama. Would you have had Amit sit at home safe and craven, ignoring Nabo's daughter's call for help? He would have lived, but at what cost?" He sent Hamid to rouse the servants, have them carry the body to the house. Then he put out his hands. "Come, my girls." Only Priya would see him weep later, behind the closed doors of his bedroom, his body so wracked with grief she feared he would not survive it. But deep in her own self she must have already known this unfortunate truth: one does not die so easily of a broken heart.

It is time to set fire to the body. The priest turns to Somnath. He does not have the words for the request, cruel, unnatural: a father to

send his son to the afterlife. But Somnath steps forward, calm again.
He says, "I will do it along with these girls, who are now both sons and
daughters to me."

Together, they light the pyre.

❁

O trickster Time. In Ranipur it oozes, in Philadelphia it flies. The fi-
nals are ancient nightmares now, the holidays packed away like Christ-
mas lights, the new semester gallops ahead like Paul Revere on his
midnight ride. So one evening Priya must force herself off Amit's
empty bed, where she has taken to spending much of her day, Jamini
having moved to the small room downstairs. She goes to Somnath,
and he, looking into her face, says *yes*. They know how lonely each will
be. Only between themselves can they speak of Amit the way he was,
stubborn hotheaded tender exasperating. Everyone else has turned
him into a saint.

They calculate the expenses of her journey to America. "I'll send
word to Munshiji to look into selling the Calcutta house," he says.

Priya, distressed, tells him he must not, surely there is some other
way, the income from the lands has fallen, yes, but perhaps she can get
a loan; with him acting as surety it should be possible. "Once I graduate, I will work awhile in America. I can earn money there quickly,
pay it back."

He shrugs. "Who will live in that mausoleum? Anyway, I never
liked it."

That night at dinner, Somnath and Priya announce their plan to
the family. Manorama and Deepa, still shrouded in their separate
griefs, are sorry but unsurprised. Bina murmurs words of good luck,
but her attention is on Sameera, who lies nearby on a quilt kicking
her legs, Sameera who might roll over any moment because she has
recently learned to do that. Nowadays Bina's attention is always on

Sameera, no matter that Pari is there to take care of the baby. Priya is happy for that.

Then Jamini says, "Leave the house be. Sell my jewelry instead, as much of it as you need." When Manorama flinches, she adds, "It is mine, is it not?" She holds Manorama's eye until the older woman nods reluctantly. To hesitant Priya, Jamini says with the confidence of a wife, "It is what he would have wanted." That night she brings a casket to Priya's room and gives her the seven-strand necklace, the waistband, the earrings studded with rubies. Finally she slips onto Priya's wrist the bangle Amit had gifted her. The sisters embrace in silence, bypassing the futility of recrimination and apology and lament.

❁

But in the Calcutta house, letters and telegrams are waiting. There are two telegrams from Arthur, weeks old. Both say, *Please return as quickly as possible or you will not be allowed to make up your final examinations. Send me your return date so I can inform the university.* The first letter is from the university committee, sent in early January. They cannot extend her leave any further. She has been away for too long and missed too many classes. Her education is clearly less of a priority to her than they had hoped. They have accepted another woman in her place. They wish her the best with her future. Their tone is polite, steely, final.

The second letter is from Arthur, sent a week later.

My dearest Priya,

I am concerned at your long silence in spite of my two telegrams. Clearly they have not reached you, which worries me further.

I hope all is well with you and your dear ones.

I am sorry, I pleaded your case to the best of my ability to the university, but I failed. In spite of that, I entreat you to come back. Since

*the time you left, I have realized how much you mean to me. Is it only
my imagination that I might mean something to you, too? You told me
before leaving that when you return, you will have taken care of past
business. I hope you have been successful in that regard.*

*If you are willing, I would love for us to get married as soon as you
arrive. There are other medical colleges here. I am certain you can gain
admission in one of them and graduate successfully. I promise to help
you every step of the way.*

Please telegram me. I will come to New York to meet you.

Yours,

Arthur

She sits in the garden with the letter until day darkens into evening
and she can no longer read Arthur's sturdy, square hand. Here is the
solution to all her problems offered by a good man, a man who made
her heart leap not so long ago. She should be thankful; indeed, she is
thankful. Why then this irresolution?

No words arise in explanation, only the flash of images so rapid they
make her head spin. Amit in this garden plucking a rose for her hair,
Amit sliding bangles onto her wrists, Amit turning his face away, saying
in a terrible voice, *You want me to follow you like the pet dog you think I
am.* Amit begging pardon for his mulish silence, Amit dreaming of
freeing himself from Jamini, of living a life of love with Priya. Amit
on the river, his chest congealed with blood, his eyes darkening, asking,
Where are we?

Her response: You are with me. We are home.

What she said that night with the storm shaking their boat and the
wind moaning around their ears is still the truth, whether she wants
it or not. And since Priya cannot make use of people, since she cannot
take where she has nothing to give, she must write to Arthur, *I am
truly appreciative of your generous offer, your kindness, your love, but I am*

no good for anyone, I am a hollow reed filled with absence, I cannot make you happy.

She could give the letter to the gateman, but she walks down the street herself. When she drops it into the gaping red mouth of the mailbox, she feels a dizziness. It is the way she had felt when, on their way to East Bengal, the boat had crossed the midpoint of the Ichamati, when she knew there was no turning back.

❀

The next morning Priya goes to the clinic and asks Abdullah to put her to work.

Abdullah is happy to oblige. From morning until night, one sick person after another, and more women coming because word is out that now there is a daktarni in the clinic with whom female problems can be discussed without shame. More Hindus, too, because even the ill have preferences and prejudices. There is no time to think and that is what she craves; she falls into bed too tired for nightmares.

Priya has not told Abdullah the details of their rescue mission in East Bengal, and he, looking into her face, has not asked. But she does tell him about Sameera, how the child wriggles her entire body when someone tickles her; how loudly she laughs when she sees a bird on a sill, a lizard on the wall; how she has learned to say Dada and hold out her arms when she sees Somnath. Abdullah wipes his eyes and says he knows it is not safe for Deepa to come and visit him, word might travel to the wrong people. So he will go to Ranipur, yes, for the first time in his life and see his grandniece, because why should Somnath have all the fun? Can Priya manage the clinic for a few days if Salima helps her?

Priya smiles. It is the first time she has smiled since Amit's death. "Indeed I can," she says.

Now the carousel of work accelerates, now there is no time to draw breath. Cut, stitch, bind. Listen to the fitful heart, the groaning bowels, the wheezing labored breath. Here is a crusted lid, a tender spleen, a leg so swollen with pus it must be lanced at once. Sell the gold ear-rings so there is enough antibiotics, vaccines, bandages, disinfectant, pain pills, cough mixture, fruits and biscuits to hand out to too-thin children with too-large eyes. The grateful faces blur into each other, *Thank you, Doctor-didi, dhonnobad shukriya.* If only they knew that they are saving her, too.

Yet like a thorn the realization pricks her: there is so much she is ignorant of. There are days the sick come to her, and she has to send them away without help because she does not know what is killing them. Yes, Abdullah will return, though not for a while, he has sent a message saying he will be delayed. He cannot leave his grandniece yet, they have become great friends, Somnath is quite beside himself with jealousy. *You will not believe it, Sameera looks just like Raza did at that age, she has all his little ways. She sleeps on her front with her hand tucked into her neck just like he used to as a boy. Your mother has made a beautiful quilt for her. She refuses to be parted from it even for a moment.*

Yes, when he comes back Abdullah will teach Priya all he knows. But it is not enough. She is shaken by longing: if only there was a way for her to learn the latest methodologies, the current procedures, the newest sciences of healing.

❧

A letter arrives from Jamini, an astonishment.

Sister, I am pregnant. I should have come to Calcutta and told you in person; that would have been the right thing to do. But it will cause me too much distress and might harm the baby—and that chance I cannot take. She follows with an apologetic explanation of how it came about, the three loveless nights she had begged for as her marital right. *I want you to know he did it only as a duty. He was not attracted to me for even one moment. You were in his heart always, he was always true to you.*

Priya believes that; she had seen Amit's eyes, heard his final words in the boat. Still, she cannot stop herself from imagining those three nights over and over, the two bodies in the bed, though it makes her so ill she has to throw up, and is that not the bitterest irony for her with her empty womb. She cannot rest although she is exhausted, she must pace the Calcutta mansion for hours, she is bloated with rage, with the fever of jealousy and the unfairness of all that life has snatched from her and deposited elsewhere. Sleepless, she writes the harshest things she can think to Jamini, the vilest, most caustic epithets.

Dizzy and exhausted in the heavy hours before dawn, she thinks she hears her father as she folds her letter and puts it in an envelope. *Priya, you are better than this.*

I don't want to be better, Baba. I am tired of it. What has being better ever availed me? What did it ever avail you?

Clearer than in months, his face rises in her mind, its sad nobility. *Life is not only about availing, daughter.*

Slowly the tidal wave of rage that engulfed her begins to recede; what remains is the last line of Jamini's letter. *I know you are furious with me, Priya. You have every right to be. But consider this. We thought Amit was lost to us completely and forever. But in this child, a part of him will live on.*

She is honest enough to acknowledge the truth of her sister's words. She crumples the letter she had written in her fist.

❀

Birth and death, serpents swallowing each other's tails. A father dies to make space in the world for the child who is coming. When a nation is born, how many must then die?

On the evening news the announcer is in tears, breathless and disbelieving; he has to go off the air midway and someone else must take his place, because in Delhi, as the Father of the Nation was on his way to a prayer meeting, he was shot to death by one Nathuram Godse, the editor of the *Hindu Rashtra*. Falling, he said, *Hey Ram*. Priya, listening, is in shock. Growing up with his stories, she had believed in her childheart that Mahatma Gandhi, older than her father, older than anyone she knew, would live forever. Now his life has ended in a matter of minutes, and Nehru is weeping, he is saying, "*The light has gone out of our lives and there is darkness everywhere.*" In the room they are weeping, too, Priya and Shefali and Banno from Lahore who knows about darkness. All over the nation people are weeping, they will weep for days, riots will break out for love of a man who prayed all his life for peace, cities will burn. But because even saints have enemies, some will be pleased. Secretly they will say, Good riddance, he was too fond of Muslims, because of him the country was broken in two.

All this Priya will learn as she sleepwalks through the next days doing what must be done at the clinic. She will keep the radio on day and night, though for what she does not know. Perhaps she wants to understand why such calamities occur, perhaps to see if what Nabakumar used to tell her is true: out of evil, good emerges. Half a million people follow Gandhi's body, wrapped in the tricolor flag, to the funeral grounds beside the Jamuna River. Airplanes drop rose petals on his pyre. Messages of sympathy are sent from across the world by kings and queens, presidents and prime ministers, writers and scientists. The leaders of India draw together in their bereavement. *A giant among men has fallen in the cause of brotherhood and peace. His supreme sacrifice will wake up the nation's conscience. A thousand years later, his light will be seen in this country, and the world will see it and it will give solace to innumerable hearts. Just an old man in a loincloth—yet when he died, humanity wept. Let us be worthy of him.*

And then, as she is stitching up the head wound of a laborer injured in a careless dock accident, she hears on the radio a beloved voice. "Far greater than all warriors who led armies to battle was this little man, the bravest, the most triumphant of all . . . May the soul of my master, my leader, my father rest not in peace, not in peace, but . . . let the powder of his bones be so charged with life and inspiration that the whole of India will, after his death, be revitalized into the reality of freedom. My father, do not rest. Do not allow us to rest. Keep us to our pledge. Give us strength to fulfill our promise, your heirs, . . . the guardians of your dreams, the fulfillers of India's destiny."

Sarojini Naidu. The announcer says that in three days' time she will visit Calcutta to speak to the people of the city the Mahatma so loved that he spent Independence Day here in prayer. Priya, jolted from the miasma of despair, rushes to her desk to write down the details: Sarojini will give a speech at the Maidan at three P.M. She will collect money for women displaced by communal riots, especially those from Noakhali, where Gandhi had spent time after the massacre of 1946. This time for certain, Priya promises herself. Let the world end, still I will be there.

What can stop her, now that all she cared for has been leached from her life?

❈

On the day of Sarojini's talk, Priya puts up a sign on the door: CLINIC CLOSING TWO P.M. She has gathered all the money she has at the house, she has taken even the clinic money that does not belong to her. She plans to give it all to Sarojini. She will sell some more jewelry later to replace it.

At two o'clock she is ready, hair combed, face washed, wearing the white khadi sari that the excited Shefali had ironed for her. Her bones are as light as a bird's as she locks the front door of the clinic; almost she could fly. *Baba, what you wanted for me is finally happening.*

But a mother rushes up the street carrying her child. Please, Doctor Memsaab, please.

Priya's heart sinks. The boy has fallen and broken his leg, there is an ugly gash, the splintered tibia sticking out. The child screams until exhausted, then screams again. Salima has already left, so Priya must do it all on her own: administer an injection for pain, sterilize the wound, straighten out the bone as best as she can, put the leg in a splint, give the child a tetanus shot. The leg will have to be operated on quickly; the clinic does not have the facilities for that, nor is she trained to perform such a surgery. Knowing what happens when the indigent show up at the overcrowded hospitals, she calls a taxi because Somnath has sold the car. She takes them with her to a bigger clinic, pays in advance for the procedure, which uses up much of her money, suffers with impatience the mother's teary gratitude.

By the time she reaches the Maidan it is past five. The speech is long over. But of course. What had she hoped for? Workers are dismantling the stage, loading bamboo poles onto a truck, folding away flags. Has Sarojini left the city? She rushes up and down, searching for someone who might have information. Finally a man in a kurta and Nehru cap takes pity on her desperation and tells her that Sarojini may have gone to the Hyderi Manzil in Beliaghata, where Gandhi had lived for a month last August.

Again a taxi that she can ill afford, again the driving across the traffic-jammed city. They pass Dharmatala and Bowbazar and Entally and Tangra, getting lost twice in dead-end alleys. Is the driver, sensing her ignorance, giving her the runaround? But no, she has maligned him, here is the dilapidated old villa, whitewash faded, precarious pillars holding up an entryway blackened with mildew, a pond covered in scum. It looks deserted.

Heaviness in her chest. She pays off the driver, who asks with some concern if he should wait for her, it is not the best of neighborhoods for a young lady. Wearily she shakes her head. She has lost her chance to meet Sarojini, but she will sit on the steps where the Mahatma used to sit, where perhaps Sarojini, too, rested earlier in the day. She imagines Gandhi coming down the steps to the pond to wash his clothes, his dishes. Nabakumar had told her he used to perform such chores himself.

There are footsteps behind her, two young women carrying books, boxes, writing materials, eyeing her questioningly. And behind them, an older woman who moves with an uncertain gait, calling to them in a tired voice, asking when her train leaves Howrah Station. Soon, says one of the assistants, we must load the car quickly, the traffic is always bad in this city. It takes Priya a moment to recognize the older woman. Sorrow and exhaustion pull at her features, making her appear far older than her newspaper photos, but it is Sarojini.

Priya stands up. Sarojini's companions—there is a man, too, coming out of the house—try to block her off. They are nervous after the recent tragedy. But Sarojini waves them away and asks her what she wants.

How to answer such an immense query? Through the blood beating in her ears, Priya can only say, "I had to meet you. I have been trying for years. I am Nabakumar Ganguly's daughter. You will not remember him, but he talked of you often, he went on the Salt March with you many years ago."

Sarojini smiles a surprisingly sweet smile. For a moment the deep grief recedes from her face and Priya can feel her charisma. She understands why so many people, including her father, worshipped this woman. Why they had walked with her into danger assault imprisonment death.

"I remember Nabo," Sarojini says. "He liked to sing. Where is he now?"

The story spills from Priya, the tears also. Sarojini sits down on the broken steps and gestures to Priya to join her. She sighs. "So much death in spite of everything Bapuji tried, everything we tried alongside him. But we must go on, carrying the vision forward. It is the only thing we can do to honor the dead." She ignores her assistants, who are trying to get her to leave, and takes Priya's hands in hers. "What do you plan to do, Nabakumar's daughter?"

Priya is taken aback at the genuine interest in Sarojini's voice, in the tilt of her head. This, too, must be what made people love this woman, the complete attention she gave to whomever life had placed in front of her. She takes a deep breath.

"I want to be a doctor like my father."

That story also spills out: the entrance exam, the unfair results, the journey to America, the family responsibilities that pulled her back, the rescue mission in East Bengal, the expulsion from the Woman's Medical College in Philadelphia, the work she is doing in the clinic now, important but frustrating, the reason she was late today.

Sarojini sits so still, she could be a statue. When Priya is done, she gestures to one of the women for writing materials, a sheet stamped with her name. "You are intelligent and focused, Priya, the kind of woman India needs," she says. "You must try again. No need to go abroad for studies, now that the country is ours. I will write a letter for you. Let us see if it gets you into Calcutta Medical College. You will have to take the entrance examination again, for fairness, but I do not think you will have problems passing. If for some reason it does not work, come to me in Uttar Pradesh. They have recently renamed the Agra Medical College after me. I allowed it because they promised they would make a special effort to educate women doctors. There will be a place for you there."

She hums a song absently as she writes. Priya recognizes the tune. It has been on the radio constantly the last few days because it was Gandhi's favorite. *Vaishnava jana to tene kahiyeje pida paraayi jaane re. Only those who feel the pain of others may be called truly good.* Sarojini sees her listening and says, "A doctor is like that, no?"

She gives the letter to Priya, she holds her hand and tells her one last thing.

Her companions are fidgety with distress, the man clears his throat twice. "All right," she tells him. "I'm leaving now." A car rushes from the shadow of the mango trees, she climbs in and like a dream is gone.

The letter is addressed to Bidhan Chandra Roy, the newly appointed chief minister of Bengal. Priya recalls hearing that he used to be Gandhi's doctor; he, too, had gone on the Salt March.

Bidhan,

I am sending you a smart young woman who wants to be a doctor. Before independence, she was excluded unfairly from Calcutta Medical College. I take it you will now give her the chance she deserves. If not, I will steal her away.

Here comes her taxi driver; he has been waiting all the while on the street. "Didimoni, I didn't want to leave you alone here in the dark." She follows him to the car. The world is full of good people, too, living their quiet workaday lives. She sees it now.

In the taxi she opens the window. The smells of the city flood her: petrol, sweat, street snacks, garbage, flowers. She holds fast to the last thing Sarojini said. *You are a daughter of independence, the country's future. Women like you are the ones for whom we fought and died, the ones who will transform India. You must carry the flag forward. You may fall from time to time. We all did. What is important is to get up again.*

Epilogue

1954

*O*n the veranda of the old mansion they are playing chess, a white-haired man and a girl of seven. The man is letting the girl win; the girl, bent intensely over the board, does not know this.

Priya, returning from the clinic, sees them and smiles, remembering. Somnath used to do the same for her when she was a girl, but then she grew up and began winning for real. She guesses Sameera, too, will do that. The girl is smart, and there are already arguments about where she will study. Deepa thinks the village school is good enough, but Priya says no, not if they want Sameera to have a career, and surely they do, so many opportunities are opening up for women in the new India.

Priya sets down her medical bag and calls out a greeting. Somnath sends her a preoccupied wave; Sameera announces cheerfully that she is beating Som-Dadu. There are rapid footsteps, a boy of five comes running. *Pia-Ma!* He holds out his arms so she will lift him up, Jamini's son Tapan, who has Amit's smile and also his temper. Both children call her Pia. They could not say her name when they were little and now it is a habit, she has grown used to it, the word no longer rakes her heart.

Jamini leaves the quilt she and Bina are working on and hurries to the veranda, scolding her son. "Pia-Ma has just come home from a long day at work, let her have her tea, don't bother her. In any case, you are too big and heavy to carry."

The boy takes exception to this. "I am not bothering her. And I am not too heavy. Am I, Pia-Ma?"

Priya assures him that he is the best of boys, incapable of bothering anyone, and light as a cloud.

"You are spoiling him," Jamini says, displeased. She is perhaps right, but Priya does not care. She loves Jamini, she bears her no ill will. Should Jamini fall into danger, Priya would willingly risk her life for her again. Still, if once in a while she looks at Tapan and sees his father's eyes, if once in a while she thinks, *He should have been mine,* who can blame her for it?

Manorama comes up from the kitchen, slower than before but still majestic in gait, her keys still proudly hanging at her waist. She calls to Pari to set out tea, the children's milk. Pari brings coconut narus, crisp singaras, puffed rice. The snacks are tasty but not lavish as in previous years. Deepa, who manages the estate as well as the household finances, has declared sternly that there is to be no waste, the Chowdhury family is not as wealthy as before. When Deepa is stern, even Manorama does not dare to argue with her.

Now Deepa joins them from the corner room which serves as her office, taking off her glasses and rubbing her eyes. When is Priya going to Calcutta next? she asks. She has papers to send to Munshiji.

After Amit's death the estate suffered, the fields lay fallow; Somnath, grief-stricken, sold off the Calcutta businesses at a loss; Priya, busy in medical college, was not there to stop him. Finally Deepa asked if she could take over. Since then things have improved because Deepa is a tough manager. When tenants do not pay their rents on time, she goes and collects them personally, taking with her Ganesh the gatekeeper, who carries an ancient rifle no one has used in years.

"Can I go to Calcutta with Pia-Ma?" Sameera asks. She wants to see Abdullah-Dadu, she will be no trouble at the clinic, she will sit quiet as a cat in the back room while they take care of patients.

"No," says cruel Deepa. "You will cry at night for Bina-Didima, you cannot sleep without her."

Sameera, affronted, appeals to Priya, who says diplomatically that she will think about it. She knows she is only an aunt; in this as in more important matters, the mothers will make the final decision, and that is as it should be.

Somnath sneaks a sweet naru from the bowl when Manorama is not looking. His blood sugar has been high recently. Priya gives him a look but lets it be. Everyone deserves a little pleasure in life, the excitement of breaking a rule or two. She tells Somnath about the clinics, how well they are running, paying for themselves; how many people she gets to heal. Her voice thrums with passion, a dream fulfilled. But she has learned from her father's mistakes. She is happy to see poor patients for free, at the clinic they never turn anyone away, but she insists that those who can pay should do so, even if it is a small amount. She has an affluent female clientele both in Calcutta and in Ranipur. Lady doctors are a rarity, and people are willing to pay Priya a generous fee for home visits. She has acquired quite a reputation for handling difficult births. The money she makes helps her finance the village clinic, which she has named Nabakumar Chikitsalaya. An assistant runs it when she is not in Ranipur. Somnath often says, Nabo would have been proud of you.

Bina, too, has joined them at the table. Though her hair has turned white, she is in good health and full of cheer. The grandchildren have done what her doctor daughter could not, Priya thinks wryly. The quilt Bina made for Sameera brought her back to her craft. Once again she and Jamini are embroidering intricate quilts that they sell at New

Market at handsome prices. Bina insists on contributing toward expenses at the Chowdhury home. Priya has convinced the reluctant Somnath to accept. She has told him that he need not always play the patriarch. *We will take care of each other.*

Manorama clears her throat, she has something important to say. Priya can guess what it is; she throws Somnath a glance of exasperated amusement. Manorama announces that another marriage offer has come for Priya; it is a perfect match, a doctor in Calcutta who is willing to let his wife continue working after marriage. She should think carefully before rejecting it, Manorama warns. She might not receive another one this good. Glumly she adds, "You are not getting any younger."

Priya only smiles. Silence, she has learned, is the best defense against Manorama's good intentions.

Tea is done; the children go off to play, followed by hawkeyed Pari. Bina and Jamini, chatting quietly, return to quilting. Deepa and Manorama go into the office to tally household expenses. Only Somnath and Priya are left on the balcony.

Jamini begins a song, "Ei Korecho Bhalo." She is singing it beautifully, but Somnath grimaces. "I wish she would sing something more cheerful. It used to be one of your baba's favorites, but I never did like it."

Priya does not care much for it either, but she now knows the truth behind the words.

You have done well, O Pitiless One,
In scorching my heart.
Until incense is burned, it does not pour out its fragrance,
Until a lamp is lit on fire, it does not give out its light.

Somnath challenges her to a game of chess.

"Feeling reckless, are you?" she taunts him. They begin.

Halfway through the game Somnath pauses. "Manorama is right. It is a good match."

"And I am not getting any younger?" Priya raises an eyebrow.

"You are not!"

Then he sighs, this man who has been a second father to her all her life. "I just want you to be happy."

She looks out toward the gate, where Ganesh is dozing on his stool. She hears hoofbeats, a horse neighing. She hears a voice calling her name. *Pia, Pia, I still have so much to tell you.* His hair falls over his eye, his imported jodhpur pants are ridiculously unsuited to village life. Something is blossoming inside her chest; it will blossom now and forever. She puts her hand on Amit's arm.

Priya holds Somnath's glance so he will see the truth of her words.

"I am happy," she says.

Here is a river. Here is a wind rising. Here is a village. Here is the year.
  The river is time, ebbing, flooding.
  The wind is memory, it can carry flowers, it can carry flames.
  The village is the world, and you are at its center. The year is now.
  What will you do with it? What will you do?

Acknowledgments

My heartfelt thanks to all listed below for their support, encourage-ment, suggestions, and blessings as I wrote *Independence*.

My agent, Sandra Dijkstra, and her team, especially Elise Capron and Andrea Cavallero.

My US editor, Lucia Macro, and her team at William Morrow/HarperCollins.

My Indian editor, Diya Kar, at HarperCollins India.

Ananth Padmanabhan, CEO, HarperCollins India, and his team.

Alli Dyer and Isaac Klausner of Temple Hill Entertainment, and Simon Lipskar and Maja Nikolic at Writers House.

My writer friends Keya Mitra and Oindrila Mukherjee.

The wonderful librarians at the University of Houston, especially Emily Deal, who procured numerous difficult-to-find books for my research.

Adish, Arun, Kasi, M.M., and Ramesh, who kept Murthy busy playing bridge so I could write without interruption!

My ever-patient and loving family: Murthy, Anand, and Abhay.

My spiritual guides: Baba Muktananda, Swami Chinmayananda, Sri Ramakrishna Paramhamsa, Ramana Maharshi, and Nisargadatta Maharaj, who point me to That from which all creativity flows.

I am deeply grateful to each one of you.